Patricia Baird.
1 McIlwraith Road,
Rhyll. Vic. 3923.

For

LIN & CLAY; LACHLAN & ROSE;
AMEÉ & HELEN; HAYLEY & CALLY

AN UNLETTERED GIRL

HER LIFE ON THE GOLDFIELDS

by

patricia stavely baird

Author's statement: This is an imagined history. The documents on which the story is based are held in the Stavely Collection, Manuscripts Collection, Latrobe Library. The Colt .31 revolver is held by the Gold Museum, Sovereign Hill, Victoria. I have tried to imagine how life may have been on the goldfields, especially for a teenage girl, and I have used those family papers and documents as well as readings of the history of the goldfields era as inspiration. But beyond the known facts I have given the characters experiences and events which are entirely imagined.

Acknowledgements: I would like to make grateful acknowledgement of all those who have taken part in the gestation of this book. The Ibis Writers for their patience in listening to and encouraging the evolution of An Unlettered Girl. My thanks go particularly to friends and perceptive readers, Sylvia Owers, Barbara Block, Sophie Maddigan and Ann Melville for their feedback and keen eyes. To Betty Osborn for her sound advice and generous response. To Peter Maddigan I would like to give special thanks for his invaluable technical skill, his creative eye for 'grace on the page' as well as his immense generosity in the gift of his time. Finally, to my family for their confidence in me; to Bob, my life partner, friend and mentor for his constant support and our grandchildren who are really the ones for whom I wrote this.

Printed by SRM Productions

National Library of Australia
Cataloguing in publication entry:
Baird, Patricia Stavely. 1930 -
An Unlettered Girl.
ISBN 0-9580934-0-7 (paperback)
AN UNLETTERED GIRL
by Patricia Stavely Baird, 2002

Contents

MAGGIE

Prologue

Strange, that after so long a time of resisting its pull, I fell almost immediately under the spell of the past as I rummaged through the sea chest. In it lay bundles of letters and tumbled boxes - a chaos of memories. Fragments from the lives of people I did not know and with whom I had no living link. Amongst the papers and letters were other things - images of a man and a woman, a writing case, a leather-bound family bible, a christening robe, a pistol.

At first I was tempted to discard everything and thought to keep only the pistol, the bible and perhaps a few of the photos. Everything else seemed too far back in time. Too fragmented. But I am a cautious person and decided to put off that drastic measure. For a while I sat there and stared at the man and woman in two large photographic plates, carefully placed on top. The man was in an arrogant pose, one arm flung carelessly across the back of his chair. He was leaning back and looking directly into my eyes as if challenging me to question his authority. But the woman claimed my closest attention. Plump and stern, she too looked directly at me from eyes so like my father's I gasped.

Carefully I lifted out the plates and leaned them against the wall, then reached into the chest and drew out a small package. It was a white paper bag and on it was written:

'Diary kept by my dear old Father when a young man of
21 years of age . . . on setting sale from Liverpool on
28th April 1853 and never sighted land again till Cape
Otway on 21st July, 1853.'

Who wrote those words? Whose was the diary? I stared at the man and woman. Suddenly their presences grew large in my mind and they seemed to stand in the room before me.

I reached into the chest and lifted out the first bundle of letters. Why had all of these seemingly unrelated things been kept?

I drew the objects from the chest, one by one, and as I did, I imagined a history for each piece.

DAVID

Part 1

THE SWEET SCENT OF PEAT

IRELAND 1845 - 1853

When I tried to recall the first time I saw the chest I realised it had been part of my life ever since I was a child and went with my father on visits to his aunts. My mother never came on these visits, discouraged perhaps by the austere, religious atmosphere that surrounded Essie and Emma.

Dad and I would set off on our adventure to Maryborough in central Victoria, he with a suitcase in one hand, limping along as always. I, accustomed to the irregular rhythm of his walk, matched my short steps to his as well as I could, and at the tram stop, I would hold his hand and wait beside him, one leg thrown a little forward, in exact imitation of his stance. A few hours later we would at last step from the train onto the platform at Maryborough and walk the last mile along the dusty footpath to his aunts' timber house.

'They're stone deaf,' my Dad said. They greeted us with thin whispers. Dry and angular as old ti trees, they did everything together, moving in a slow dance, each anticipating the other's next thought, next movement.

The house was scattered with fragments of their written conversations, words, underlinings, exclamations, crossings out. Their dry voices had no rhythm to my young ears, and they gave no answers to my questions.

As I recalled those childhood visits, my memories are of the silence of the house, and the names I heard the aunts whisper in their soft voices. A confusion of names. And photographs standing in rows on tables and sideboards and mantel pieces. Pieces of furniture burdened with silent memories.

Aunt Emma would lift a photograph and show it to me and name the faded figure in its silver frame. 'My sister Mary' or 'my brother Atch.' Then, 'this was your father's real mother,' she murmured and her eyes strayed to the window, 'poor Agnes and Willy.'

An-gus I thought . . . 'Who's Angus Dad?'

Dad smiled. 'Agnes was my mother, Love. But I don't remember her.'

11

I tried to fit Agnes' awkward vowels into my mouth. 'Ag-nes. It's a funny name.'

'I was only two when she died. She was your grandmother.'

'But what about Sunshine Nanny? Isn't she my Grandma?'

Dad crouched down to my level and explained carefully. 'Willy was my father and Agnes was my mother. After our mother died Dad needed someone to help him look after us and so he married Nanny.'

Aunt Emma said 'Willy should never have married so soon.'

Dad gave his slow smile to Aunt Emma. But he spoke to me when he asked, 'Do you remember your grandpa? He died when you were three.'

'Was he old?' I asked, trying to recapture a picture in my young mind.

'Seventy one.'

That was a big number, it sounded old to me.

'He wasn't really old but he was deaf too.' Dad's eyes were a bit shiny when he said 'He was riding his bike to work and forgot to look out for the train.'

'Did he go to heaven?'

'I think he probably did.'

And from some deep part of my childish memory a wisp of tobacco scent wafted across my mind together with the feel of gentle arms in rough cloth.

Much later I wondered what so occupied my grandfather's mind that on that fated morning that he forgot to check for the 7.15am train. Had he mounted his bicycle and ridden off to work with hard words lingering in his mind? After all, Dad had shown me scars on his legs where, one day in a fury at some misdemeanour, Sunshine Nanny had pushed him into the fire. I have little doubt Dad would have tested her patience, but to push him into the fire, that seemed beyond the pale. But although I remembered her as sharp and strict and critical, she was never cruel to me.

Poor Dad, death and illness seemed to have shadowed his life. His three little sisters had died when they were babies and at the age of two he contracted polio, although they did not know what it was at the time. Then his mother's death. And when Dad was nineteen and the Geelong Road was just a narrow strip of bitumen, his brother Bill had a fatal motorbike accident. Followed so soon by his father's accident. Little wonder he was preoccupied with death. Finally, his last remaining sibling, his sister Mary, died suddenly at the age of thirty five, just as her mother had done. So that by the time he was forty there was not one of his family remaining. But in spite of these losses and his profound conviction that he would never make old bones, he lived to seventy four.

Dad did not even know Nanny was his stepmother until he was twelve. On a visit to his cousins, his maternal aunt had said to him as she held out a photo of her sister's wedding, 'Do you know who this is Hugh?' she asked, pointing to the pretty young woman in the wedding dress. Hugh shook his head. Putting her hand on his shoulder and shaking him gently his aunt said. 'This is your *real* mother.'

In the aunts' house was a room which was seldom opened. When I was good, or if it rained, I was allowed in there to open boxes, to find treasures. Ribbons and buttons, buckles, wool, knitting needles and sewing needles, crochet hooks, reels of cotton, gloves, rolls of material, strange looking corsets, (my mother was so modern, I'd never seen stays before). Everything new in its box, I didn't realise until decades later that these were the left overs from the family drapery store.

In the corner was a large wooden chest. It looked like a treasure chest to my young eyes with its iron handles and metal strapping. It had two keyholes like elliptical eyes looking at me. Part of me knew it was not to be opened but one day, hoping for jewels, I dared to lift the lid and look inside. I was bitterly disappointed at the dull looking papers with their musty odour, but I spied a tiny purse and was just reaching for it when I heard Aunt Emma's steps coming to the door. I closed the lid and forgot it for forty years.

WRITER'S NOTES: *The Sea Chest*, stands 900 centimetres wide, by 500 centimetres deep, by 600 centimetres high. It is made from some timber I am unfamiliar with, possibly oak or elm. In patches the timber is eaten away as if by sea worm or some such pest, although that damage has long since ceased to progress. It has a lid some 10 to 12 centimetres deep, overlapping the main body of its bulk. All of its corners and edges are reinforced, not with tin strapping, but what appears to be thinly beaten iron, nailed into place with forged nails. On either end are iron plates with forged handles attached and at the front, a few inches below the lid, are two elliptical brass plates with keyholes. There is no key. It is lined with zinc and so it is very heavy even when empty. It gives the appearance of being made by a careful man. It is robust, double locked, well constructed yet not without a certain sturdy attractiveness in its choice of materials, the fashioning of its metal parts and its proportions. Whoever made this chest was both skilled and had an eye for balance and harmonious detail.

Piece of slate, wrapped in the remains of an old linen jacket. Perhaps it is a roofing slate, although smaller than any I have ever seen. It is about 15 centimetres by 25 centimetres and one corner has been broken away. One surface is quite smooth but the other side is slightly ridged where it has been split away from its matrix. Once it must have been finely cut and split but now the corners are chipped and a crack runs along the grain. It is extremely fragile and the way it is wrapped suggests it's intended to be treasured.

Bundle of letters, with photograph of a church on top. The church is a small stone building with buttresses supporting the walls. Wind bent pine trees surround it and beneath them, tilted gravestones stand in an overgrown graveyard. There is barely discernible writing on the back of the photo. With a magnifying glass and some patience I find the writing says: 'Rureagh Presbyterian Church built 1777. Grandfather and grandmother Stavers are buried here.' But it is unsigned and I don't know who wrote these words.

Tiny maroon velvet purse, Inside, a lock of hair and a small, smooth stone, shaped a little like a pair of lips. How strange. The hair is curled around the stone. There are one or two grey hairs amongst the dark ones. I believe that in the days before photography, a lock of hair was the only memento available to those who could not afford a likeness to be drawn or painted. Except for its shape the stone appears unremarkable although its smooth surface suggests that it has been polished in some way. I almost tossed it in the garden, then hesitated. Instead, I put it in my pocket and that night as I undressed, it fell out. I picked it up and decided to sleep on it. It was still there in my hand in the morning but warmth seemed to have changed it, so that now I knew that it belonged. It fitted my hand, but more than that, it fitted my . . . mind. And as I held it, I fancied I could hear Maggie's voice as she murmured to her children in the firelight.

BALLYEASBORO, NORTHERN IRELAND 1845.

In the later years of her life, when Maggie recalled her childhood on the Ards Peninsula, her memories were vivid and detailed. Seated on a stool in the spring sun, or beside the fire, she would tell her children of the stone cottage of her youth and innocence, of her mother's Irish songs, and of her own life later, on the goldfields and in Majorca. And always her story would begin with the unforgotten green of Ireland, the sun glimmering on the lake, or the mountains beyond.

It was not raining that day, and the sun was warm on me back as I hurried home from the fields. I was hurrying because as we climbed over the stile my friend Sarah said to me as she planted her hoe over the wall,

'Maggie, did you know there's a meeting this evening? At Benson's barn.'

'And what would I want with a meeting at all?'

Sarah announced grandly, 'There'll be a master there. Teaching reading and writing!' She knew I had a hunger to learn, and when

15

she said, 'It's called a Hedge School and my Da says anyone may go,' I was caught entirely.

Sarah trudged away down the hill with her hoe over her shoulder, but I was just standing there, me mind racing like a little breeze runnin' over the surface of the Loch. She turned and called 'Mind you, Maggie, you must bring a slate and some chalk.'

I'd never had no chance to go to school - I'd worked in the fields with me Mam and Da since I was a small thing. Now I was twelve it seemed to me that a body that can write and read could do almost anything. The thought of that Hedge School was like a big sunbeam came and shone down on me life. Straight away I forgot how weary I was and leant my hoe beside the wall and I ran up the hill to the chalk pits and gathered some pieces from near the rocks. I was dancing down the hill again feeling pretty pleased with meself about the chalk, when I remembered Old William's cabin. It had been empty since Old Will died, and I seemed to remember seeing slate on the roof before it fell in. So I got me hoe and me chalk, and I ran fast as me skinny legs would let me to Old Will's.

When I got there, I was going very careful through the door, hoping there'd be no ghosties, for I was very superstitious in me youth. As I pushed the door it creaked and cobwebs stretched out tight. Beyond it was dark and I could feel the wind blowing cold through the empty windows. Suddenly something flew past me head and out through the open door. I was shaking so much I made the door rattle, but I made meself stand still with both me hands holding on to that door and then the feathers floated down and I laughed to think wasn't it only an old owl that gave me such a fright. Then soon, I was thanking that owl because there in front of me, under a hole in the roof, sure enough, there was a piece of slate, just sitting there waiting for me. I bent down and picked it out of the rags and litter on the floor. It was only as big as a skillet and covered in grime but I took it out into the light and rubbed it on the wet grass and dried it on me skirt and soon enough it started to look like a real slate.

I didn't want to show meself up by being entirely ignorant so I sat on the wall in the slanting sun and practiced making marks on the slate with a piece of chalk. I felt as cack-handed as a babby. Each time I pressed the chalk, it made a fearsome squeak and the marks I made looked for all the world like the chickens had walked through the milk. I spat on the slate and rubbed it with me sleeve and tried again but still it wasn't like real writing to my eye. When the cold of the stone wall started to make me back end go numb, I thought I'd best be moving meself if I wanted to go to that Hedge School that night.

I knew me Da would never let me go out in the evening lest all me work was done so I hurried meself along, hoping MaryAnn hadn't been able to find any fleece. When I got to the door I washed me hands in the pannikin beside the barrel and I was just coming in when our Mam called.

'Hurry yourself, Maggie. MaryAnn's gath'red a basket of fleece here to be carded.' Bother MaryAnn I thought. Mam panted as she moved about, the way she always did, while I was shaking me hands and drying them on me skirt. 'Where've you been this last hour?' she asked.

'Up at the chalk pits, Mam. Why can't MaryAnn do it this time? What's she been doing all the day?'

Mam patted me on the shoulder 'Tis a good hand you've got with it Maggie. Don't you be arguin' now.'

It was dark inside and me hands was cold and cracked, but I knew the fleece would clean them and make them warm soon. I sat on the stool near the door with the last of the sun slanting through and pulled the basket of fleece to me and I took up the paddles and began the pull, pull, pull that turned the wool from greasy fleece to fluffy strands ready for me and MaryAnn to spin. All the while I was telling me Mam and MaryAnn about the Hedge School at Benson's barn, about the chalk and how I found me slate. I could see me Mam looking at me all the while, like she wished she could come too and I knew she would let me go when I had finished, for Mam always favoured me.

There was no hurrying with the carding so I just went at it steady. But all the time I was pulling at it I was thinking about that piece of chalk, and the slate and I could see meself sitting and writing, and reading a book out loud, such that I might be sitting in a schoolroom and reading to the teacher. Soon my little sister Susannah wanted to help and pulled at the paddles. I pushed her away with my elbow and she tumbled into the heap of wool and rolled in it and rubbed her face in its sheepy smell.

It was a good big heap I had when I'd finished and MaryAnn climbed up the ladder to help me to hoist it up into the loft. I remember I had me arms up holding the basket up the ladder to her and Susannah was hanging on me skirt, and the chickens was flapping and our Da was grumbling. MaryAnn tried to grab the basket, but didn't she miss one handle, and didn't the entire fleece fall down again around me legs. We was laughing so much we couldn't do anything. And the chickens all squawking and running around and Lizzie chasing them and our Mam coughing and MaryAnn and me laughing fit to bust. Sure, it was like trying to blow a bag of feathers up a hill.

While we was picking the bits of fleece off the chicken's backs, I asked our Da if I could go to Benson's barn that evening.

Da was sitting on his stool, tapping his pipe out on the hearth, 'What do yeh want to be wasting yeh time with such nonsense? Singing and the like.'

'It's not the singing Da. It's reading and writing. It's a Hedge School for learning. Oh please, Da. I've got me chalk, and I've found some slate. Me and MaryAnn have finished all the cardin'. I'll be home before full dark, I promise.' I was scrambling round the floor gathering the last few bits of fleece and dancing from one foot to the other praying our Da would say yes. 'Please Da, please.'

Mam poked at the coals and gave them a good shake. 'Let the girl improve herself, Father.'

'Just an hour then.' Da grumbled and I quickly grabbed me slate and me chalk and started to leave before he could be changing his mind. Mam pulled a potato out of the coals and wrapped it in a corner of her shawl before she put it round me shoulders. I held its warmth against me skinny chest as I hurried out the door.

Mam leaned over the half door. She was gasping, 'Now mind you're home before full dark, Maggie.' As I hurried down the hill I could still hear me Mam coughing. She always said it was the smoke from the fire.

I was eating me potato as I walked and I was almost finished and still I had the hunger on me. It was but a scrap of bread I had that morning before I went to the fields and a slice of bacon would have been a fine thing. But it was seldom enough I had that. Just cabbage and potatoes every day, and sometimes the lid off me Da's egg if he was feeling generous. The day the cock lays an egg, that'll be the day I get one to meself, I thought.

'Halloo' Hugh called from the bottom of the hill. Now my brother Hugh, he can read. He went to school once for a whole year when he was ten. That was six years ago. He can write his name and he can write 'Ballyeasboro', and he can write my name too. He wrote it once with chalk on the wall but our Mam rubbed it out again and clipped his ears for it.

'So it's strollin' out in the evenin' are you now?'

I started to tell him about the Hedge Master and Benson's barn and me chalk and how the slate was there as if it was waiting for me.

'Whoa now Maggie.' he said. 'What's all this about readin' and writin'? Next you'll be wantin' to go college in Belfast.'

I wondered how it was that Hugh always seemed able to read me mind entirely, but I just told him, 'You know I wouldn't be doing that, Hugh. Although I would like to see Belfast. Sarah told me the girls in Belfast wear pretty hats and the ladies are very grand - they ride about in coaches and wear little boots with buttons on them.'

As he walked on by Hugh told me if I paid attention I'd soon be getting the way of it. Then he asked if there was any supper left for him.

'Little enough.' I called as I went on down the hill.

When I got to Benson's barn Sarah was there. She had a whole slate with a wooden frame around it with a little string holding her crayon. I very much wanted a slate like that but I knew our Mam would say we have no money for boots, no mind such things as slates. I held my bit of slate very tight because it was thin at the edges on one side and I knew that if I dropped it, it would break and

I wouldn't be getting another one so easy. And that slate was somehow special, coming to me as it did.

All the boys and girls from the village was gathered. We sat on rocks and logs under the pine tree by the barn, waiting while the master leaned his board against the wall and wrote some letters on it. He began showing us the letters, giving a name to each one. A. B. C. There was 26 of them to remember and they all made a different sound. I remember I liked the M because it sounded like the beginning of my name. And I liked the B. Sometimes it was sounding like a bee in the flowers and sometimes it was quick, like in 'but'. They looked such funny little marks to me- all lines and curls and loops and so many shapes to remember. I was getting very confused at first, but I would learn it. I knew I would.

I remember hearing everybody's chalk scraping on their slates and Biddy Jones was sniffing all the time. By the end of the lesson I could spell my name. M A R G A R E T M C F A D E N . On my way home, I said it out loud and in my head I could see the letters written on me slate and it gave me a feeling like I was bigger, and I ran up the hill and the wind was blowing in me hair and I felt like I could run forever.

It was near dark when I got home and I crept in so's not to wake me Da and all. I curled up in the corner beside the chimney next to MaryAnn and me little sisters, but I couldn't sleep. I wanted to tell someone about the letters, but I knew by their breathing they was all sleeping fast, except me Mam who was coughing something terrible. So, I was lying there in the darkness with the chickens cooing softly and the moonlight shining through a crack in the window and all the while the little letters kept dancing across me mind.

MaryAnn was already up next morning when I woke with me knees all stiff and me toes cold as stones. I knew our Mam hadn't lit the fire for the chimney was cold and I could hear her still coughing her heart out. Da and Hugh weren't nowhere to be seen. Susannah was on her knees trying to light the fire with a couple of twigs and there was ash flying out all over her as she blew down low on it. Little Lizzie was wailing. I picked her up and put her on my hip. 'Be still Lizzie' I told her. 'Where's our Da, MaryAnn? And Hugh? Is there no grits?'

MaryAnn was throwing me a dark look, 'Hush Maggie, do you never think of anythin' but your stomach? Our Mam's ailin'.'

'God preserve us from all harm' I cried. 'What's wrong?'

MaryAnn's hands was twisting strands of hair. 'She's been coughin' and spittin' blood all night long and now she's not answerin' me.' She whispered, 'Our Da's gone to get Aunt Moore and Hugh's gone to Mrs Collins for a physic.'

I squatted down. 'Lizzie, help Susannah with the fire now.' I tried to put her down but she clung to me, pushing her little face into my neck and holding her skinny legs tight around my waist. I looked at Susannah and she was biting her bottom lip and her eyes was full of tears. I turned to MaryAnn.

'She'll be gettin' better, won't she?'

MaryAnn took a deep breath 'Oh Maggie,' she sighed, 'I'm scared half to death meself. Our Mam's breathin' strange, and she's so hot, I can't tell what might happen. And I just wish Mrs Collins would come, or Aunt Moore, or someone.'

I saw the dark stains on the bedclothes and I felt terrible sick in my stomach. Biddy's Mam had died of the coughing. What if our Mam died too?

Just then Mrs Collins came in and she pulled her shawl from her head and stood looking at our poor Mam, clicking her tongue and shaking her head. Lizzie was still whimpering in my arms. Then Aunt Moore came in and we all gathered together at the side of where me Mam was laying. Mrs Collins came over and took Lizzie from me and told her to hush, and that our Mam needed her to be still now. She patted Lizzie and settled her down in the corner with Susie then turned back to our Mam. She knelt down and held me Mam's hand and felt her forehead and she seemed to be listening very hard to her breathing and she put her head on me Mam's chest and her fingers at the side of her neck. After a while she stroked Mam's hair and looked up and sighed. 'God preserve us. We'll just have to wait and pray.'

Outside the door I could hear the village women murmuring.

21

Aunt Moore was telling MaryAnn and me that we would have to be the mothers for now. That we would have to look after our little sisters and cook for our Da.

We waited. Praying didn't make no difference. Nothing made no difference. Hugh was sitting outside holding his head and our Da was walking up and down, not saying anything, just groaning. We was all scared.

Lizzie was whimpering again and us four girls was all gathered together, holding each other.

'MaryAnn, I'm afraid.' I whispered.

MaryAnn shook my arm. 'Be quiet Maggie. You'll frighten the wee ones.'

Our Mam's breath was rasping in and out, and then stopping. And then starting again. And I was watching her lips all blue, with the dark blood at the corners and a little bubble of spit. Shining pink it was. I held me own breath in time with hers and I watched her face and her lips was all blue, and even though her eyes was pointing at me they wasn't looking at me at all, and when I held her hand, it was cold, and the ends of her fingers was all blue too, just like her lips.

'Mam! Mam! Look at me Mam!' I cried.

'Maggie. Maggie.' MaryAnn said to me, quite kindly. 'She can't hear you. Maggie. Please. Be still.'

And I looked at MaryAnn and thought how she never said please to me, never. And even though she was older than me, she looked so small and crushed like, and her voice was thick. 'I think she's dyin' Maggie.' And big tears filled up her eyes and splashed down her front and she looked at me and I looked at her and there was a whole world of nothing between us. And I knew that it didn't matter what MaryAnn asked me to do, even if I tried for the rest of me life, whether I did it or not, nothing mattered because still, our Mam'd be gone.

After our Mam died, we each took a lock of her hair as a remembrance. We had no such thing as scissors then and as Aunt Moore cut the curls from her lovely dark hair, I could hear the knife rasp and the sound of it was more than I could bear. Like cutting the flesh from her body it was. After they'd finished cutting her hair, and wrapping her in a sheet, I folded me lock of hair and put it into a little purse me granmam had given me and I tied it on a string around me neck. I tucked it into me bodice and I ran away by meself to the old pine tree and climbed up into its branches and held me arms around it and wailed for me lost Mam. And wondered how I could live without me Mam and only having MaryAnn who hated me.

The day of the funeral it was raining a fine mist as we walked to the graveyard behind the cart, and I thought even the sky was crying for me Mam. I remember the church bell was ringing, one toll of the bell for each of the 42 years of me mother's life. And with each toll of the bell, and each step I took, I could feel her moving further and further away, and I couldn't remember her face at all. All I could remember was her coughing. And her hair. Her dark hair, warm against me heart.

RUREAGH, NORTHERN IRELAND, 1853.

David's father was waiting for him at the church gate before the evening service. It was dusk and as they walked past the gravestones David could barely see the names he pointed out. 'My father and mother are here,' his father said, 'and my sister Lizzie and her two babes. Uncle Sam - well, I've no reason to grieve his passing,' David recalled much bitterness between Uncle Samuel and his father over the years. Father and son did not exchange many words as they walked from stone to stone, but David's skin prickled as he was walked through the generations of his family. The oldest stone, fallen and broken, lay near the church wall. On it in moss covered letters was carved the name David

Stavers, 1696. David had seen that stone often enough before, but suddenly, on this final, gloomy night, he felt as if he was looking at his own memorial.

His father's voice broke through his thoughts. 'He was my great grandfather. He fled from the persecution in Yorkshire in 1660 and came to Ireland. His manor house in Ripon, called Stavers Hall, still stands. Remember when you are far from home that you come from a long line of Stavers.'

'Where does the name Stavers come from? I've never heard of a Stavers that wasn't our kin.'

'And neither you will lad. 'Tis a singular name and comes from Staver - a gatherer of staves. Such as might have been used in the old days to build walls around a village.'

'I never knew that before Father.'

'Aye, well.' And his father turned and began to walk back to the church.

As David walked down the aisle to their family pew, he thought of how he had done this each Sunday of his life, with his family around him, ever since he could remember. He remembered the warmth of Mother and his eleven brothers and sisters sitting beside them from the smallest to the tallest. The cool walls of the kirk glowing in the light from a hundred candles, held them together, in their family, their church, their village. Their shadows danced across the stones. And when they sang, their voices sounded clear and gentle, and seemed to spiral up into a single sound, hymning their souls towards heaven.

At the end of the service the minister told everyone that David was going to join his brother in Australia and offered up a prayer for his safe journey. It was a comfort to him.

As David hammered together the timbers that would form his sea chest, in the tiny hamlet of Rureagh in Northern Ireland in 1853, the rhythm of his hammer blows lulled his mind into thoughts of the day Sam had left home. David thought Pa should have known Sam would never be a farmer - ever since we were small lads Sam had wanted to sail away to another land. He had made just such a sea chest seven years previously and David remembered how he had envied him, how he too had wanted to go adventuring, to sail away to America or China and return with his pockets full of gold. Later when it was Will's turn to sail away, David knew their father had driven them out with his rigid demands, his determination to rule their lives.

He hammered the last of the zinc lining into the chest and dragged its dead weight steadily across the field and down into the stream where he left it till the next morning. He woke early and still in his nightshirt, ran down to the water's edge and lifted the lid of his chest. Not even one drop of water. Triumphantly he closed the lid again and thumped it firmly into place and dragged the chest back to his parents' cottage where his eight younger brothers and sisters were just waking.

'It looks handsome enough. Will it hold out the sea?' Father asked, as he leaned on his stick and tapped at the corners with his doubting boot. He tried to lift the lid. David smiled a little to himself when he was unable to move it.

'I tested it, Father and I am sure.' David was proud of his workmanship, and proud also to demonstrate its quality to his demanding father.

'My advice to you my son is that you should put in the bottom those things which will best stand the ravages of the sea and to preserve the most important things by packing them near the top.'

'Aye, Father. I have thought of that.' David replied with some satisfaction and thought how remarkable it was that his father unfailingly reminded him of what he already knew.

David could not say when he first knew that he would leave Ireland. Perhaps it was in that beautiful summer when he was seventeen and revelling in the strength of his body. When for day after day he pulled the flax and laid it, in shining swathes, in the pond to ret. But at the end of that summer the flax lay there still, rotted beyond recall. The linen mills were closed. His father's loom was still. Hunger had come to their village. That was in 1848, the year Will had sailed away, determined to become a sailor. Since then they had but one letter telling how he had been shipwrecked in the Bay of Biscay and rescued by fishermen and was on his way from Marseille to America in search of gold. Five years passed before the second letter came, sending money for David's fare to Australia. Now Father said he must go before the end of April.

Two weeks previously David had walked with Eliza beside the Loch, his heart thumping with agitation. He straightened his jacket and tried to still the tremor in his voice, 'I've a good trade now, Eliza. And I'm sure Mr Maxwell wants me to continue in the drapery,' he paused, watching Eliza's face for some small sign of encouragement. She glanced up at him and smiled.

'Ah, that's surely a fine thing. Are you thinking one day he might want a partner?'

David turned and faced Eliza, walking backwards, his voice full of excitement. 'He has no sons, nor nephews either, so he will need help as he gets older. If I can just save a few pounds, I could buy an interest.'

Eliza laughed at his enthusiasm 'It sounds like the best thing for you David.'

'I hope it will be the best thing for us also Eliza,' he said, taking her hand and looking into her eyes, willing her to understand. But she had flushed and turned away, and pretended to notice the birds sweeping over the Loch. Still, though Eliza did not answer him directly, he had hoped that it was settled between them, even though they must wait for a few years.

David's voice sounded harsh to his own ears when the time came for him to tell Eliza that all was changed. He hated it that his father's decision should interrupt his life at so profound a level and could not keep the anger from his voice when he said.

'Father says I must go to Australia.'

'But David! Why?'

He felt the touch of her concern and put his hand over hers. 'Things have been bad for my family. I must meet my brother Will on the goldfields to try our luck.'

'But it's half way round the world!'

'Will has been there for almost a year and has profited from digging for gold. He has sent the money for my passage. Father says I must go too.'

'Isn't that where they send all the convicts?' Eliza asked.

'Will says the convicts are all in Van Diemen's Land but in Port Phillip there are only free men.'

'How long will it take to make your fortune?'

'I should return within two years if all goes well. It's not so long.' David knew he could no longer delay and taking Eliza's hands in his, asked, 'Will you wait for me Eliza?'

Eliza looked down and drew her hands away, then put them to her hair and brushed it back behind her ears. David's heart sank for a moment as he thought she would turn away, but she looked up again and flushed a little and smiled sweetly as she said, 'Yes. Yes, I will, of course I will, David.'

Eliza gave David a small painted likeness of herself. It showed her standing beside the Loch. She was wearing the same blue dress and was looking over her shoulder towards the viewer. Her expression was a little surprised, just as she looked when he first told her he must go to Australia. David believed that painting confirmed Eliza's promise that she would wait for him.

His mother had held his hands tightly when the time came for leaving. 'Such strong hands . . . ' she said. Her voice broke a little but she straightened and said, 'I cannot imagine what this Australia may be like, David. You must write and tell us. I will be waiting for your letters.' As she spoke, she patted his hand as if to fix the memory of her words in his mind. 'Remember to keep your faith; and take care what company you keep. You may meet evil strangers in that place - I beg you, be cautious my son.' Lifting his hand to her face, she whispered, 'I fear I shall not see you or Will again.'

David wordlessly put his arms around his mother's tiny figure and bent his head to hers to still the first chill of doubt in his heart. His voice betrayed him 'God Bless you Mother.'

'And God's Blessing on you too my son.'

'I can hear the horses!' Father called from the doorway. He and David's younger brothers struggled to drag the sea chest out onto the roadside in readiness. As the coach wheels crunched to a stop outside his home David could hear his father calling 'Heave it up lads!' and their grunts as they struggled with its weight. He grasped his bag and told his brothers and sisters that he and Will would make their fortunes quickly and return within a year or two, hoping his words would prove true.

He embraced his sisters. The twins Robert and Mary Jane were clinging to his coat tails, pulling him back from the door. 'Don't go, Davey. Who will take us fishing?' In that moment his young courage almost failed.

His father's lips were tightly closed as he grasped David's hand. 'Write as soon as you are able, Lad. Mother and I are depending on you. Goodbye! Goodbye!' They stood at the door waving as he hefted the weight of his bag upon his shoulder and climbed up beside the driver to begin his long journey. As the coach lurched away, he looked back to the small cottage. A wind was blowing the branches of the trees towards the coach and their leaves seemed to reach out to him, as if to hold him back, to prevent his departure. And framed within those yearning branches, his parents stood in the doorway of his home, his mother's hand to her face, his younger brothers running behind, calling to him, waving. The image burned itself into his mind.

Before him yawned the unknown. How many years before he would see them again?

He was twenty one.

I pulled up roots of violets from the thickets along the roadside as I walked up the hill to the churchyard. It was early on a Sunday morning and I was on my way to visit me Mam's grave before going to church. It's almost five years past since Mam died, and it's hard years they've been. MaryAnn is always angry and tries to take Mam's place and she orders me around, and me Da's lost heart, and we's all full of misery.

Every spring I pull a few more roots of violets to plant around her grave. They was flowering near her grave when we buried her and now, when I see them lift up their little heads and greet me, I know it's near the time of when she died.

I pushed past the briars and climbed the fence instead of walking up to the gate, and I found the small mound where me Mam lay and I knelt and began to clear the weeds away from the ferns. I pushed the roots of the violets in, patting them down firm in the peaty soil. Oh Mam, I still miss you so. And now our Da says we must go to Australia. I don't want to go and leave you anam cara, me soul's friend, for how will I be able to care for you and speak to you when I am half way round the world? It's been so hard since you left. MaryAnn is always driving me and Da doesn't seem to see it at all. And the 'taters are rotting in the ground worse than ever and we never seem to have enough to eat. I'm so thin Mam, me skirt is falling off me, for I've nothing to hold it up.

I looked up at the big oak tree and I could feel me Mam. Close as a breath. I ran me fingers through the soft earth and it seemed to be warm and I dug down a bit deeper to put in the last bit of violet root. It was then I felt a stone with me fingers. I held it and drew it out. It was a flat stone, shaped like a leaf and as I brushed the dirt from its surface a shiver went down me spine and me hair stood up entirely. I turned it over and over, brushing the dirt from it and it seemed familiar to me, yet strange. It looked like granite it did, but it had been smoothed and its sharp edges worn. I remembered how my Gran told me before she died about the elf folk and the wild ones and how they carried stones that they polished with their fingers. And she said those stones remembered something. Then I wished I'd listened more careful because I couldn't recall her words about what it was that they remembered at all. I put the stone to me cheek and I shivered a great shiver, like something moved through me from me toes to the ends of me fingers. It was like me soul held out its arms and gathered in Mam's soul and held it.

From that very moment I knew I'd keep that stone always. It was a message from me Mam and every time I held it, I'd think of her. It would be my piece of home to take to Australia. I spat and rubbed and cleaned the stone and held it in me freezing fingers. When the church bell began to toll, I went to the barrel at the back and I dipped it in the icy water to clean it properly and held it in me pocket while I listened to the minister telling us all about our Heavenly Father and how he would watch over us and that if we was good always we would go to a better place after we died where everything would be happiness entirely. And I hoped that was where me Mam was now where nothing at all could hurt her or harm her ever again.

After the sermon I walked home with me friend Sarah. 'When Mam died, wasn't it the beginnin' of me troubles entirely? She was the one who always stood by me.' I sighed and Sarah put her arm through mine. 'That MaryAnn thinks she can take Mam's place, but she's not like Mam, Sarah. She's bone hard. She drives me every minute.'

Sarah nudged me with her shoulder. 'She'll be married soon, Maggie. She'll be so taken up with James, she won't even think about you.'

''Cept to clip my ears!' I laughed, 'But just sometimes I wish she'd give me a little please, or a smile. Other times I feel like I could sit on her back and push her face in the mud,' I shrugged my shoulders 'but then, maybe she misses our Mam too.'

Sarah swung around so that she faced me and she smiled a tight smile and pushed her hair back the way MaryAnn always did and said 'Please Maggie, don't push me in the mud!' And we laughed and Sarah ran ahead with me close behind. When we stopped at the corner where we went our different ways, we was out of breath, and leaned against the stone wall. I picked some curls of lichen from the wall and I wound them along strands of Sarah's hair, and looped them over her ears.

'There now, I've made you a pair of earrings!' Then I took my stone out of me pocket and showed it to Sarah for there wasn't another soul I could tell it to. She knew what I meant when I told her it was like a message from me Mam.

'And Sarah. Our Da said ever since Mam died we've had the

devil's luck - whatever we've planted, everythin' went bad, what with the blight and all.' Then the tears came and made me nose run and I had to wipe it on me sleeve. And then I told her 'And now he says we must go to live in Australia.'

'To Australia! To live! But Maggie, I won't see you ever again!' Sarah threw her arms round me and we hugged each other there beside the cold stone wall.

I told Sarah, Molly Ferguson says Port Phillip is entirely a tent town filled with savages who eat people. I saw Sarah's eyes grow large again at this horrible information. 'At first it seemed excitin'. Goin' over the sea to a new place. But now I'm afraid, Sarah. I'm afraid of leavin' Ireland, and I'm afraid of leavin' you, for you're the only one that really understands me.'

'We'll always be friends Maggie.' Sarah looked at me and pulled at my sleeve, 'if only your Da hadn't stopped you from going to the Hedge School . . . we could send letters!'

'But how can I?'

'Maggie, Hugh will help you. I promise to write as soon as ever I know where to send a letter. He will write for you, and he will read mine to you. Promise me.'

'I will Sarah. I will. I promise.' But I had no faith at all that a letter would take the place of me friend. And me Mam. And me home, such as it was. I swallowed and tried to blink my tears away at the thought of me terrifying future.

Sarah put her arms around me 'You are my best friend Maggie and I shall never forget you, no matter how far away you may go.' She reached up to her neck and undid the ribbon that held the favour she always wore. 'You must take this with you Maggie.' And she tied it round my neck and tucked it inside my bodice. 'In remembrance of our friendship.'

That was in the deepest part of the winter in 1853. In April we left our poor cottage for the last time, waving goodbye to Aunt Moore and Mrs Collins and all the folk as we climbed into the cart taking us to Belfast and the ferry to Liverpool. And I've still got Sarah's little favour you know. Through all me troubles I've always kept it.

I've travelled further in the last week than ever in me young life. I thought back two days to Belfast and how I had clung to Hugh's coat tails when first we got off the cart, and how Susannah and Lizzie had clung to me in their turn. I had never in me life seen so many people. So many houses! Big houses! So many shops, streets, lanes, roads, buildings. So many people shouting, walking, wheeling, carrying, flying past in coaches and carriages and carts. I dragged Susannah and Lizzie along behind me gawping and staring at everything.

'Hugh! It's so noisy. Do you think it sounds like this all the time? Where do all these people come from d'ye think? Look at that carriage. It's shinin' like the sun on a puddle. And the horses too. Oh it's surely the grandest place I've ever been.' I remembered how Sarah had told me about the ladies with buttons on their boots and sure enough there they were, and I would have liked a pair of them meself they was so pretty. I laughed and thought how innocent Sarah must have thought me.

Before we left Belfast I did not know that to go upon a ship could be such a misery. I shuddered when I remembered how I huddled down below for hours. I was afraid down there. And afraid to go up to the deck. After a few hours, me bladder was near to bursting but I would never go to that stinking closet again. The first and last time I went, it was slopping vomit and worse, and to even go near it made me heave up me stomach. I thought I'd throw up my very vitals. I was half dead from vomiting when Hugh came down and dragged me up on deck.

'Come now Maggie. You must come outside. You'll be feelin' altogether better up there,' Hugh said and half dragged me up the ladder and out onto the pitching deck. I staggered to the railing and hung on it like a wet rag on a fence. The ship plunged down and down and I thought it would go to the very bottom of the sea and then it would surge up and up and me stomach didn't know where it was at all. Hugh made me look up, over the heaving sea, and then I saw it. A light glowing in the east. Each time the ship rose to the crest of a wave I could see for a moment a shining world. Like a gate it was. The sun, between two towers of cloud, was rising all pink and gold and making a path that looked like it might lead to the very gates of heaven. I forgot the pitch and roll of the ship and I fixed me eyes on that golden gateway and made up me mind that from that day on I'd never look down again.

After we crossed from Belfast to Liverpool, even though it took us all the long day to sail up the Mersey, I had nothing but gladness to be in sheltered water. And then, there I was, shivering on the docks in Liverpool, with Susannah and Lizzie clinging to me skirts trying to get a bit of shelter behind me that's only as wide as a broom! The river at the dock was very wide and it had so many ships upon it, I think I could have almost crossed it entirely by jumping from ship to ship.

'Where's our ship then Maggie?'

'I'm starvin' Maggie!'

'Oh hissht the two of you!'

'Maggie! Me drawers is falling down again!' Lizzie said, hitching at her clothes. Susannah giggled behind her hand.

'You'll just have to hitch them as best you can Lizzie, I can't be helpin' you all the time.'

'Why is our Da lookin' so black?' Lizzie asked and I turned to look at Da and my brother Hugh, 'Don't mind Da, he's probably thinkin' of our Mam.' I felt for my special stone. My piece of Ireland. I held it tightly and thought about Mam's hair in its little fold of cotton next to me chest. It seemed to warm me.

MaryAnn was away a bit, with James' arm around her shoulders, and I wished I had a husband to keep me warm. But I wasn't hoping for too much with me two young sisters clinging to me skirts.

I pulled my shawl closer about my shoulders 'You two go along for a walk now. See if you can recognise a body you know.' I walked over to the edge of the dock where there was a gap between two ships and I looked across the river. It was wide and grey and had none of the prettiness of Loch Strang at all and I wondered if the entire world except Ballyeasboro was like this - grim and grey and dirty looking.

All morning there was people and families everywhere on that dock with their bundles and baskets and boxes, and their children. And all the piles of provisions heaped and spilled all over the wharf. And stevedores with their trolleys and cranes all bundling goods onto the ship. I was beginning to think that ship would sink they were putting so much into it. 'Sure and they can't all be going to Australia, now can they?' I asked me Da.

'The agent was sayin' there'll likely be four hundred on our ship.'

'Four hundred! Da! The boat'll sink entirely!'

'Let's pray the captain knows better than to overload.'

Susannah and Lizzie was pulling my sleeve again.

'We're hungry, Maggie. We've had no bite to eat all day.'

I asked me Da, 'Are we going aboard at all? They said we'd board this mornin', and still we're standin' here with the sun almost fallin' into the sea.'

Da rummaged in his pockets for a coin, 'It's right you are Maggie. I doubt we'll board this day. Here Hugh, I believe I saw a brazier settin' up outside the female depot. Maybe he'll have some hot 'taters.' Da handed Hugh a shilling. 'See what you can get.'

I knew my Da was troubled. That he was doubting his decision to emigrate. Not wanting to leave his brothers and sisters. He did not seem to remember we was leaving Ireland because of the hunger. If we'd stayed we would have likely starved to death. I don't know how I knew, but sure as I held my stone in my hand I knew we would eat better once we got to the new land.

Hugh came back, juggling a dozen hot potatoes 'Here now Maggie, this'll warm your heart.' And he passed a hot potato on a stick to each of us.

I nibbled my potato to make it last and walked to the edge of the wharf and looked down at the water while I ate it. I felt as if I was on the edge of the world, about to step into an unknown place. Nothing I saw was familiar to me. I looked at the ship. It was clean and new, and much bigger than the one that had brought us from Belfast to Liverpool. I was praying that I wouldn't die of the sea-sickness. And I was holding my stone and thinking I was scared and I was excited and I was sad all at once.

As David drew further and further from his home and all that was familiar, he looked about him, eager to see everything. He had never previously travelled more than the few miles that separated his family, his apprenticeship, and his church, and now every new prospect filled him with excitement.

Once arrived at the docks, to conceal his nervousness, David adopted what he thought was a confident air as he strolled along searching for his ship.

'Would you take a look at that crane! It's gigantic!' Involuntarily, David spoke out loud, to no one in particular. The bustle of the wharf had made him forget the apprehension he'd been feeling ever since the crossing of the Irish Sea, which the seamen declared had been the roughest they'd had for many years. But now, his seasickness gone, he watched the wharf men as they manipulated their machinery. David stared at the shining wheels and cogs and levers. He leaned on a crate and studied the way the machine worked, as two men put their weight behind a great wheel that turned the crane and swung a bulging net in an arc from the wharf to the hold. He admired the easy way the sailors grabbed at the load's bulk to still its swinging, and felt a small thrill as the lever was eased back, releasing a brake, so that the load spun slowly down, down into the waiting hold.

He'd never seen such a huge and complicated machine before and his hands itched to try those levers, to have that skill, to deftly let the net down, guide it smoothly into the hold. He thought of the long, hard days he and his brothers had toiled to build just one heap of peat, no larger than that bulging net. Plunging their square spades into the soft rich peat, and stacking each sucking spadeful with air between, to dry slowly over the summer. These men with their pulleys and cranes were moving just as much in a few short minutes with hardly a drop of sweat on their brows.

David strolled on. Amongst the forest of ships and rigging around him he looked for the latest acquisition of the Golden Line, the Miles Barton, 995 tons. She was a three masted barquentine, built by W. & R. Wright of Liverpool. This much David had learned from the ship's agents, who also told him that there would be twenty cabin passengers and 367 in intermediate and steerage. David wondered how 400 souls could be cramped into one ship for a voyage that could take more than six months. And how they might be provisioned?

He wondered too, how much space he could expect to get for his ticket in steerage. He picked his way between the barrows and boxes and small groups of people with their heaps of belongings and bundles surrounding them, nodding and greeting those who had some air of familiarity about them. He gazed up at the tall masts with their trim furl of sails, as a sailor scampered through the rigging.

'Hoi! Watch out there!'

David jumped as a crane angled into his view, and a slinged horse, head down and stiff legged, swung across in front of him, towards the deck of a battered old trader tied up to the wharf. He gaped at the dejected horse and, stepping back for a better view, stumbled over a heap of sacks.

'Have you never seen a horse afore?' a red-faced Yorkshireman asked, grinning.

David flushed as he got up and hoisted his bag onto his shoulder before he asked, 'Can you tell me which ship is the Miles Barton?'

'You shipping out on her then?'

'Yes. Yes, I am. I'm from Rureagh, near Belfast. And you?'

'From Ripon in Yorkshire, bound for Melbourne on the very same ship. There she is, over there. The new ship. The one with the slim lines.'

'My great grandfather came from Ripon.' David thought it a great coincidence that almost the first person he should meet was from the very county of his forbears before they came to Ireland. He turned to look at the ship. 'What a beauty!' Momentarily the clamour in David's stomach eased as he took in the sleek and efficient lines of the ship that was to carry him halfway round the world. 'She looks very new,' David said as he stepped to the edge of the wharf and peered over the bulwarks into the cook's cabin, where someone was making a great clanging while clouds of smoke issued from the chimney.

'Sure enough. Neat as a new pin and she's well fitted out, too.' The Yorkshireman flicked a lucifer into the murky water beside the wharf and drew on his pipe.

'Has she been tried in the open sea, then?' David asked doubtfully over his shoulder, his eyes taking in the bridge and the neat set of the sails, all tightly furled.

'Liverpool built and launched only a month ago. I believe she's sailed once across the Irish Sea and back, but this is her maiden voyage to Australia.'

A rumble of uncertainty returned to David's stomach when he heard the words maiden voyage. He walked the length of the Miles Barton, to closer inspect her hull. The Yorkshireman talked on behind him and David nodded in his direction a couple of times hoping he would find someone else to talk to. He thought the ship looked modern and well built. But then, Will's ship had been wrecked on its maiden voyage. David prayed the captain knew his craft well.

The last few nights had been sleepless, a sixpenny space shared with hundreds of others for the privilege of being kept awake by their grunts and snores. Now the day for departure had come and he was on the wharf with his sea chest and other baggage just as the thin sun came up on a grey and uninviting sea. David jostled along with everyone else as they began climbing the gangway to the deck.

David struggled to maintain his place in the crush. The Yorkshireman, who seemed to know everything, had told him to get into the line early so that he might ensure a good position but his endless talk had delayed David and now he was well down the line.

The man in front of him was carrying a bag over his shoulder and it pushed into David's face as he tried to squirm into a more comfortable position. His own bag was in danger of being wrenched from his grasp as he pulled it behind him. Down on the wharf he could see a family group clustered together and suddenly in the midst of that great press of bodies, an immense loneliness swept over him and in that moment he would have fled back home to his family if he had been able.

Slowly they inched forward, each few minutes a couple of men erupting from the end of the narrow gangway to the space of the deck where crewmen checked their papers.

The best hammocks were taken by the time he got below decks where the single men were quartered, but he found one not too far from the hatchway. David stowed his bag in the area allotted to him and looked about in the dim light. He thought his companions a mixed lot, with quite a few who looked as if they might cut his throat while he slept, or steal his meagre possessions. He was glad his chest was to be stowed in the hold - at least it would be safe from these villains for the length of the voyage. Two or three hammocks away he heard a brogue very similar to his own and pushed his way over to three men who were talking together.

'My name's David Stavers. You have a sound of the Ards about you.'

The three men turned and saw a slim, dark young man with a pleasant open face and an intense, blue eyed gaze. 'It's right you are there. We're from Ballyeasboro. And you?'

David felt comforted to find someone from a nearby village. 'From Rureagh, not ten miles distant I believe. I have a cousin at Ballyeasboro, name of James Stavers. He has a small farm near there.'

'Ah yes, a fine fellow. Well, my name is Robert McFaden, this is my son Hugh and this is my daughter's husband, James Ennis.' They shook hands and stowed their gear as they spoke and when all was in place, together made their way up through the hatchway. David followed behind them to the deck where all was noise and confusion as passengers milled around, anxious to be settled in their places.

Robert turned and leaned against the bulwarks and David saw a thin, rather red-faced man before him, sweating and short of breath after the brief effort. He was gaunt and hunched, his face lined. David guessed him to be about fifty years old, and his son to be a few years younger than himself and James a few years older. Their dress was plain and much worn, they appeared both humble and poor, yet they were gently mannered, if a little rough in their speech.

'What is it, brings you to be sailing to Australia, then?' asked David.

Robert muttered, 'A man without a wife might as well be unhappy in Australia as in Ireland.' and turned away hunching over the side of the ship, looking down into the sloshing water.

Hugh explained, 'Havin' no mother, the last five years have been very hard for us. Da thinks we might have a better chance at Port Phillip. But even on the ship havin' no mother is makin' things difficult for us.'

'Why is that then?'

'Because we can't be travellin' as a family. Me sisters Maggie and Susannah and Lizzie have been assigned in the single women's quarters, and MaryAnn, she's married to James, so they're in the married quarters and me and Da, in the single men's quarters. It's provin' very difficult, bein' in three different parts of the ship.'

David was embarrassed by this knowledge of their situation, but could not resist remarking, 'I hope then for the sake of your sisters, that the passengers in the single womens' quarters are of a better quality than in the men's.'

'Aye. 'Tis hard on Maggie, carin' for the others, and her so young.'

'How old is Maggie then?'

'She's just seventeen. She's small but I don't think Lizzie and Susannah will be comin' to any harm in her care.' Hugh laughed.

Just then a bell rang and the Captain announced that all passengers must assemble to hear their instructions on the messing arrangements for the voyage.

Part 2

THE RHYTHM OF WATER

THE VOYAGE, APRIL 21ST TO JULY 26TH, 1853

ST. KILDA 1951

In the last months of Aunt Emma's life Dad visited her often and then in the winter of the year I was to be married, she came to live with us. Even though she had lived alone since her oldest sister died a few years previously it must have been a huge wrench for her to leave the house in Maryborough where she and Essie had lived for over thirty years. But stern and sharp as ever, she came to my parents small suburban flat and filled it with her quick mind and firm presence.

There were many lectures delivered from Aunt Emma's invalid bed on the evils of smoking and gambling and painted faces. My mother was driven to lies and fanning away of smoke fumes and furtive cigarettes in the lavatory while Dad tried to keep the peace.

Unaware of the tensions and dramas, I was in a state of bliss and excitement that obliterated all else. Absorbed in my own world I hardly paid her any attention at all, except to tell her the details of my coming marriage. At that time Bob was living up north and only came down to Melbourne about once a month. When I told Aunt Emma this, she said,

'He must be running pretty hot by then!'

I was affronted and astonished. This was Aunt Emma as I had never heard her before, and hinted at a life beyond the cold and distant spinster image I knew.

By the time we returned from our honeymoon, she had died. There were many nephews or neices to whom Aunt Emma might have left the sea chest. But my Dad was her favourite. To Emma, he was the son she never had and to Dad, Emma was a link to the mother he had lost when so young. So she left him not only the chest, but made him the main beneficiary of her will and thus gave my parents an opportunity to establish themselves more securely in a home of their own.

It was only after a couple of years had passed and my parents had moved house that the chest appeared again and my father tried to engage my interest in it. It saddens me now to think that I was so unresponsive to his delvings. But strangely there were odd things that registered in my mind. The Aboriginal artefacts which he mentioned. The revolver. Dad's words, 'My grandfather was a Gold Escort.' And the needlework.

Dad was by profession a tailor and had in fact made my wedding dress. I was a 'bit of a stitcher' myself and I was intrigued by the lovely work in a christening robe that he had shown me. I guess he showed the revolver and other things to Bob and me, but I don't remember.

So the years drifted on and the chest waited.

In the year following my dear Dad's death in 1982. I found myself the unwilling possessor of the family history. Even then I looked on the chest without a great deal of interest, except perhaps to appreciate its manufacture. I polished it up and put it in the hall where it reproached me every time I walked past. 'Look in here,' it would say and I would answer as I hurried on with my busy life, 'One day.'

On the very day Dad died a letter had come to him from a distant cousin, Paula. In the months of sadness that followed, the letter slipped my mind and it must have been years before, one dull winter's day, I phoned her. It was a fateful call because she was a genealogist who had almost given up hope of ever getting access to what she understood were 'the family papers'. We agreed to catalogue the contents.

In the chest were many things. Amongst them were mementos, bundles of letters, photo albums, greeting cards spanning sixty years, two writing cases, a Colt .31 revolver in a rosewood presentation box, a handmade leather holster, a child's christening robe, some gold cufflinks and a silver fob watch. And a tiny pulse.

The cataloguing, the transcribing of the more fragile letters from the nineteenth century, the sorting out of which Maggie, or Will, or Mary or David was who, proved to be a task which took years. There were over eight hundred letters. All written to Aunt Emma and coming from branches of the family in all parts of Victoria, in Ireland, England and U.S.A.

In times before the telephone became common, letter writing was the main means of communication. Aunt Emma wrote to all her nieces and nephews and through her the threads of family were gathered together. As Paula and I read these letters we began to have a sense of these individuals, not just their names but their feelings, their personalities. And from their celebrations, hints of disquiet, their depths of despair, and from the daily patterns of their lives, we began to know these people from the past. We pored over the letters, deciphering the idiosyncratic handwriting, puzzling over faded words and had moments of high excitement when some small insignificant notebook or scrap of paper presented us with a vital piece of the puzzle.

I found the diary in one of the writing cases in the chest. It was small, about the size of my hand, and very faded and frail. The first and last few pages were missing. The stitches that had once bound it firmly were now loose and as I turned the fragile pages fragments of paper flaked away like confetti. I learned much of how a sailing ship worked. How far they could expect to sail in a day; how the storms were endured; how the passengers were fed. I thought of the young man who set out to sail half way round the world one hundred and fifty years ago. And I thought it some kind of miracle that this small book written in the midst of storms and tempests, had withstood not only the storms, but the years. Born in a young man's hopes, protected by an old man's memories.

I settled down to read it through. The writing was rather quaint and old fashioned and somewhat difficult to decipher. His words told me little of himself, the entries dealt largely with the management of shipboard life and the weather. But coming through the 'reporting voice' was the character of a serious young man, an observer and recorder. I was a little disappointed by this. I wanted to know more of what happened to him, how he felt, who he met, what his experiences were. The young writer gave no hint.

But as I read I began to like this young man - he knew what was right and was prepared to take a stand for just treatment - I saw him as an eager participant and a principled observer, even though he was so young. And I wondered too about young Maggie McFaden. What were her feelings and experiences on that ship so long ago.

WRITER'S NOTES: *Small sketchbook*, containing a drawing of a three masted ship. I looked up sailing in the encyclopaedia and the ship in this sketch is very like the American clippers that achieved the fastest sailing times in the days before steam. These three masted barques were built from about 1840 until steam came in about 1880. This coincides with the influx of gold seekers to Australia. The ship carries a lot of sail and the hull is not high and clumsy as ships like the Endeavour always appeared to me, but long and sleek and very businesslike, with an elegant prow. In 1853 there were few photographs and, there being no other way, most people learned to draw or paint a picture in order to share their past experiences with others.

Page torn from a notebook, written on it in pencil is a treasure of information about the mysterious people who left these remnants of their lives in the chest. It says: 'Our people, father Robert McFaden aged 52, (his wife having died some years previously) and his married daughter MaryAnn 21, (her husband James Ennis), his son Hugh, 19, and his daughters Maggie, 17, Susannah 12, and Lizzie 9, left Ireland in 1853 to sale to Port Phillip on the Miles Barton. Never sighted land until Cape Otway on 23rd July, 1853. David Stavers on the same ship.' Again I do not know who wrote the words but now at least I know which names to look for. After a bit of research I found that the fact that they did not stop anywhere meant that they sailed by the great circle route, via the roaring forties, to take advantage of the westerlies in those southern latitudes. And I found myself wondering how Maggie and her family had made the trip from Balleyeasboro to Liverpool and what it must have been like to leave all that was familiar, no matter how poor, and venture to the other side of the world.

Rather bulky box, decorated with fine strips of wood inlaid in geometric patterns on its lid and round the sides. When I first saw the delicate working of this box, I was full of admiration for the handiwork of its maker, and at the same time regretted that it had not been better preserved. But that was all. It had no pull. No mystery. But now, I feel differently because I think I know who might have used it. It is very handsome. To open it I have found that I must put the lock to the back and open it towards myself so that when the lid is flat the two halves make one agreeably sloped surface for writing. Each half is itself hinged near the main axis of the box and forms the lid of another compartment with space beneath for letters and papers. The whole of this flat surface is covered with worn, dark blue leather, once tooled in gold of which faint traces remain. At the top of the writing surface are a number of small compartments such as might hold an inkbottle, pens, seals and wax. I know now that it is called a writing desk. If only I could glimpse the many pages that must have been written on that deep blue surface; the words of love and loneliness, the frustrations, anger, grief, joys, happiness, and exultations that must have been expressed. The everyday tedium of accounts and bills, of business matters, of debts and richness. What pattern of their lives these would show me. I have so few fragments. Scrawled words written with a lead pencil in a small notebook. Accounts for medicine, gloves, super phosphate, whiskey and brandy pipes. Scraps of newspaper cuttings, a note scrawled on a paper bag, a birth notice, a death notice. What I want to know is their lives, their dreams, their tragedies, their triumphs. What I have is an empty, ink stained wooden box, with a small key and a broken lock. No secret compartment. No note of illicit love. Just a faint whiff of history as I open the lid.

APRIL 21ST TO JULY 26TH, 1853

There was so much pushing and shoving to get down below that Lizzie and Susannah was torn out of me hands and I lost one sack entirely and I didn't find it again until after supper. The ship's officer had given us bunk Number 97. When he looked us over I could tell he was thinking we was so skinny he could put all three of us in one double bunk. And he did too. Then he told us where it was and he said it was altogether a good bunk with a wall at the head and down one side and all. It took us a terrible time to find it because someone else had all their sacks on it and we had to wait for them to move. I didn't think we'd ever fit ourselves in. Three feet by six feet, all the space we have to live in for the next three months. And a narrow shelf to put everything on. Less than a coffin each I thought and shivered.

'Here Susie, do you think now you can find a corner for your bag?' I said, 'and Lizzie, would you be putting the treacle and our pannikins on the shelf there. No, not there, up the other end.' Lizzie shoved the treacle to the other end of the bunk and while I had my head down she disappeared like she always does. Investigating she calls it. In a few minutes she was back, pushing between the other girls. They was all clamouring and struggling for space and there was even a couple of fights with girls pulling each other's hair and screaming at each other.

'There's a privvy over there Maggie, and it's stinkin' already. It's a big bucket with a lid, but someone's been missin' their direction and it's all mucky.'

'Oh hissht Lizzie, what do you want to be lookin' in there for? We'll all have to put up with it soon enough. Now get your blanket and put this bag under . . . no, no, put the bag on the shelf and the pots under the bunk. If water comes in it won't hurt the pots.' That was what I said, but I was praying that the sea would stay out of our space altogether for I wasn't wanting to get to know it too closely.

At last we had everything stowed away but I was feeling nervous about looking after those two for the whole voyage. I even wished MaryAnn was here to help me. Susie was gawping about as usual, while I patted the last of our goods into place. Da had bought some extra food for we had heard that sometimes the rations was barely enough to keep a body going. We had a good slab of bacon, two tins of treacle, and a box of tea and as I pushed the bacon under the bunk it seemed like a sort of treasure. I didn't want to lose that bacon so I got Susie to tie it to the leg of the bunk. Then I changed me mind and tied it to a peg by the shelf so it wouldn't get wet. At home we'd not ever had bacon more than a few times that I could remember. Lizzie was running her fingers round the rim of the treacle tin as if she could taste it already.

'Now girls, remember what our Da said. You have to mind what I tell you and stay close by me.' Lizzie and Susannah stared at me as if they didn't understand what I was going on about at all. I flopped down on the bunk, pushed my hair back. I didn't much want to be mother to these two all the time. If they was proving difficult I did not even know if I'd be able to see me Da because the captain said women wasn't allowed to go to the single men's quarters. And here's meself not even feeling like a woman, much less a mother.

Just then a bell rang and everyone rushed to the ladder up through the hatchway. Once again we pushed and shoved to make our way up on deck and when we did, there was the second mate assigning mess captains, whatever that might mean. I pushed through the crush until I was beside me Da and me brother, 'What's a mess captain, Hugh?'

'Girls aren't allowed near the galley, Da says, so he'll be mess cap'n for you. It means he's the one who takes our food ration to the galley to be cooked and then brings it back to us again.'

'So, I'll have to meet him at the hatchway with our pot of supper?'

'That's right Maggie, and he'll bring it back later when it's cooked. It's going to be hard for him 'cause instead of just taking it to one place, he'll have to bring it to all three of us at our separate hatchways. And it means you'll have to be waitin' at the hatchway for him too. But he said it's the only way he can be lookin' after everyone, since we cannot travel as a family at all.'

I could see it would be hard for me Da but I was feelin' most relieved that I'd be seeing him three times a day.

Da said 'It's no more'n cruelty, not lettin' us in the married quarters. It's hard enough to bear that yeh mother is not with us and now they'll not even give us the comfort of bein' together,' and I could see the water comin' in his eyes again, 'but if I'm Mess Cap'n for all of us, at least it'll be givin' me a chance to speak to you all each day.'

Now meself's feeling sorry for me Da again, trying to look after us all, and him not even knowin' how to hold himself together.

When me stomach had stopped heaving I wished with all me heart there was someone I could talk to. If I could write to you Sarah I'd tell you that to be in a ship upon the wide sea is very frightening. It was days before I could even think about anyone but meself. If I had known how fearful it was, I would not have come. But for the fact I was starving. For the first week everyone was so seasick you cannot imagine how terrible it was. We was all locked down below, vomiting in our bunks and no hand to help us. For five days we endured our own stench and the tossing of the ship before we was allowed up on deck to clean our bedding and ourselves as best we might. We have had storms and tempests unlike anything we might have at home. The wind screamed and the seas was like mountains which crashed down upon the ship and she was leaning over so that we could not walk on the decks at all and the bulwarks was under the sea and the waves washed down between decks and we and our beds was soaked. Many times I thought the ship was sinking and prayed that we might be preserved.

At night it was worse. There were the most fearful noises. The ship groaned and the sails cracked like a tree falling and I could hear the captain calling his commands. And the sailors cried out in the darkness to each other and their feet pounded as they ran about above. And when the storms were bad we were locked below to prevent the sea coming in and swamping the ship. At first I was grateful the hatch was closed because the sea would be altogether pouring in if it was open. But later I wondered what would happen to us if we struck a rock or foundered. Then I was thinking they would be forgetting to open the hatches and we would all be drownded and no one to save us at all.

I can tell you that I smelled very bad. The men washed themselves up on deck with salt water, but there was no private place for the women to do likewise and since we were not allowed to wash down below, we must do without. And Sarah, to make things even worse, in the second week I became a woman and then I had to wash me rags. The captain said we must do no washing of clothes below decks neither, and I thought I would die of the embarrassment if I had to do me washing out on the deck in view of all. He said that next week when we come to the warmer weather we will be able to get our boxes from the hold and get some clean clothes before we get to the equator. Until then we must all put up with ourselves and each other altogether.

I will remember today for the rest of me life. For ten days we have had terrible storms but today the sea is calmer. Susannah and Lizzie and me have washed as much of our clothes and ourselves as we can. We all stood in a circle holding our skirts out to make a sort of tent and then we took it in turns to wash under our skirts and take our tops off and bathe ourselves in buckets of salt water. After, it felt very strange with me skin all tight and rough from the salt. And me belly's tight too. Today I had porridge for breakfast and meat and potato biscuit for lunch. I couldn't remember at all when last I had two meals in one day, with another promised before bedtime. And meat too. Susannah and Lizzie are still pale but they spend most of their days off investigating every corner of the ship they're allowed into.

The air is feeling crisp and the sea is shining blue, with altogether the whitest foam blowing from the tops of the waves. Only last night the ship reeked something terrible but now that we've cleaned ourselves and scrubbed and cleaned below decks, we're feeling like people again instead of the dregs of humanity locked down in the hold. The sailors are tossing buckets of water down the scuppers and it's all bright and shining.

I leant on the poop rail looking to the deck below, and learnt how to let my body roll with the movement of the ship, to plant me feet firm, to bend me knees. I began to like the fresh salt taste on me skin, the wind in me hair, even the creaks and groans of the ship as it rose and fell with the roll of the sea. Sometimes the seamen sang together as they pulled on the ropes and then, when the sails were full with the wind and the ship was speeding along, I thought we'd be in Australia very soon.

I could see MaryAnn and James. They was leaning on the rail, looking over the sea, and he had his arm round her waist. They looked as if they was enjoying themselves. Da and Hugh must be down in the single men's quarters with not a care at all, and here's me with two young sisters to look after entirely. I'm feeling a bit put upon.

I'm wishing I could be like MaryAnn. To have a husband put his arm around me shoulders and look down into me eyes. Or even a young man courting, who would smile at me and give a little bow

51

when we met unexpected, then take my arm and we would walk along the deck together. And then later the ship's master would marry us.

I looked down at me bodice and me tattered skirt and pushed me hair back and wondered what did I look like? I've only ever seen me face in the water in the barrel, or in a pond on a still day. I've heard the girls below talk about a thing called a looking glass. One of the fancy girls has one - it's like a little glass she looks in and she can see her face. I felt me face and tried to imagine how it might look to that Mr Stavers me Da told me about. Which one was he anyway? I was wondering if that's him there, the tall one with the big chin, or maybe the neat one with the wild looking eyes? I felt me face again, and went over to the cabin window and tried to catch me reflection. The sun was shining on it and it was dazzling me but I could see me dark hair and I could see I was looking just like Susannah with her dark eyebrows and the little bump on the end of her nose, only me mouth is wider and I still have me teeth entirely. I laughed when I looked at me hair for it was just like a tangled mop and me clothes hung off me like rags off a picket, except on top where I could feel my little titties pressing against the cloth.

Just then Susannah and Lizzie found me again. Lordy, those two never give me a moment's peace, I thought, as I shepherded them back down the hatchway to prepare our supper.

'Pea soup tonight Pet Lambs, and a bit of biscuit to sop it with.'

'Put some bacon in too Maggie' Lizzie suggested while she struggled to pull the mouldy bacon from under the bunk. I rationed out some dried peas, put an onion in with them and cut a couple of rough slices of bacon into the pot then sent Susannah up the hatchway to give it to Da. Now, don't you talk to any of those ragamuffins up there Susie, just come straight back here. 'Come now Lizzie, help me find a corner of the table and we'll have a game of jacks.'

Straight away Lizzie was under the bunk rummaging in her basket for the knucklebones she and Susannah begged from the cook last week.

'Here they are Maggie. I can do it already. Better than you!'

Look!' Lizzie took the handful of bones and tossed them carefully in the air, turned her hand and caught all five on the back of her small hand. 'See. I got them all!'

'Isn't it the smart one you are? You go first then, Miss Clever.' While Lizzie and I tossed the bones and they rattled on the table I watched her. Wasn't she all flushed and excited? I'd never seen her so lively and I knew that it was the three meals a day was doing it; that and not having to work every day in the fields.

Soon Susannah came back and joined in and while our supper was cooking, we played and laughed and tried to beat each other's scores and for a while we forgot that each hour was taking us further and further from our home.

Last night there was a baby born and she is to be called Emilia Barton. I do not think it a pretty name for a girl at all. If I had a girl baby I would not want it to be named after a ship. Da pointed out Mr Stavers from the Ards and I saw him again this morning when I was shaking out me blankets. He's got dark silky hair and his eyes are as blue as the skies above us. He looks very intent at me. Me Da says I must mind my manners and talk gentle to him when I meet him. It's amazing now isn't it? Here's me coming from Ballyeasboro, and him coming from Rureagh, and they're only ten miles apart, and here we are sailin' round to the other side of the world together. He looks a bit like me brother Hugh, not so tall though, and he's got side-whiskers more than Hugh has. I was noticing his hands too. They're small for a grown man, and I think he doesn't do too much hard work, 'cause they're so pale and don't have callouses at all, like me brother's.

One night I dreamt that I was running across the sea, my feet touching lightly on the surface of the moonlit waves. I saw cloud wreathed lands, green and mysterious, fading before my eyes as I ran and I came to a ladder of light across the sea, rising to a mysterious island and it seemed to me that the ladder was swinging on a cobweb in space and I was climbing and climbing the ladder but never coming any closer to the island of my dreams.

The next day I was leaning over the ship's rail and watching the deep blue of the sea slipping past. Last night was the very first time in my life I have slept without a single covering entirely and not felt cold at all. Sarah, can you imagine the pleasure of it? Already when I awoke the sun was warm like a summer's day at home, and it made me feel as I might be entirely dreaming, it was so cosy. You would not know me now. Already me skirt is getting tight round the middle and I've had to move the button so it was easy to believe me Da when he said that Captain Kelly is a good captain who doesn't skimp us on our rations like many do.

We have been almost three weeks upon the water and not the least sign of land during that whole time. Each day I look out upon the sea, and all around there is nothing but the sea, and it is hard to tell if we are even moving, it is so large around us.

The skies are clear and every day the sun pours down in an empty sky. There's just the endless sea and the endless sky and our small ship - nothing changes. I cannot tell whether we move forward or not. There's only the readings of the captain to reassure us that we move at all. I long for a cloudy day - anything else to look at but this endless, unchanging horizon. I like it best when we have a few clouds for then there is something to look at. The clouds make pictures for us and when they are on the horizon we make believe that Port Phillip is just behind the clouds and we will be landing the next morning. But mostly it is just the sea and waves and wind. I can tell you there is not much to be looking at, at all.

One day, and I'm not even knowing what day it was, but there was meself sitting down below when I heard MaryAnn screaming for me as usual.

'Maggie! Maggie! There's another ship!' I looked up as MaryAnn almost tumbled down the hatchway and cried out as she ran towards me.

'Maggie, There's another ship on the horizon! The captain is puttin' little flags up on the mast. The sailors say it's a message he's sendin' and that soon the ships will meet!'

It was all buzzing between decks as the girls dropped whatever they was doing and rushed up the ladder. I pretended not to be in such a haste, but I was surprised entirely at MaryAnn bringing me good news, so I gathered me blanket to shake out in the morning breeze and to see the other ship while I was about it. I turned to tell MaryAnn I was coming but already she was flying up the ladder with her skirts all hitched up.

When all the passengers was running to the one side of the ship it started to tip over so that I hung back and I tried to climb up onto the top of the hatchcover so I could see better but the mate told me to get off. And he told me the other ship was the Elizabeth Grange bound for New York in America.

I asked him wouldn't you think they'd be sending the letters to Ireland instead of New York! He said after they had been to New York and picked up some more letters there, it would go on to Liverpool and they would send them to Ireland from there. It's a very complicated world entirely I was thinking. As the ships drew closer our captain called through a trumpet and told their captain he would send a boat over with our letters and that we would take any he wanted sent to Australia.

Just then I saw Mr Stavers leaning on the hatch cover and writing very busy like. He always carries a little book with him, and a bottle of ink on a string about his neck and a pen in his pocket. Usually he wrote in the book, but this morning he was writing on some loose pages.

I told him 'Good mornin',' and, feeling a bit bold-like, 'Mind you the wind does not take your papers.'

'I'm hoping the ship will take them, Miss McFaden. There is a ship passing, headed for Liverpool. We signalised her about half an hour since to come alongside. I have been writing letters to my father and my brother.'

I wished I could send a letter to you Sarah, for I have so much to tell you, but Mr Stavers was going on,

'Those who have letters ready will be able to send them over in a few minutes.' And then it was like he read my mind the way Hugh does, 'cause he said, 'Do you have a letter you would like to send back to Ireland? Could I perhaps give you a page here and the use of my pen?'

'Oh. No. Thank you, Mr Stavers. You're most kind but . . .' and I began shaking out me blanket right in front of him, to hide me red face.

What good was his paper and his little ink bottle to me? I couldn't tell him that I could barely write my own name, no more. And that I'd never used a pen and ink.

'Surely you have a friend who would want to know you are well?'

I thought how stupid he was that he could not see, then these words came out of me mouth, 'She'll be waitin' a long time afore she gets a letter from me, for I cannot write any more than me name.' And me face was burning red and I was so overcome with the embarrassment that I turned away and shook me blanket again and thanked him kindly and ran straight away down below and hid in me bunk and cried. I didn't even see the changing of the letters at all. And you can imagine how I was thinking that all my good manners was being wasted entirely. He'd think I was worth nothing at all if I couldn't even write me name with his sharp little pen.

After the other ship had gone on its way and the girls was all back down below, they was all teasing me, laughing at meself as they played cards, or did their embroidery and sang their songs. They called, 'How's your Mr Stavers then?' or 'Mind your manners Maggie!'

I turned away from them and lay across me bunk, with me face to the timbers. We was sailing quieter now after the tossing of the last few days and I was rocking gently with the ship, thinking how close the sea was, so close, on the other side of that wood that was once a tree, just a few inches from my face. How beautiful it is to feel warm, I thought and closed my eyes and put my finger in my mouth like I always did, ever since I was a babby. How soft my lips are. I was playing with my lips, feeling them a bit tingling and of a sudden there was another tingling down between me legs. I put my other hand down there and it felt warm and tingling all the while. I pressed again and the tingle darted right up to me heart. Me breath came quick and me cheeks was flushed and I rubbed a bit more cause it felt very exciting but then I thought perhaps I shouldn't be doing it at all. But it felt so beguiling that my fingers was soon back in their own little boat and rubbing some more. I drifted away into another world, so warm, rocking in me small waves of pleasure, when suddenly a big wave, a really huge wave, washed through me. And it swept me away altogether. It was like nothing I'd ever felt before and me body gave a big shiver all over itself and I sank down into the rolling of the sea.

From far away I could hear MaryAnn's voice.

'Maggie! Da's waiting for you! Hurry yourself along!'

I opened my eyes to see MaryAnn's face frowning above me. I blushed and scrambled out of me bunk thinking she's cross as two sticks because she's been fighting with James. 'Oh hissht MaryAnn, I'm on my way this very minute. You'll not starve to death in the next small while,' and I hurried up the ladder with the family soup pot in me hand, a smile on me face, feeling on top of the world.

I like watching Mr Stavers. He's not so tall, but he's nice made, with his dark hair and wide brow and his eyes looking about him, sharp and quick. Each morning when it is fine, he comes up on deck very business like and makes a space well away from everyone else, which is not so easy to do. He cut up an old shirt yesterday into strange shapes and then he measured, and planned and lay the bits of shirt on some linen. He concentrates so hard he doesn't even see me when I come up close behind him and watch. When it came time to cut the linen I could see he was hesitating, as if he was afraid. He ran his hands along the linen then held it to his nose, as if he was breathing in a memory. And I was wondering what it was he was thinking. Maybe he was remembering the days when he cut the flax, or his mam was spinning it or his da weaving it.

I came a bit closer and said 'What is it you're doing Mr Stavers?' I think he must have been surprised because he looked up into the sun and squinted his eyes and tried to see who was speaking to him.

'Oh Good morning. I am attempting to make a jacket, Miss McFaden. My parents gave me this length of linen, and I feel a great responsibility in the making of it, that I should not waste it, nor spoil the results of their labour.' As he spoke he smoothed the linen out on the deck again and made it straight.

I reached out and touched the edge of the linen 'It's very fine Mr

Stavers. I should not like to put a pair of scissors to it meself for fear of spoiling it. But I'm sure you will make a fine jacket from it.' And I thought to meself how clever he was to be reading, and writing and making his own coat.

'I wish I had your confidence,' he smiled, 'but I shall do my best and hope it will help to pass the time.'

I was just feeling as if we was getting along fine when Susannah and Lizzie came up behind me and pulled at me sleeve.

'Maggie. It's time for our soup, Maggie. Our Da's waiting at the hatchway for you. You must come now.'

'I'll be along straight' I said, wishing they was anywhere but with meself and thought I'd come again the next day when they was busy at something else. Each day after that I would sit near and watch as Mr Stavers stitched. It was fascinating. I'd never in me life had a shift or a dress made special for me. Always passed on from MaryAnn or cut down from me Mam's.

'Where will this bit fit in Mr Stavers?' I pointed to a piece of linen that looked like part of a kite.

'That's the part of the front which folds back when the jacket is on.' And he flicked one corner of the piece back and suddenly I could see it entirely. It was a like a sort of magic to me, the way he fitted the pieces together.

He moved a little to avoid the sun coming into his eyes and went on with his stitching. Tiny, tight stitches, one by one up the side of the jacket. Each time he pushed the needle with the thimble and drew the thread through and tugged it tight. And best of all when he came to the end of the thread he nipped it off neatly with his teeth before measuring out another length. Then he ran the thread over a wax tablet to make it stronger and smoother he told me, then threading his needle he would draw both ends until they was equal, and giving a little roll of his fingers, a twist and a pull and sudden as if by magic there appeared a little knot at the end. It was altogether thrilling.

Then one day he said, 'Would you like to know how to spell some words Miss McFaden? Perhaps while I'm working I could spell them for you and you can remember them.'

When I'd got over me shock, I said, 'I know all me letters and I can spell me name.'

'Well then, let us begin.'

He could spell anything it seemed and I repeated the spelling after him and I remembered them 'cause it's a good memory I had. And even though I wasn't writing them down I remembered them all. But one day he asked me to spell learn and I said L U R N and he laughed at me.

'You needn't be laughin' at me Mr Smart Stavers for you yourself told me to spell T U R N and B U R N and surely 'learn' would be almost the same?' And though he tried to explain, he didn't make no sense at all to me and I marched away and told him I would not come again to be laughed at.

But I remembered his hands, small and strong they was, and brown after the sun, and the nails neat, not rough, nor the palms calloused like Hugh's, but smooth. And the rhythm of his stitching, the push, the pull of it. The way his arm drew the thread through in one long pull, and the way the needle went in exact, and out exact. Each time a perfect stitch, the same as the one before. And as I marched away there was something in the way I could still see his hands in me head, and the way I wanted to see them, that made me angry with meself.

After we passed the Cape of Good Hope, the weather got bad and the winds began to blow again. Da says we're going very fast but we've all been down below all the time and the girls are fighting with each other for there's nothing to do except stop your body from being tossed from one side to the other. I tried to go up on deck but it was slippery wet and the sea was stinging me face and me eyes so much I soon came down again.

Me teeth are chattering and me fingers are blue again. These last two weeks we have spent almost entirely below decks. It is bitter cold. I have not seen Mr Stavers since he laughed at me and I am regretting now that I was so proud. For a few days I went up on deck hoping I might see him again but it was raining and cold and then I slipped down the hatchway and hurt me wrist. It pains me a lot. The ship's doctor has put a bandage around it but that doesn't stop it from paining. We are beginning to stink again. There is no way to keep warm except to huddle together in our bunks and everyone is cranky at the confinement. Yesterday two of the girls had a great fight. They was pulling each other's hair and calling each other the most terrible names. Screaming and biting and scratching they was, like a couple of alley cats. And when they was pulled apart one of them had the mark of teeth on her cheek and the other had two long scratches on her neck as well as her bodice torn. I was ashamed of those girls behaving like wildcats.

Meself and Susannah and Lizzie has decided that we would like to work in a grand house in Melbourne town. We pretend that I will be the chief cook and Susannah the housekeeper and Lizzie will be our kitchen maid until she can cook better. And our mistress will give us pinnies and little white hats to wear and we will have a room with our own beds and a table.

I think I can smell the land. It's coming like a soft movement of air across the sea. Warm it is, after so much cold, and it smells sweet and spicy. I wish the moon would come up and light it for me. I cannot wait to leave this heaving ship. I want very much to stand on the earth and smell trees and flowers. Last night there was dancing all the night and we threw the last of the bacon into the pot and we poured the last of the treacle onto our biscuits and had a great party. We had tin whistles and accordions and we all beat out a rhythm on pots and pans and oh we had a grand time of it altogether.

Then this morning I saw it, and I was never so disappointed in all me life. Like a great cowpat it was, sitting there on the horizon all brown and lumpy looking. It's not green like home, but an awful drab brown all over with nothing to break the sameness of it all, at all. And we've been sailing past it all day and still it's looking the same altogether without a bit of change. This afternoon we sailed almost up to the entrance to Port Phillip but the tides was against us and now Da says we must spend another night before we meet the pilot boat.

Three days we've been drifting up and down with the tide waiting to get through the entrance. Now we're all tired of looking at the sameness of it all and a few days ago we was sick of looking at the sea and now we're sick of looking at the land.

Mrs Oliver is poorly and not likely to live. Imagine coming all this way and dying before you even landed. She's been sickly all the while and I think she must be dying before she even sets foot on the shore. It made me think of me Mam and I took out the little stone I found at her grave and held it and put it to my cheek and cried a bit when the girls wasn't looking. MaryAnn came down and caught me. She's left me alone these last weeks and now I know why she hasn't been up on deck at all. She is with child. She said she's feeling sick in the mornings and she's looking pale and thin, not like the rest of us. I don't feel sorry for her, it's no more than she deserves. Maybe if she's got a babby she'll not be nagging at me.

Just now the deep-water pilot came aboard and now the captain is shouting out orders and the crew are busy fixing the sails and we're going through the entrance at last. It's very narrow and the waves are conflicting and toss us about something terrible but the wind is strong enough to keep us heading through and we can see the little pilot boat waiting for us inside.

And inside its all calm and pretty and not so dull as I was thinking before, for the sea is a such a pretty green and blue colour and it's all sparkling, and there's white banks at the edges and little huts and some few cattle and such a fine sunny day for us to be landing at last.

Meanwhile, the young men on the ship have been equally restless, coming up on deck to sniff the air, walk about and peer into the darkness whence the soft wind blows. Locked below decks for their own safety, they can hear the Irish girls singing and dancing, a wild excitement in their voices, a jagging rhythm tapped out by their feet, eager in their waiting to dance down the gangplank onto the new land.

A tallow lamp burns dimly in the galley as the cook rattles the stoves and builds the fires to do the last bake of the voyage. For the past hour David has been standing by the ships rail, his face turned into the wind. He has been watching the unfamiliar patterns of the stars, bright and brittle in the southern sky. He turned and spoke to the man next to him.

'Have you noticed the path of that group of stars there? The ones shaped like a kite?' and pointed low to the south.

His companion searched the sky for the shape David had described. 'There?'

'Aye' said David. 'The captain has told me that group forms the Southern Cross and that its bottom star always points south. I've been watching it for the last few nights and it swings around in a great arc as the night passes.'

David tried to accept these foreign stars into himself. To be familiar with them as he was with his home stars, which led him through the dark of night. How would he find his way in the night if he could not recognise these unfamiliar patterns? And that moon, all about the wrong way. He felt both triumphant and fearful, like an explorer. Excitement stirred him as he thought of completing the first step of his journey. His first step into his new life, his first step towards the unknown future, in this strange world full of mystery and potential.

A slight breeze strengthened and with it came an aroma of land. David turned and sniffed again. Such a strong and delicious, spicy scent. It made his head buzz and he leaned into the darkness and drew the scent into himself as if it might give him some knowledge of the land, as he peered into the blackness, seeking some form, some outline to confirm its presence. As if in response to his longing he felt a flutter at his neck and a moth landed on his shoulder. He gently put his hand up and captured this fluttering fragment, this land life, this fragile evidence of the land they could not yet see.

He stayed thus for another hour while all around him two hundred pairs of eyes willed the land to appear.

Suddenly the watch called out 'Cape Otway Light! Port Quarter!' The ship listed a little as all the passengers rushed to the side, delaying the sighting of the light by a minute or two, but soon it could be seen, shining steadily, a small golden gleam just above the horizon, their first light of humanity for ten weeks. A mighty cheer went up from the men on deck and in response the cries of the Irish girls below pierced the air as they screamed their answering delight.

As the sky in the east began its first faint lightening and the Otway Light faded behind them, the land began to shape itself into their peering. Dense, forested hills plunged to the sea's edge, unrelieved by any sign of man or building. Rocky headlands were passed. With each passing, another would appear without break in the impenetrable coastline. Gradually the headlands became smaller and further apart, and white banks began to appear, long pale crescents of sand with sometimes a tiny filament of smoke drifting into the dawn. David went below and fetched his writing box and began a letter to his parents.

> *My Dear Mother and Father,*
> *We can see the land. Everyone aboard is full of excitement, and a little fearful that even so close, we could meet with disaster. The Captain has told us that the narrow passage into Port Phillip is one of the most treacherous he will ever have to negotiate and it is called The Eye of the Needle. However, he has my full confidence for he has brought us through storms and tempests, the fury of which you would hardly believe.*
> *We have sailed by what is called The Great Circle Route. We did not call in at the Cape to reprovision but sailed much further south where the westerlies blow and though it was colder and much more stormy it was faster and therefore cheaper for the ship owners. For us passengers it has been very trying and frightening although it has been but twelve weeks since we left Liverpool instead of twenty or more. It required a captain of considerable courage and good judgement because of the severe weather conditions and the need to aim for Bass Strait. Aiming for this fifty-mile opening from so far south was truly an amazing feat of navigation and Captain Kelly has earned our great respect.*

Today it is the 23rd July, but three months since we left Liverpool and we are within hours of breaking the record for the fastest voyage to Melbourne.

A few minutes ago, one of the sailors sighted the Cape Otway Light and now it is come into sight for us on deck also. I cannot tell you what a welcome sight it is to see some sign of habitation after so long a time upon the sea.

I have kept a diary during the voyage, and a second copy for you, which I shall send with this letter. I hope it will give you some idea of the privations we have had to suffer and the many times when we prayed to God for deliverance.

I have been bold enough to cut for myself a jacket from the linen which you gave me and have three parts finished the stitching. I think it will be suitable for the climate here for even though I am told it is mid winter, the air is moderate.

I trust I shall be able to find William at Richmond. There is a man aboard who told me that Melbourne is growing at an enormous rate and what was true six months ago, may no longer hold. There are said to be many thousands of 'Diggers' heading for the goldfields. Pray William and I are not too late to make some benefit from it.

Many of us will have some sadness on leaving the ship despite the hardships for it is our last link with home and we have made friends amongst the other passengers. I have met a family from Balleyeasborough. Robert McFaden is travelling with his son and four daughters. They have been very kind.

I must conclude now for we are nearing the entrance to Port Phillip and there will be much bustle and busyness for the next day or so. I pray this letter find you both in good health.

Your affectionate son, David.

Three days later the ship still rolled at anchor outside the entrance to Port Phillip Bay. Many times during those three days the Captain had attempted an entrance. The excitement and frustration of the passengers was tangible. For the whole of those three days they have been tantalised by the land winds wafting from the shores and frustrated by their inability to make any progress towards their destination.

Three times David packed his below-decks gear in anticipation of disembarkation only to be frustrated by the insistent northerlies. He thrust his hands into his pockets and strode around the decks a dozen times, telling himself to be patient, to be grateful to have survived thus far, that he was not ill, that his brother awaited his arrival, that he had much to be grateful for. Then resigned himself and went below to spend an hour with the Yorkshireman who lay listless in his hammock.

'How are you feeling George?' David sat on a box at the side of George's hammock and looked at the Yorkshireman's gaunt face.

'Ah, I have no strength in m'limbs David' sighed the stricken George. Nor much in your will either, thought David who told himself he would not have allowed a simple fever to lay him so low.

'Well you must be getting up soon for within a day I believe we will be at Melbourne town.' David briskly got a bucket of water and set about bathing George's head and hands to revive him a little. 'It's not so cold you know. Now that we are in the lee of the land it's warmer and it would refresh you greatly to smell it. It has a sweet spiciness about it I find most attractive and I can see the smoke from many small fires along the shores. But though it's wild, it has a softer look about it than I expected.'

'Be they settlements d'ye think. Those fires? Or natives?'

'Well the scrub is so thick I doubt it's settlers.' David squeezed the water from the cloth, 'More likely natives, for I've seen no sign of buildings.' David found it curious that George could be so brought down by a simple fever and concluded that his usual bluster was a cover for a weak personality. Under the pretext of smoothing George's hair, David probed the contours of his head, feeling for the telltale flatness at the back which denoted a weak character. His suspicions were confirmed by George's unbulging cranium and David gave a small inner nod of satisfaction at his own perspicacity while dabbing the last of the moisture from George's brow.

Later that day the pilot ship finally got them through the narrow heads and into the safety of Port Phillip. As they sailed up the bay the light was crisp and clear and the air sharp. David and the ship both seemed to strain forward, as if she too longed to step upon the land thought David as he quickly scribbled the last entry in his diary. All about him scrambled and jostled together, eager to be first aboard the lighter which would take them ashore. At last it was his turn and he tossed his bag onto his back and climbed down the ladder to the steamer. There were a hundred or so ships at anchor, the sky like a forest with their masts. He had intended to farewell the McFadens but in the crowd and the bustle he lost sight of them. As the boat scraped on the sand he leapt out with his bag on his shoulder and stumbled straight away at the firmness of the sand after so many months at sea. As he waded to the shore his heart swelled in his chest and he fell to his knees.

'Thanks be to Almighty God for our safe deliverance.'

Part 3

PROSPECTS ON LANDFALL

GOLDFIELDS, VICTORIA, JULY 1853 TO 1860

I had never thought that I would be interested in writing history but the engagement is gradual, like a new garden it grows on you until one day you find you have surrounded yourself with a shape and a form and a place. Likewise with family history, suddenly one fine day you find that the curiosity that led you to look into the papers is the lure that pulls you on and on until one day it becomes imperative to write it all down. There is no escape. The old ones inhabit your mind and speak to you, in obscure whispers, of their lives. Of their triumphs and disasters. Of their daily toil, and small pleasures. Your body begins to feel their injuries, their illnesses. You experience their loves, their despair, their joy. I suffered with Maggie in her terrible hours and could hardly bear to write about what happened to her. And experienced too David's boldness and determination and his self inflicted humiliations. At times I was so close to Maggie I felt I might wake in the morning to find myself in the same humble room where she slept, or could feel her strength in my hands as I kneaded the dough in the coldness of the early morning, as she must have done so often.

As the story grows I find that they are writing it for me and in the end, what I put down becomes the real history whether it bears any resemblance to what actually happened or not. And when I compare notes with other history writers, real historians, I find myself telling them what happened to my forebears and suddenly remember that maybe that didn't happen like that at all, that maybe the line between fact and fiction is so blurred that there is neither fiction or reality, just story.

I read everything I can find on the gold rush era. I immerse myself in those times. I visit the places, try to get a feel of the land, the creeks, the towns, the streets, the old buildings. I smell the land and wait for it to rain so I can smell it again. I puzzle over all the odd little things that I find in the chest.

There was that time when I almost discarded all these seemingly disconnected objects, but gradually I began to see that each and every item, no matter how obscure it appeared to me at first, had significance. There was so much. Christmas and greeting cards, beautifully embossed and lettered, some hand painted; postcards by the dozen from all over Victoria.

There was a series of letters from Ireland from a cousin who wrote to one of Maggie's daughters. Her life seemed hardly any better than the life Maggie left behind decades before, but the connection that existed between that sad Irish woman and her cousin in Majorca, who was the only one she could confide in, was deep and durable. Please don't tell anyone what I have told you, she pleaded. I have no one else I can speak to. And across the seas, a friendship was formed and nurtured and lasted for thirty years.

There were albums with photographs of graceful girls in high necked Victorian dresses, their hair also fashionably high. At the front of each album were photographs of the same two people and eventually I realised that these were Maggie and David. What pleasure it gave me to see their faces. To know them. It's as if at last I had visited them, and seen the faces of people who were already friends even though far away, like that distant Irish cousin.

WRITER'S NOTES: Today I went to the State Library of Victoria. As I approached the library I tried to imagine how grand it must have looked when it was opened in 1856. How proud Melbournians must have been then of their fine new library with its splendid dome. It must have dominated the scene. What wonderful aspirations they had in those days.

I went to the newspaper collections and soon I had in front of me a microfiche copy of the Argus Newspaper dated 29th July, 1853, a day or two after the McFadens and Stavers arrived in the colony of Victoria. It is very different from today's papers for there are no pictures, not even any illustrated advertisements. Below the paper's banner are headings such as Shipping News, Arrivals and Departures, Government Reports, Public Notices and many columns of Personal Notices. I find details of the arrival of the Miles Barton, but what I am looking for is some message from Will Stavers to contact his brother. I read many of these personal notices and am moved by the desperation in some, such as the plea for John Brown to 'please meet with your wife Aggie as soon as possible as I am desperate for money.' Poor Aggie. There are horses for sale as well as every desirable item from the simplest of foods to a whole house. There are warehouses advertising everything from sardines to ships anchors. I can see the McFadens, feeling strange and a little afraid in this new land, huddled together as they scanned this very edition of the paper, seeking a place to live. But I find no message from Will Stavers in this copy of the Argus, or any other copy published during that week.

Scrap of newspaper, with a few other notes and fragments. It is a small advertisement. The ad has been marked with a pen stroke. It is only one of many columns of similar pleas. It reads:

> DAVID STAVERS. Will any ship mates of this gentleman, please tell him to go to the Golden Age Hotel where he will receive news of his brother William.

So there *was* an ad! I wonder how long it was before David found it. I've read that in 1853, with so many immigrants flooding in every week, the new colony was stretched to the limit to provide basic services such as mail and roads. People depended much more on word of mouth and of course newspapers, to contact those they had lost touch with. I can imagine how bewildering it must have been, trying to find a particular hotel when all you had to go on was a name, when there were no street maps, and probably not even any street signs. And Melbourne must have had hundreds of hotels then.

Leather letter-folder, which opens out to show compartments for letters, envelopes and stamps. It is black on the outside and the inner parts are fine buff leather or kid. In the very back I find, folded away a brief note: To Whom It May Concern: Maggie McFaden and her sisters Susannah and Lizzie have been in my employment for two years. They are good workers and of sober habits. It is signed B. Tarleton, Plenty, and is dated December, 1855. This is the first indication I have found of what happened to Maggie and her sisters after they left the ship. What could it have been like at that time, before trains and phones and electricity? Before decent roads too, probably. How isolated they must have been. Letters their only means of communication over distances. If Maggie couldn't write, how did the family keep in touch when they found themselves separated by circumstance?

Leather holster, found pressed flat between a leather bound bible and a photograph album. When I examine it I find it is hand stitched and unlike most holsters I have seen, the sleeve where the barrel slides in is closed off at the end with a small round piece stitched in. There are two vertical slots near the top for the holster to be threaded onto a belt. As I handle it I reminds me that my father often told me that his grandfather was a gold escort at one time and that a revolver was presented to him in connection with this. I wish I had listened more closely to my father, that I had asked him more questions.

Note, written I believe from the handwriting, by David's daughter, Emma . . . Cryptic as always, she says only 'Father and Uncle William mined for gold at Amherst, Back Creek (Talbot) and Pleasant Creek.(Stawell). Then later had a tent store selling picks and shovels.' How I wish she had written more. It's very frus-

trating. Since I have become captured by this history I have often wondered why she did not record more about her parents and their early experiences. She was an educated and intelligent woman who must have been aware of the historic significance of their lives.

Pair of pottery boots! They are about the size of a baby's bootee (the pair fits easily on my hand) and each little boot has a rose on the front. They are made of pottery of a mossy colour and are roughly textured as if some kind of beach grit has been placed on the surface before firing. Apart from the rose they look a lot like the illustrations I have seen of 'pampooties', the traditional Irish shoe made from a rough circle of hide, gathered much as moccasins are, and with three holes on each side of the opening for lacing, but having no tongue. An Irish friend has told me that the pottery is a type unique to some part of Ireland, but she doesn't know where unfortunately. I'd really like to know more about these - their lack of identifying marks and rather rough style and appearance make them seem either very old or of a particular tradition. They make me wonder whether Maggie even had boots at all.

Miner's Right, this made me stop and look! This small sheet in the form of a certificate is about half A4 size. It has an elaborate heading typical of the mid 1800s, all swirls and curlicues. Written across the top is COLONY OF VICTORIA, and below that the rampant Lion and Unicorn stand on either side of an oval picture of, I presume, Queen Victoria with a supplicant miner on each side of her. Or maybe it is Britannia. The Queen figure is holding what looks like a large twist of fleece in each hand and behind the figures of the miners, ears of corn sprout forth abundant heads of grain. The certificate was issued in the county of Talbot and is dated September 1853 so David must have obtained it not long after he left Melbourne. It is issued to D.Stavers and was current for one month, for the sum of thirty shillings. Across the bottom is written in bold letters NOT TRANSFERABLE.

Boomerang, elbow shaped. I can see that the branch it was carved from was chosen very carefully as the grain follows its elbow shaped form, with one arm longer than the other. It is very finely carved and decorated with lines and dots. It feels beautifully balanced and when I hold it back over my shoulder I almost know how to throw it. By the feel of it I'm sure it would throw well if only I knew someone who was able to do it properly. This piece feels very old. The timber is heavy and dark and has a light sheen on it as if it has been much rubbed with oil. How did it come to be in the chest?

Revolver and powder flask, in rosewood case. Best pieces in the collection so far. Here is hard, heavy evidence of lawless days and desperate people. Its official description reads: 'Samuel Colt's Pocket Revolver is known to collectors as the Model of 1849. It is a single action pistol in .31' calibre. This Model was made in barrel lengths of 3in, 4in, 5in, and 6 in., usually as a five shot weapon. Particularly suitable for horsemen as it was designed to be holstered.'

To my surprise it fits my hand snugly which makes me think that men's hands must have been smaller in those days, in spite of historic heroes. It is however, a little too heavy for me and its six inch barrel points rather dejectedly down when I hold it. It is such a complex piece of machinery - the trigger curved and elegant, the barrel with its five chambers, the smoothly articulated rammer.

When I heft it, it feels great, heavy but balanced, the handle smooth, the steel parts cool, and as I walk about with it in my hand, it is difficult to remind myself that it is a killing machine. A killing machine with a finely engraved scene on the cylinder of wagons and horses and men, reminiscent of the Wild West.

The powder flask is made of steel and brass. Its pouched shape also fits my hand. It has a brass band around the neck with a little brass lever fashioned to fit the finger, and from the top a tube emerges from which the dry powder would have been shaken. There is a wonderful fineness in its manufacture. The finish is impeccable. Tiny screws hardly bigger than a pinhead secure the brass band at the top and embossed on the pouched sides, are American eagles with wings spread.

I hold the pouch in my left hand, the revolver in my right and think of my great grandfather whose sons were gentle men, and how I had always imagined the gun as inactive in its velvet lined case. But then I look more closely and find, with a small shock, that it is polished and worn around the trigger.

Mirror, oval, frame carved from a single piece of timber, native cedar perhaps, smoothly curved with small decorative insets of mother of pearl on either side of the handle. Inlaid strips of light and dark elegantly frame the glass. Someone has spent many hours engraving the back with a design of intertwining vines and leaves. At first I did not notice, but then I became aware that twined amongst the leaves and vines are the words 'I love Maggie'. How I long to know who wrote those words.

I look at my reflection in the mirror, at hints of my father's face in my own heavy brows. If only I could look back through the generations and see all the faces that have looked into this mirror. Maggie brushing her long dark hair, David combing his beard, or perhaps a child dreamily looking into the glass at the world reflected in a dust moted gleam of light from the window. If it could tell me what it has seen, what smiles, what anticipations. How often did Maggie hold this mirror to her face? I lay it gently down on my dressing table, where each time I pick it up, I pick up the past, in its weight, its smoothness, its scent of wood, its modest decorations and its memories.

Carte de Visite, one of those cards used in the 1860s as a calling card. It shows a photograph of a woman aged about forty I suppose, with an open, pleasant face and slightly wistful expression. She is plump, but well dressed in a black, high necked gown which is made from what looks like taffeta. It is tucked and ribboned on the bodice and fits well. She stands slightly side on and looks across her shoulder to the viewer. One hand rests on the back of a rustic chair and behind her, some drapery has been hung to create a background. On the back of the card is written 'Mrs Armand, the first woman David Stavers met on the goldfields' And below that, in different writing as if it has been added later, 'Jones Creek'.

This photo could not have been taken at the time David and William were at the Jones Creek because there were no photographic studios at the diggings when they were first there. But it does place them in time, because the Jones Creek rush was in late 1853. Perhaps the photo was taken later. All I must do now is find out where Jones Creek is and what happened to them while they were there.

Tiny letter, it fits into the palm of my hand. It has no stamp, just Jack Weir, C/- D. and W. Stavers, Jones Creek. (Waanyarra) I read it and find it is from Jack's mother in Ireland. She pleads with him to return home, that she and his father have more than enough worldly goods to share with him, that the goldfields are dangerous and they would give anything to have him back. My heart goes out to her in her longing to have her son home again. I can almost hear the fiery words which must have precipitated Jack's furious departure and his determination to make his own way in Australia, against his parents' better judgement.

Mails in the early days of the gold rush were very uncertain. A moving population of fifty thousand diggers, many without well developed writing skills, did not make any easier the task of those who were attempting to deliver. In the absence of proper post offices, bags of letters were simply left with whoever was available at the time. This little letter had crossed the hazardous seas, then the even more hazardous miles from Melbourne to Jones Creek but the last few hundred metres were the most hazardous of all.

Notes about Eureka Stockade. There are several scraps of papers mentioning such things as 'Father gathered signatures,' or 'Father was at Eureka Stockade', but without any additional hints or information. I have checked early records to find any mention of his name, but without success. But this does not convince me. Aunt Emma had told me he declined to have his name on the Pioneer Register because he did not consider himself a real pioneer! So it is quite likely he did not consider registering his name for the Eureka Stockade either.

Map of the main street of Pleasant Creek. Across the top is written:
'Names on blocks are of the original occupants of the buildings. The buildings shown in black are of wood.' Both the scale of street outlay and the printing are tiny and I must use a magnifying glass to read them. The page has been folded and is torn and indistinct at the fold so that some details are missing. Of the approximately three hundred named blocks about ten percent seem to be general stores. There are lots of hotels and ironmongers, the usual sprinkling of solicitors, chemists, auctioneers, photographers, bakers, saddlers, blacksmiths, drapers,

banks, newsagents, brewers, hairdressers and a scattering of schools, churches and banks. It gives such a lively picture of life at that time.

Right in the middle, just above the frayed part, I find D. & W. Stavers (General Store) and since the building is shown in outline only, I know it was a canvas structure. I have been to the town and walked the path where this canvas store stood, and breathed the air of the town. On the site where David and Will carried on their first permanent business there now stands a double fronted store, built in 1859. It is a graceful building with wide front windows and a recessed doorway. It happens to be occupied by the local Historical Society so that its contents are sympathetic to bygone days and retain an atmosphere of the past. The town's historical records were destroyed in a fire in the 1850s so I cannot check the name of the builder, but something tells me that this is the very store that David and Will built.

Lovely, simple gold locket, quite unadorned. It is a perfect, flat oval, and relies upon its simple form and the quality of the precious metal for its beauty. It is a particularly lovely soft pinkish gold colour. Its surface is slightly dented here and there, as if it has been much worn. It is hinged so that it opens out into two separate frames and there is a curl of hair in each frame, one black and one brown. It must have been in the chest for over one hundred years yet its lustre is undimmed. I wondered who wore this locket? And I wondered too, whence came the beautiful golden pink colour? Was this alluvial gold, washed from the edge of a stream, or auriferous gold, dug with every pick stroke from the unwilling earth?

PLENTY - 1853-1860

Maggie and her sisters scrambled one after another down the ladder into the lighter, skirts flying, while the sailors tried to hold the boat steady in the choppy sea. Maggie stretched to look over the sailors heads towards the shore and, impatient to see, attempted to stand in the heaving boat.

'Siddown miss, you'll have us all capsized.'

She blushed and sat down quickly but still fidgeted and stretched to see the mysterious shores beyond the straining shoulders of the sailors, and the hundreds of ships that had arrived before them. Spray from the dipping oars flew across their faces and quickly drenched them but the boat soon settled into a steady progress as the men pulled strongly, singing with each stroke 'So now we're bound . . . for Melbourne town . . . beware young girls . . . of thieves and churls . . . who'll steal you all awa-ay.'

'What do they mean Maggie?'

Maggie hardly knew herself but said 'Don't pay no heed to them Susie. We'll meet our Da on the shore. He'll take care of us.'

Maggie was bursting with curiosity. There was so much to see - the bay full of ships, the disappointingly barren landscape of the port, the crowds of people. At the far end of the beach, a group of natives with fur capes about their shoulders were huddled round a small fire.

Her fears of the ship now gave way to a different set of fears. Here were strangers, black people hardly more than savages from what she had heard. And a crowd which seemed to be made up almost entirely of men with here and there a few hags screeching at each other.

The boat crunched up on the sand and in their turn, the girls tumbled out into the shallows and waded ashore with their bundles. Maggie's feet stepped on air as she stumbled behind her sisters, shepherding them away from the waters edge.

'Maggie! The ground's so hard, it keeps comin' up to meet me! Me legs is all wobbly!' Lizzie was staggering and stumbling. About half the passengers were already disembarked and a scatter of boxes and baskets littered the whole length of Sandridge beach. Rough looking men touted for business.

'Come on me Pet Lambs' Maggie urged them along the beach, past the ruffians, relieved to see a familiar face nearby.

'Mrs Thomas, have you seen me Da anywhere, at all?'

'I think he's down there by that green wagon Maggie. Good Luck my girl, I hope I'll be seein' you in Melbourne town. You be lookin' after those sisters of yours now. Goodbye!'

'Goodbye Mrs Thomas. Thank you for bein' so kind to us. I was altogether lonely in those first days out of Liverpool, missin' me Mam an' all that.'

'You'll be alright Maggie, just you be keepin' cheerful now. Goodbye dearie.'

Maggie and the girls struggled along the beach with their bundles, saying their goodbyes as they passed each family group. Maggie looked for David Stavers but could not see him in the moil. She wondered how all these people and all these goods could possibly have fitted on the ship.

At last, at the same moment, she saw both David and her father, and with uncharacteristic guile, sent the girls on to their Da. 'Good mornin' Mr Stavers. 'Tis a pretty mornin' to be landin' in Australia, though the wind's a mite cold.' Maggie's wet skirts were flapping round her ankles and the water squelched in her boots.

'Why, good morning Miss McFaden. It is a great relief to be here at last. And where will you be lodging? Do you have someone to meet you and give you some guidance?'

'Me Da'll manage. We'll find somewhere. Will you be goin' to the goldfields at all?'

'In a while. I must find my brother first. Or hope that he finds me!'

Maggie was holding her shawl as the wind tried to take it from her shoulders. 'I hope you find gold, Mr Stavers. An' that we do too. I don't suppose it's much diff'rent diggin' for gold than it is diggin' for praties! Me brother and me Da'll be goin' soon enough.'

'I hope we may meet again Miss McFaden, and that you and your sisters may find employment quickly. I hear domestic service is much in demand, so perhaps it will go well for you. I hope it will be so. I wish you good luck.' And he gave a little bow to her. In her self-consciousness, Maggie bobbed down, said a hurried 'Good luck to you too Mr Stavers!' and holding her bedraggled skirt at her sides, she ran towards her family. With her face hot and flushed she turned at the last moment to wave and flash him a smile. Then raged at herself for behaving like a servant, even if I am to become one, she said to herself.

'A shillin' for you and your box to Melbourne!' a man with a cart called out as Maggie rejoined her family.

'A shilling? Each?'

'Ninepence each here! And I'll 'ave you there in 'alf the time!'

Da negotiated the last places on an already overloaded wagon, and calculated in his mind the profit the driver would be making for just one trip. ''Tis no less than highway robbery!'

'Five shillin's for the seven of yeh then. Them twos only as big as one.' They all climbed aboard the wagon and found themselves a place to sit and began rocking their way into Melbourne over the muddied and rutted roads.

Maggie sat on top of the parcels and packages at the back of the wagon with her feet dangling. She looked back, seeking one last glimpse of the Miles Barton. Her heart contracted when she could not pick it out from the masts and rigging of the hundreds of other ships riding at anchor in the bay. And Maggie huddled down, feeling like a crab without a shell. Me last link with home, she thought, and I can't catch no sight of it at all.

All around her was outlandish. The air, the sun, the colour of the land, the small straggling bushes, everything was strange and different, even the voices all babbling and gabbering. So many ships she thought, it's no wonder there's so many people here. Every one of them ships has spilled its load of people just like me. Where are they all going? Where are we going? I don't much like those rough looking men. And there's mud everywhere. I thought the streets was paved with gold. I haven't seen no gold paving. I haven't even seen no streets, never mind gold paving. There's no real trees, and no hills, and no green. Just mud, and people and tents and horses and carts and noise. What has me Da done? I think I'd rather be safe and hungry at me home back in Ireland than here. Even if we have had enough to eat these last three months, I didn't think it would be like this, so grey and bare and ugly, without even the shelter of a tree. There's a house at last! At least it's looking like it might be a house when they've finished building it.

'Look Da, they're buildin' a house without a scrap of a stone in sight. What do you think they're building it with Da?'

'It looks like iron. Big iron sheets, the driver says. Bolted together and then a roof put on. Amazin'!'

'I don't think it's amazin', I think its ugly. There's no stone to build walls and cots. Not like at home in Ireland. And not a tree in sight at all, at all.'

Hugh McFaden bit his bottom lip and ran his stubby finger down the advertisements in the Argus and carefully drew a line below one with his pencil.

'Here's one Da.' He read out slowly 'A one roomed cottage, furnished or unfurnished, at Colling Wood, opposite Rising Sun Hotel. They don't say the rent. Can't be more'n two shillin', or more'n a mile or two. I'll walk up straight and try my luck, and I'll look for anythin' else on the way back if that one's gone.'

Robert McFaden panted and dug reluctantly in his pocket for one of their last few shillings in the world and eyed Hugh, 'Mind yeh're not cheated.'

'The wagoner said to make sure to get a place with a water-butt if there's no water close by,' Maggie could see herself and her sisters lugging bucketsful, 'and a privvy, Hugh!' she called to his retreating back.

'Lord save us Maggie, we won't be gettin' a palace!' Hugh pocketed the precious shillings. 'But I'm hopin' to better this place!'

Robert McFaden and his daughters sat by the roadside and waited for Hugh to return. They were accustomed to sitting on the earth but it was difficult to find a place that was not mired in mud and impossible to escape the stench of the streets. James and MaryAnn strolled arm in arm over the bridge, unaware of the others, in their own world.

They had all slept poorly the previous night in a scrofulous hotel where Robert, Hugh and James had shared a room with boozing, snoring companions. Beds were so hard to get that MaryAnn, Maggie, Lizzie and Susannah had been forced to sleep in with the landlord's woman. They had huddled together in a tumble of ragged blankets, kept awake all night by the sounds of men fighting, bursts of gunfire and dogs barking, not to mention the thuds and groans from the adjoining bedrooms.

'It's the worst night I've ever spent in me life.' Susannah said as they prepared to leave in the morning. 'A rat ran through me hair!'

'And the mice was nibblin' me toes.' Lizzie joined in.

'Did you hear that woman screamin? I thought she was bein' murdered!' Maggie scratched behind her knees and exclaimed 'Ugh, and there's bugs too!'

Hugh was outraged when he returned an hour later. 'They're askin' fifteen shillin's a week for no more than a hut. I think we'll have to try across the river Da. Maybe we can get something there.'

They finally found accommodation in canvas town at South Melbourne where they muddled around in their tent, with water seeping in through the walls and under their feet, in the wettest winter anyone could remember. Before leaving for the goldfields, Robert knew he and Hugh must earn enough money to buy tools and provisions. Nor could he go to the goldfields with an easy mind unless his daughters were settled.

James and MaryAnn were first to find a place to go. James had a cousin at Bunninyong with whom they could stay until they found something for themselves.

From the Argus Robert had read out to Maggie. 'Wanted, Girl about 16 or 17 to care for two children and make herself useful. Apply Mrs Tarleton, at the Lions Head Public House, Smith Street

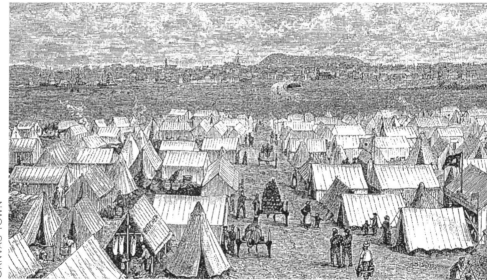

CANVAS TOWN

Collingwood. That one sounds all right, Maggie. But you must ask Mrs Tarleton if Susannah and Lizzie can come with you.'

Maggie had stood up straight and minded her manners when she had gone to meet Mrs Tarleton, who seemed very tall, and did not look at Maggie when she spoke.

When Maggie said she could not read or write Mrs Tarleton muttered 'An unlettered girl! Really! Well I don't suppose I can expect any better. This is a most peculiar situation to be in. When most people cannot get a good girl at any price, I am in the curious position of having to take three! I shall pay for only two, since your sisters are so young. I expect they can make themselves useful, looking after the children.' Mrs Tarleton paused and looked up. 'As well as looking after Bertrand and Horace, I shall expect you to do all the washing, cleaning and cooking. You must bake bread every day - I can't abide stale bread - and since there are three of you, I will expect you to do the milking and make the butter, as well as look after the kitchen garden, the chickens and any other tasks necessary to run the household.'

'Beggin' your pardon Mrs Tarleton. We've never made butter afore.'

Mrs Tarleton sighed. 'Well I suppose I shall have to show you myself. You know how to milk a cow I hope? And weed the garden?'

'Oh yes Ma'am.' Maggie lied a little; having seen a cow milked often enough but not had her hands on an udder.

'If I am to take all three of you then you will have to sleep in the kitchen. I shall pay you and Susannah 10/- each per week, payable at the end of the year and I will provide your food.'

'We's all good workers even though Lizzie's only nine Mrs.'

'*Mrs Tarleton*, if you please. I shall be leaving for Plenty at 10 of the clock tomorrow, Miss McFaden.'

'Beggin' your pardon Mrs Tarleton. For plenty of what?'

With a pained expression Mrs Tarleton explained 'Plenty is the name of our homestead on the Yarra Yarra,' obviously exasperated by Maggie's ignorance. 'It's about 30 miles from Melbourne. I shall expect you and your sisters to be ready to leave at that time.' Mrs Tarleton glanced down at Maggie's bare and battered feet then took several coins from her purse. 'Here are your first week's wages in advance. Please buy yourselves decent skirts and a pair of boots each.' And with these words Mrs Tarleton dismissed Maggie and left the room.

Maggie held the coins tightly in her hand. She could hardly believe that they would be earning 10/- a week. It seemed like a small fortune. When she got back to the tent she said, 'Da. Mrs Tarleton gave me a pound to buy boots and skirts for all three of us!' When Maggie told her Da that Mrs Tarleton had also said they could all work for her, he nodded in satisfaction. 'Then she's a decent enough woman. What other family is there?'

'She said Mr Tarleton's gone to England and her cousin Mr Wesley will be stayin' at Plenty until he returns. I'm glad Susannah and Lizzie are comin' for I don't think I'd be managin' those boys too well without them. But Da, where is Plenty? And how will I know where you are?'

'I'll have to be askin' about to find out where Plenty is. And as soon as ever Hugh and I are settled I'll be sendin' a message to yeh.'

It was two months since David's arrival at the Port of Melbourne and each morning since then, he had woken wondering what new experience the day would bring. After the confinement and restriction of the ship, Melbourne was a cauldron of activity. Everyone in haste; shouting, carrying, travelling, building. It had taken him days to adjust, not only to the firmness of being on land after the motion of the ship, but to the noise, the activity and the sheer numbers of people everywhere. He could never have imagined so many people all in one place. And everyone in a hurry. Not at all like Ireland where people stopped and greeted each other in a civilised manner.

David and Will had not seen each other for five years and David barely recognised his brother. In spite of ruddy cheeks and a sense of well-being, David felt somewhat puny beside his older brother. 'You've put on some muscle then.'

'Ay, well I've been digging these past months - that soon shows a man how to work.' Will remarked wryly. 'A man's no good here if he can't work. Come, let's share a pint.'

'I don't touch liquor, Will.'

'Bit of a namby pamby eh? We'll soon knock that out of you.'

David was lucky enough to get work with Carson's Boot and Shoe Store almost straight away. The wages were good, almost thirty shillings a week and he was able to save most of that by sharing Will's room at Mrs Starling's boarding house.

By the end of August he had accumulated enough money to buy a horse and a saddle and some few basic tools. David had never ridden a horse before he reached Port Phillip. As soon as he arrived Will had insisted it was the first thing he must learn. He was a strict and impatient teacher and whatever nervousness David may have felt had to be concealed in spite of the falls and the bruises he endured in those first days. After two weeks Will selected a gelding for him and advised him to ride at least ten miles a day in preparation for the long ride that lay before him. Once Will felt David was competent enough on horseback he had departed for the goldfields ahead of David to secure a wagon, well past the bogs and morass immediately north of Melbourne town.

Will's words before he departed hadn't done much to ease David's apprehensions about travelling alone in the bush.

'I'll be waitin' at the Digger's Rest; that's two, maybe three days ride.' Will had cinched his horse's girth and quickly mounted his lively little mare.

David had held her bridle for a few more moments, reluctant to let his brother go. 'How will I know the track?'

'You'll be safe if you start out in the afternoon on the Mt Alexander Road. Just follow the mob north west.' David reminded himself that as he walked north the sun would be shining into his face, not warming his back as it did at home in Ireland. Will's voice came back into his consciousness. 'The Keilor Plains can be boggy after rain so watch out. Don't be stoppin' to help every johnny who's got his wagon down to its axles or you'll never arrive. Try to camp alone, keep a look out and don't trust anyone.' Will had wheeled away then and called back over his shoulder, 'You should be managin' alright but likely we'll be needin' each other's company afore we go through the Black Forest. There's many a bushranger there. Just waitin' to kit himself out with new gear.' This was more than his older brother had said to him in the last two months and after watching Will gallop off into the distance, David had spent some hours digesting his words.

On the first of September, the first day of spring, David was on his way to the goldfields at last. He turned the words over in his mind. Goldfields. He envisioned fields of golden grasses spreading to the horizon. Silvered streams with golden pebbles gleaming beneath the surface. Glittering fragments flashing their golden light from amongst gravel at the water's edge.

As he rode through intermittent gusts of wind and rain towards Castlemaine, he found it difficult to match his vivid images to the mud smeared, work-weary men he rode past. They glanced at him with red-rimmed eyes as they trudged along their way back to Melbourne. They did not look like men on whom luck had smiled and the sight of their sagging shoulders weighed heavily on David's buoyant mood.

There were others of course, who rode past on fine horses with polished bridles. Or sat in coaches with ladies of fine dress (but dubious reputation) leaning back and taking their leisure while the driver pushed the horses along and the coach rocked and bucketed over the ruts.

The muscles in David's back and legs still protested as he rode out on his long ride and it took several hours for his limbs to loosen up. Late in the afternoon, following Will's advice, he had gradually angled away until he was separated from the other hopefuls pushing their barrows towards their cup of gold. He dismounted stiffly, his knees barely able to function. Uneasily, acutely aware of his solitary state, he tethered his horse to a tree and unsaddled him. He

ate sparingly and using his saddle for a pillow spent a fearful night filled with the strange rustlings and unfamiliar sounds of unknown creatures slithering and creeping through the darkness.

He rose long before dawn and after eating some bread and cheese approached what he thought must be the Keilor Plains Will had told him about. As he trotted along in the cool grey of a light misty rain, as far as he could see before him, was a vast marshland filled with struggling men and horses. To David it looked as he might have imagined a battlefield. He saw hundreds of wagons and carts, mired in mud. As men heaved and flogged and struggled and swore in their efforts to move their wagons and carts forward a few feet, David felt himself to be an observer in the nightmare of a vast and endless battle. A flock of white birds flew screeching overhead, and then wheeled away, their wing beats flickering in the pale sunlight.

He picked his way where the wheeled vehicles could not go, grateful for Will's foresight in riding ahead to buy a cart some days further up country. Beyond the mud. Even so, there were times when his horse sank deep in the bog, and was forced to lunge end-lessly through the sucking morass. At these times, when they reached slightly higher ground, both blowing hard and sweating with effort, David was obliged to halt and rest both the horse and himself for a time.

85

He looked about at the dun coloured landscape with distaste, at its treeless monotony of mud and rank grasses. The sun was harsh in his eyes. They said it was spring, yet to David's eyes everything was the same dull green. No flowers sprang from the winter bare earth, no lark sang, nor any blackbird, and the ragged trees still carried their winter burden of leaves without any sign of fresh new growth.

As he rode, his thoughts returned to Ireland. To his own green land, and its mountains sweeping in a green spill down to the lake. And in its still and mirrored surface a reflection of every mountain, every tree, every detail doubled so perfectly he could hardly tell one from the other. And recalled how as a boy he had imagined himself a bird, and had flown, wing tip to wing tip with his reflection, into the world beyond his imaginings. He had not thought the other side of the world would be so unlovely.

He longed for an Irish spring, with winter's coldness still in the air, mist rising from the lake in the morning, bare trees veiled with softest green, and sappy leaves pushing through the peaty earth. Green against peat; tender, unfurling buds folding out in the thin sun. His spade cutting through the earth, its moist, rich odour in his nostrils.

He thought of his sisters and their teasing laughter, the kirk and the oak tree where Eliza stood when he last saw her. He could still see his home growing smaller and smaller as the coach drew away and he looked back from its window. It seemed now as if he looked back upon the pages of a book and saw this picture of his family and his home in Ireland. His father at his loom, humming a rhythm to the clickety clack of his shuttle hurtling to and fro. His mother in the soft light of evening, as she greeted him when he came home, the kettle clicking on the fire, the smell of bread and soup. The rushes on the floor. The skittering of mice at night in the roof. His trundle where he dreamed the wondrous dreams of a boy. His mother, still and cold in her chair.

David woke from his reverie with a shudder and dismissed the thought. But it stayed there, like a small piece of ice at the back of his mind. To distract himself he resolved to attempt a pot of soup when he and Will were settled on the goldfields, it would be good to have such a homely meal as a change from boiled mutton.

David rode on, skirting the worst of the morass and drifting further and further from the main track. His legs were chafed and blood was beginning to ooze into his boots. He tore some strips from the bottom of his shirt and bound his calves then remounted painfully, regretting that he was not more hardened to riding.

After several hours he could see ahead a fringe of trees. At first he thought he was dreaming again for they were clothed in golden light. Was this the gold field they spoke of? As he drew closer he saw they were flowers. Golden flowers. Trees covered in tiny golden globes. Bunches and branches and millions of golden globes. He stopped beneath one of these trees and shook a branch. A shower of gold cascaded down around his shoulders and the most beautiful soft perfume surrounded him. He laughed and again shook the branch and tiny stamens showered into his hair and his beard and floated softly on his skin bathing him in their lightness.

He rode on and came to places where wildflowers bloomed in purple profusion. Where creepers spiralled around tree trunks, pushing tendrils behind the bark as it dried, and bushes with red flowers like curled grubs sprawled across his track. As he picked his way amongst the honeyed blooms, flowers of enamel yellow, cream and pink, mauve and white tumbled all about. His horse's hooves crushed blue orchids. All day long he rode through this garden, drunk on the perfume of an Antipodean spring. At the end of the day he lay down, no longer afraid, and fell into a deep and dreamless sleep.

At first faint glimmerings of light, David woke to the sound of a thousand squeaking windmills, marching across the landscape like some otherworldly army. As the myriad skreikings tore at his sleep like metal on metal, the crescendo of sound drew nearer. He opened his eyes and sat up, alarmed again at what new torment this terrifying country might be sending him.

Gradually the sound materialised into a cloud of pink and grey birds, wheeling and swooping above him, in a vision of sound, shrieking and screeching, wheeling and changing colour, until they settled squabbling on the branches of a dead tree, clothing it in a mass of pink, chattering blossoms.

David's heartbeat slowed to its normal rhythm. He sat up and leaned against the tree trunk and watched bemused, as the birds swung and tumbled from the dead branches, still screeching like demented spirits. He could not reconcile the pink and grey beauty of these birds with their harsh and strident cries. They did not behave like the birds at home. They seemed more like wild children at play. So noisy, so abandoned. He lay back and watched the birds scream at their mates, swing from a twig by one foot, or hang upside down with their wings outstretched like so many tattered rags, their breasts like pink flesh, warm, in the sunrise.

Mrs Tarleton insisted that Maggie set out the dishes in a most particular way, and the bread be baked just so, and the cow milked and the vegetables kept in rows, and the weeds not allowed. And breakfast always at eight o'clock, and young masters, Bertrand and Horace have their faces washed and their beds made, and their bums smacked, thought Maggie as she gathered the dishes and carried them out.

The three girls had laughed and struggled and finally learned, with a bit of help from Mr Wesley, to bail the cow and coax the milk from her. Susannah and Lizzie set the cream in dishes in the rough little kitchen away from the main house then poured the whey from it and churned it in the wooden butter churn, taking turns, one holding the churn, the other at the handle. They turned and turned until the butter separated from the milk, then washed it, and salted it, and patted it into blocks.

'I don't mind so much makin' the butter,' said Susannah, 'even though the handle is hard to turn, it's the cleanin' of the churn after, that takes so long. All that scrubbin' and rinsin' and scrubbin' and rinsin'. Even a speck of cream left behind will turn the next lot.'

'But Susie, don't you just love butter on your bread and potatoes? It's just the best thing.' Lizzie ran her fingers round the inside of the churn and licked them. 'We never had no butter at home.'

Every day they carried water from the river, for washing, cleaning, cooking and drinking. Lizzie mostly carried the water, two wooden buckets hanging from a yoke over her thin shoulders, up and down to the river, a dozen times a day, while the boys followed behind. She hated washing day. Up the slope she would stagger with washing water, and starching water, and rinsing water while Maggie and Susannah stood beside the tubs, sleeves rolled up, and scrubbed and washed and rinsed. At last at the end of the day when all the sheets and towels and petticoats and shirts were hung over shrubs and branches, well away from the main house, so Mrs Tarleton didn't have to see them, she would fall into her rough cot and be asleep in a minute, often without her supper. And since it was also her job to feed the chickens, they too often went hungry on washing day.

When Maggie wasn't cooking, she scrubbed and cleaned and polished, while Susannah mostly worked in the kitchen garden, weeding and digging, pruning and raking up the leaves and tried to look after the boys. All three girls sang as they worked and Mrs Tarleton's tight heart was unbound by the sound of their singing.

There was the cow to be milked twice a day, preserves to be made, and jams, and pork to be salted, and bread sometimes twice a day when there were visitors. That was the chore that Maggie most enjoyed. Mixing the flour and water into a smooth ball, kneading it in the soft glow of the fire - the firm push of her arms, the soft pliability of the dough as it warmed in her hands. She would set it aside in the bowl, covered by a cloth, and the next morning before her sisters were awake, she would take the bread from its place and punch it down. Maggie hummed as she worked, pulling the dough towards her, pushing it away, until it warmed and softened again, and squeaked like a living thing beneath her small, strong hands. Then she would mould it into loaves and taking her sharpest knife and, to keep the devil away, with a little shudder she would slit the doughy flesh across the top before taking it out to rise in the morning sun.

Mrs Tarleton, in spite of their isolation, demanded a high standard in all things, particularly in caring for Horace and Bertrand. Three for the price of one, Maggie had said that first day right enough, but for all that, they were glad to have a place to sleep and enough to eat and a mistress who was not too harsh.

Maggie longed to tell Sarah of her new life and how Da and Hugh had gone to the goldfields and that they heard nothing from them even though Da had said he would send a message. To tell her that the work was not as bad as working in the fields at home and that even though it was not so cold and the sun was often shining, it was strange and lonely without a bit of family.

Maggie did not much like Plenty. The trees crowded in around the house in a way that was wild and frightening, like a dark wall beyond which the strange noises of the night sounded. Maggie feared the ghosts and goblins, which might lurk in those dark shadows. She did not like the way the towering trees kept out the sun nor the cold shadows that came so early. And there were times when bands of natives wandered through the nearby bush and Maggie's hair would rise on the back of her neck when she could feel their eyes upon her.

One day Horace and Bertrand came to Maggie and urged her to follow them down to the river. A family of natives were there, laughing and playing in the water. The boys had been drawn by simple curiosity but Maggie hung back, afraid of their strangeness, their wildness. But as she watched from behind a screen of trees, the image of that dark family fixed itself in her mind. Never in her life before had she seen such freedom. They frolicked in the water, splashing and diving, their bodies lean and glistening in the sunlight. Parents and children together, all playing. Maggie longed to experience their innocence, their joy. But they were so strange. So black, so naked. And still the fear lingered in her.

As the months passed, Maggie watched Mr Wesley chopping down the trees, heard the sound of his axe ringing, saw his hands blistered at the end of every day, but saw little progress for all his work. Sometimes it took him three days to fall just one tree and when it came crashing down, for a time, there was a little more light but it seemed to Maggie the bush soon crowded the gap again as if it could not bear an emptiness and grew all the faster to fill it. After Mr Wesley had felled a tree he sawed it into different lengths, some for fencing and some for building, and it was Maggie's task to split the shorter lengths for the kitchen and house fires. As she swung the axe and the wood split clean, she felt strong and was glad enough to keep warm twice.

There was one tree, which to Maggie looked like a giant fern. She stood in its lacy shadow and wondered at its green fists pushing into the spring sky like a crown at the centre and watched the birds pull strands for their nests from its hairy trunk. She fancied it as a giant parasol and in her mind as she knelt and polished the floors, she worked out the patterns of the bobbins she would use to make a piece of lace just like the giant fern with its spreading green ribs and curled fronds.

All three girls slept in the kitchen. It was a small hut separate from the main house and was now their home. Mr Wesley had hammered forked sticks into the earthen floor of the hut, then laid long, straight branches from one end to the other, and large sheets of bark on top to make a tolerable bed for each of them where beetles and spiders and snakes could not easily reach them. Maggie was terrified of snakes. Every rustle in the grass or the wood heap threw her into a trembling fit of fear that she did her best to conceal but which transmitted itself to her sisters and the children.

It was a special day. Maggie had to make extra bread because today Mrs Tarleton's cousin Flora was coming from Melbourne. And the mail. Mrs Tarleton had been twitchy all morning, hoping for a letter from Mr Tarleton. The bustle throughout the house was continuous with the girls dusting the furniture, shaking mats, and arranging fresh flowers and Maggie in the kitchen cooking legs of mutton and making fruit pies while the boys tried to distract her and steal the fruit she had prepared.

About a month previously Maggie had had a letter from Hugh. It was the first letter she had ever received and in spite of her spelling lessons with David Stavers, she had to ask Mrs Tarleton to read it out to her. Ever since, she had carried it in her pocket.

'*Da And I are at Amherst.*' Mrs Tarleton had read. '*we have been digging for about six weeks and until last week found only small nuggets only enough to keep us going this week we found a nugget worth about 25 pounds if we have more luck like that Da says we will be able to buy a house in Melbourne and get work down there closer to you Da saw David Stavers and his brother Will they are going to Back Creek soon and hope to have a wagon store selling picks and shovels they are doing well MaryAnn and James have a daughter named Eleanor after our Mam*

your loving brother Hugh'

Maggie put the letter to her cheek as if she might feel the warmth of Hugh's hand in its writing. She thrilled at the news of David Stavers, brief though it was. And tried to imagine MaryAnn with a baby and hoped she would be kinder to her baby than she ever was when Maggie was a bairn.

When cousin Flora eventually arrived Mr Wesley called to Maggie 'There's another letter for you Miss.' Maggie almost fell over herself in her haste to get it and called to Susannah and Lizzie, 'There's another letter. It must be from Da. Come and we'll get Mrs Tarleton to read it to us.'

Mrs Tarleton and Flora were laughing and talking. 'Later, Maggie,' Mrs Tarleton said as she waved Maggie away and walked into the parlour, 'we're just having tea now, and we've so much to tell each other.'

By firelight in the kitchen that night Maggie, Susannah and Lizzie puzzled over the page, running their fingers over the letters as if they might feel its meaning in their fingertips. They passed the letter from hand to hand and peered at the words. Though Maggie thought the writing looked in some way familiar, still it did not look to her like her father's hand.

'And Maggie, it don't look like I remember Hugh's writing at all.' Susannah agreed.

'I think I can see 'Hugh' written here, and down here, 'MaryAnn'. What does it mean? Who can it be from?'

'Who else would be writing to us?'

They could get no sense from it at all.

The next morning Maggie asked Mr Wesley 'Where's Mrs Tarleton?'

'She's gone riding for the day with cousin Flora.'

Maggie's face must have shown her disappointment for he asked 'What is it, Maggie?'

'It's my letter Mr Wesley. The one you gave me yesterday. I . . . I don't know who it's from.'

'Can you not read then?'

Maggie blushed as she looked down and shook her head.

'Give it here Maggie. I'll read it to you,' and he took the letter from Maggie's hand.

'Can I call me sisters, Mr Wesley?' Not waiting for an answer Maggie rushed out of the room to get Susannah and Lizzie. In a moment they were all there breathless and excited as Mr Wesley spread the letter on the table.

My Dear Misses McFaden, he read.

'Who's it from? It's very fond!' laughed Susannah as the girls gathered close around.

Maggie saw Mr Wesley's face sag and a stab of fear sent her heart thumping. Urgently she begged 'Go on, please. Go on.'

'It's signed, '*David Stavers*' and he says, *I am writing to you because Hugh has asked me to convey to you the sad news of your father's death. He was took bad last Friday evening with a coughing fit and a fever and in spite of being physicked by the doctor, he never improved and passed on, on Sunday morning. Hugh was with him all the time and he was most moved by your father's sad concern for yourself and your sisters. It is particular sad because Hugh and your father have just begun to get some better reward for their labours.*

Hugh has asked me to tell you that he intends visiting you at Plenty in the next week or so after he has been to see your sister

MaryAnn.

I am sometimes at Melbourne staying with Mrs Bellamy at Fitzroy when I am not at the diggings. She has been a most kind landlady even though we have cabbage almost every night for dinner. If I can help you in any way you could leave a message with her.
Your friend in consolation,
David Stavers.'

'Maggie, I am very sorry this is such sad news for you and your sisters.' Mr Wesley folded the letter and handed it back to Maggie, who clutched it to her chest and ran from the room, followed by Susannah and Lizzie.

Maggie felt a dark void before her. 'It can't be right. Our Da dead! He can't be dead. What will happen to us?'

'Orphans. We're orphans.' Said Susannah.

'What's a orphan?' asked Lizzie.

'It means we have no mother and no father, Lizzie. And MaryAnn gone to Buninyong, and Hugh far away, and us with only strangers round us,' Maggie sobbed. 'What will happen to us? Where can we go? I don't want to be stayin' here forever.'

A week or so later Mr Wesley approached Maggie and suggested that perhaps he could teach her and her sisters to read and write. From then on, in the evenings, Mr Wesley and the three girls were to be seen crouched round a candle in the kitchen practising their letters and stumbling over the words on the pages of a small book. He was a patient teacher and though the girls learned quickly, their spelling was always erratic and original.

It was almost a month later, at the end of October, before Hugh finally arrived.

'Hugh. How can you be thinkin' of goin' back to Ireland' Maggie pummelled Hugh with her fists. 'Since Da died . . . an' I was left here with Lizzie and Susie, you was the only one I could count on. You can't know how lonely a girl gets in this country, without a friend or anyone to call family at all.'

'Maggie. I must go. Uncle Hugh McFaden, he's written a letter sayin' he's leavin' his farm to me if I go back.'

'What about us?'

'You can come in a year or two.'

'I don't want to go back to Ireland.'

'When Uncle dies I can run the farm my own way.'

'And when might that be? I'd be an old maid by then.'

'But there'd be plenty of room for you and Lizzie and Susie. Helpin' out.'

'Diggin' and starvin' agen. If only I could find a husband I could stay here and be happy entirely, as long as I had a bit of family round me. But I'll not be marryin' just any gold digger. I want a proper husband and a proper house, not just some tent up on the diggin's.'

When Hugh made up his mind to return home it seemed to Maggie that Sarah was her only connection with her mother, with Ireland, with the past. That night she struggled to write her first letter. Though short, she knew Sarah would welcome it and hoped that before many months she would receive a reply. All that she held dear seemed to be falling away and with Hugh's departure she dreaded the aloneness that loomed ahead. She knew Hugh would write but rarely, and clung to her memory of Sarah.

> *Deer Sarah,*
> *well as you can see i can now rite much good it will doo me it was bad enuf loosing our Mam now our Da has gone too and Hugh back to Ireland MaryAnn is marrid and living at Bunninyong and i am with Susannah and Lizzie at Plenty it is very far from Melbourne and we are very lonly but theys plenty to eat and we all has got some flesh on our bones now pleas tell my cusins we are not dead*
> *your loving frend Maggie*

Susannah came rushing into the house one morning, 'Maggie! Maggie! Mr Wesley says there is a beast with two heads! Come and see!' The three girls hurried out onto the verandah where Mr Wesley pointed out a creature like a crouching deer. And to be sure, it had one head on its shoulders just as you would expect, and another lower down, coming from its belly. The girls stared in amazement as the two headed creature continued to crop the grass with both its heads.

'What is it? Mr Wesley, what is it?' they clamoured. To their amazement as they watched the smaller head withdrew into the belly and the creature hopped away. Mr Wesley laughed and slapped his thigh.

'It's a kangaroo with a baby in its pouch!' he declared and laughed at his joke.

'Oh Mr Wesley, you rascal! You tricked us. I'll never believe another word you say!' Maggie laughed.

'We can't have that Maggie. Come on, what say I teach you to ride the pony. Come along, I'll get her ready.'

Mr Wesley lead the small mare out of the stables and tied her up to the hitching rail. The mare stood quietly, giving an occasional lazy stamp of her rear hoof. Having been released from the stable, a few minutes later she raised her tail and deposited a heap of steaming dung.

'Come now Maggie. Watch me put on the saddle. You must know how to ride.'

'I'll not be puttin' me leg over that beast!'

Mr Wesley spoke gently to Maggie. 'You don't have to m'dear. You can ride side saddle if you want to. But it's considered a bit old fashioned in the colonies.'

'I'm not old fashioned! But that beast is not knowin' that. I can't be talkin' to it and tellin it I'm only twenty years old. How old is she?'

'Maggie she's fifteen. She's an old horse. She's not going to be kicking her heels up!'

'I don't need no horse to help me kick up me heels - I can do that perfectly well on me own.'

Mr Wesley shook his head at the wonderfully twisted logic of his young pupil.

'Come on Bertie, show Maggie how easy it is.' Young Bertie climbed on the fence and clambered over to the horse's back. Without bothering with the stirrups he kicked his little heels into the horse's sides and trotted off round the yard bouncing in the saddle like a drop of water on a griddle.

'It's easy Maggie. Don't be afraid.' Bertie said.

'I'm not afeared of that beast. I just don't especially want to be ridin' it!'

'But Maggie, you can go fast on a horse. And you don't get tired.'

'A bit of walkin' never hurt a body. That's what your legs are for my lad. Not for spreadin' over a horse's barrel belly.'

'Come now Maggie. Just one try. I'll give you a boost up.'

'I'm only doin' this to prove to you that I'm not afeared at all.' Maggie flounced to the side of the horse and presented her foot for Mr Wesley to give her a lift into the saddle. He lifted, and Maggie fell, leaning across the saddle, half on and half off.

'Put your leg over the saddle Maggie. Push yourself up with your arms and get your leg over the saddle.' Mr Wesley instructed patiently. He held the reins with one hand and with the other tried to guide Maggie's foot into the stirrup while the mare stepped sideways away from him.

With a great effort Maggie pushed herself upright with her arms while one leg felt around for the stirrup and the other tried to crawl over the back of the saddle. At last she managed to be seated.

'It's not natural, spreadin' me legs as wide as this!' Maggie laughed then blushed at what she had said.

Mr Wesley discreetly looked down and adjusted the stirrups. 'Now how does that feel? That's right, now off you go!' He gave the mare a pat on the rump and she began to walk around the yard.

Maggie was just getting the feel of it when Mr Wesley gave a click, click with his tongue and the mare broke into a trot.

'Stop that! Stop it! Make it stop!' Maggie was bouncing around with arms and legs flailing, making the mare go faster. She clung to the pommel, her mind full only of what she would do when she got off this devil of an animal. Murder, she thought. I'll murder him for this, her hand tight on the pommel, as if it was Mr Wesley's throat.

He laughed and ran over and grasped the mare's reins and pulled her up. 'Not bad for a beginner!'

'And that's the end of it, you beast! I'll never be gettin' on a horse again, you can be altogether sure of that! If I want to go any place I'll be walkin there on me own two legs as the good Lord intended.'

One sunny Sunday afternoon Maggie decided to take a walk while Susannah and Lizzie were racing twigs down the creek with Horrie and Bertie. She was tempted by the flowers which tumbled in profusion as spring grew into summer. She tucked the bottom of her skirt into her waistband to make a place to carry the wildflowers she had gathered and after an hour or so, had a wonderful collection. She was entranced by their variety, and determined to ask Mr Wesley if he knew the names of them.

She had come across a patch of violets, small and lacking the perfume of those which grew at home in Ireland, but violets nonetheless, and she sank to her knees amongst them. She picked a bunch and held them to her nose and suddenly remembered that morning twelve years before when she had hidden in the loft and heard below her mother's moans, like the cow when the calf came out. She had peered through a crack then, she remembered, and saw her mothers legs, white and writhing, and she had hidden there afraid of what was happening, not knowing, thinking her mother was dying. She had put her hands over her ears and crouched down and made herself small until sleep claimed her for a time. She was wakened by a single drawn out scream which pierced her heart. She squeezed her eyes closed even tighter, waiting, she didn't know what for. Then it came, a thin and tremulous, wavering cry, like a cat mewling. And she had looked down again and seen it, small and red and howling. Her sister Susannah.

Maggie smiled to herself at this memory of Susannah's arrival in the world and gathering her violets and flowers, turned to walk back to the homestead.

A subtle change in the bush made her feel uneasy. The path she had followed seemed unfamiliar and as she went further it grew fainter. Her boots scrunched through dried leaves and sticks. Beetles and spiders fell into her hair and she brushed them away with a shudder. The mad jackasses laughed at her. And all their laughing brothers cackled a chorus across the gully. Surely she was going in the right direction? It all looked the same. No matter how far she walked, the same trees appeared before her, the same rocks slid beneath her feet, jumbled and unformed into any track.

Then she ran, her flowers scattered. Stumbling and falling she clambered up the slope through the crackling, prickling bush, in hope of seeing where she had come from, then fell again and lay, panting and her heart thumping.

'Dear God. Help me to find me way back for I cannot be doin' it by meself.' She flinched as a flash of parrots wheeled past her, so close she could hear their wing beats and her heart leapt again. In an instant they disappeared into a tree, their brilliant colours lost amongst the foliage. Maggie slumped against the tree and wiped her face on her skirt. How can they disappear like that. They are so bright and pretty. Have I vanished like they have? Will anyone ever find me? The bark was pressing into her back, and swarms of ants trickled onto her ankles and legs and she brushed at them, stamping her boots to shake them off.

Into a small sunlit space a few feet away a snake came. It stopped in its small space and looked at her with its snake eyes. It was a ragged snake, its scales lifting and dry. It looked very old. Maggie froze, shivered, held her breath, and drew back into the trunk of the tree in terror, trying to become part of it. She kept very still as the snake lay quivering in its patch of sunshine. Fervently, she hoped it was dying. It began to contort in death throes, throwing itself in aimless motions like some ungainly dancer, then lay still again. In fascinated horror, Maggie saw that the skin at the sides of its mouth had split a little. It contracted, then slid forward, stopped, and shuddered. Again it slid forward and fixing its body between small clumps of grass it shuddered and shucked itself forwards and eased itself from its papery sheath, to emerge gleaming, from its own mouth. Shining in the sun. She could see its heart beating rapidly at its side, its head and back striped dull yellow and brilliant black as it slid silently away beneath the bark and leaves, its tongue darting from between its new lips.

Maggie was both fascinated and repelled. After a time, when she was sure the snake had really gone, she crept to where the discarded skin had grown dry in the hot sun then bent, and touched it with the end of a twig. With the twig she lifted it to look more closely. Tentatively, and with trembling fingers, she touched it. It was not slimy as she had expected, but dry and papery. She was surprised at how strong it was, how light and perfect in every detail. Each scale's shape left behind in pattern. Even the head, the eyes, the lips. Snakes lips, tongueless. Snakes eyes, sightless. Maggie lifted the skin to her eyes and looked through the empty eye scales to a world of snake seeing, blurred and indistinct. And wondered how it might be to shake off your old skin. To slip scales from your eyes and see, freshly and sharply. To peel your skin and emerge, new and beautiful.

As she looked through the snake's eye scales she saw a shadow of movement, then heard a rustle and stopped. Quietly she drew herself in behind the tree and peered into the scrub, the snake skin fallen and forgotten. She heard strange, high pitched, jabbering voices and the laughter of a child. Her heart beat harder as she tried to make herself small. A breeze blew her skirt and she caught it and held it between her knees to stop its flutter and put her hands to her face, as if she might hold her breath back.

Two women and a child appeared. They were black, with wild hair and deep, dark eyes. And naked. They carried sticks and had woven bags over their shoulders. Maggie had heard they carried parts of people's bodies in those bags. Fingers, and hair, and dried up ears and bits of flesh, which they ate. They used those sticks to poke into people's eyes. Maggie shrank behind her tree, not wanting to become a grisly piece in one of those string bags. But curiosity drew her eyes back to the two women who did not cover their nakedness with their hands or with leaves, but walked as if they wore the finest clothes. She wondered how it felt to walk about with sticks in your hair and only a string about your waist, and your titties all bare and scratched by the twigs. Then as she looked, suddenly she perceived that the younger woman's body was a darker, mirrored image of her own, with small tender breasts, with shoulders and hips angular above a dark wisp of hair, with slender legs, and knees as knobby as her own.

Maggie looked down at her arms. They were scratched, and the flies which the dark girl brushed from her eyes, flew and settled on the cuts on the backs of Maggie's hands. The dark girl had no scratches on her arms or legs, Maggie observed, but her feet were large and spread, and along the sides, deep cracks split the flesh. And Maggie remembered such fissures on her own feet in the deep of winter in Ireland, when she had no boots, when her feet were numb from walking in the frozen mud, when they burned and itched with chilblains and when she scratched them until they bled.

The two women did not seem to have seen her for they stopped and the older woman put the child on the ground and they both began to dig vigorously with their sticks, until with a burst of laughter the girl pulled a lizard from the earth and holding it by the tail, slapped its head hard on a rock. She then pushed the bloodied head through the string around her waist and bent to wipe her hands on grass. As she straightened, her eyes met Maggie's and for a moment she froze, then grabbed the child quickly, and jabbering and pointing, she and the older woman held each other and backed away.

They're afraid of me! thought Maggie. 'Please. Don't go away' she begged, 'I'm lost. Which way is the house?' Muttering to each other they looked at Maggie and then arms extended, they tossed their hands as if they might shoo her away and throw their hands after her, 'Go. Go.' they called, 'Follow sun.'

'Please. Please show me the way.' But already they were disappearing like the parrots, their dark bodies melting into the shadows amongst the trees.

Maggie faced the descending sun and pushed her way through the scrub, praying the dark women had directed her truly. As she began to despair of ever emerging from the endless scrub, the sky seemed to lighten and soon she could see the open fields and beyond them, a wisp of smoke from a chimney.

Afterwards she would remember the snake and the dark girl. The snake, beautiful under his old skin. The dark girl and her own body in that strange moment of affinity - as if their bodies were the dark and light of each other. And in the darkness of the night when all around was black, Maggie stroked her own body, and in her stroking wondered if the dark girl felt as she did.

One morning not very long after this, Mrs Tarleton bustled into the kitchen. 'Maggie, tomorrow morning I want you to get together all the tins you can find. Boragee told Mr Wesley of a tree down by the lagoon that he called a honey tree. Mr Wesley thinks there might be a hive there. We're going to collect the honey.' Next morning at first light Maggie, Susie and Lizzie were up and ready with two kerosene tins each when Mrs Tarleton and the boys and Mr Wesley trotted out with the dray.

'I'm sorry Maggie, but Susie and Lizzie must stay home with the boys. I don't want them to get stung.'

'Boragee said the bees don't sting, Bertha,' reminded Mr Wesley.

'Well you don't believe an ignorant savage like him. I know perfectly well that bees sting and Bertie and Horace must stay home.'

Maggie looked at Susie and Lizzie, shrugging her shoulders and pulling a face behind Mrs Tarleton's back.

'We'll be alright, we'll take the boys fishing in the creek.'

'Mind they don't fall in now, girls.'

Mrs Tarleton handed Maggie a veil to tie over her hat. 'Put this on when we get to the tree - if the men are going to chop holes in it I'm sure the bees will be very angry.'

They followed Boragee as he went ahead, his boomerang and woomera held in his right hand as he ran. Maggie knew he would be looking for a wallaby or a kangaroo to knock down for a meal by the campfire; an unpleasant habit Mrs Tarlton was never able to dissuade him from.

After pushing the dray through dry scrub and crackling undergrowth they came to the tree at last. It was a huge old red gum, its canopy filled with a host of birds that flew up into a noisy cloud on their arrival.

Boragee stood still and looked carefully up into the tree's lower branches, tapped around the trunk and branches for a few minutes before pointing excitedly to a small hollow in the second branch. Quickly he climbed the tree and had his hand down in the hollow when Mrs Tarleton called out 'Come down Boragee. Mr Wesley will chop the branch off!'

Boragee climbed down. 'Don't chop 'im tree Mr Wesley.' He begged, crouching with his back to the trunk, his arms outspread. 'This fella tree, 'e my father.'

'Move away Boragee' Mr Wesley said as he pushed the small dark man aside. 'Come now, what's this nonsense about the tree being your father?' He climbed up into the lower branches.

With every stroke of Mr Wesley's axe Boragee shuddered. With each stroke he held his side as if the blows were falling on his own body. He began to cry and retreated to the shelter of another tree nearby, inconsolable.

'Don't be ridiculous Boragee - it's only a tree.' Mrs Tarleton sniffed.

With a last blow the great branch crashed down. A golden stream of honey poured out of the gaping wound and Maggie and Mrs Tarleton ran to the tree with their tins and put them beneath the golden flow.

Boragee was still weeping 'That tree, 'e my father.' He beseeched. ''E never cut. That tree die. I die.' And he hugged his body and wept afresh.

They filled tin after tin and staggered with their weight to the dray. Boragee refused to help. At the end of the day even the baby bath was full and everyone was covered in honey from head to toe. Maggie licked her hands and arms. Mrs Tarleton delicately confined herself to fingertips.

When they were ready to leave, Boragee insisted on closing up the wound in the tree. He made a paste of clay and chips of wood and began to push it into the hole.

'It's almost dark. We can't wait Boragee.'

He didn't even look around. His whole attention was on the wound in the tree and he tended it as one might have tended a severed leg. He applied layer after layer of clay dressing until the gaping wound was closed and then put more clay over that to make sure.

Boragee then sat down at the foot of the tree and began a chant that was to last for several days.

As they rumbled back to the homestead Maggie wondered at Boragee's devotion to the tree, then suddenly remembered her own feeling of comfort when she sat in the arms of the old oak tree the day her mother died. She decided she too would have wept if anyone had wanted to cut down her tree.

Within weeks of his arrival at the goldfields David applied to ride escort with the gold consignments once a week. Most diggers were too busy looking for gold to sacrifice a few days of their week to ride down to Melbourne and back, acting as guards for the gold as it was transported to the bank in Melbourne. But David and Will hadn't had much success with their digging. There were others much more experienced than they who always seemed to strike it lucky, while they got only minor returns for their efforts. When the commissioner called for men to act as guards, and when he mentioned the pay, David decided it would be more profitable even if it was more risky.

Will thought him a fool but with his youthful enthusiasm, David went to the commissioner's tent and registered his name. That night he told Will

'I've been issued with a carbine and a uniform but I have to ride my own horse. They pay five pounds for every round trip and a bonus of a pound each to us guards when the consignment arrives intact.'

'Aye, it's generous enough. And what does it pay if you get shot?'

'There's eight of us on every consignment Will! All armed. No bushrangers are going to attack eight of us!'

Only two weeks later David was not quite so confident when he heard that a consignment had been held up at Heathcote and two of the escort fatally wounded. A large amount of gold was taken by the bushrangers. It was the second hold up in a month.

On the next escort, David was in the saddle ready to depart, as the last of the gold, packed in chamois bags, was loaded in boxes onto the wagon. Finally, the load was secured and the drivers flicked their whips and the four horses began the long haul from Castlemaine to Melbourne. The escort made a colourful picture in their red jackets and blue caps as they ranged themselves, four on either side of the wagon, and began the long steady journey, trotting smartly along. The weather looked set fair to make it a quick and safe journey, with clear skies and a light breeze.

As they drew away from the town the road deteriorated and slowed them a little, but soon they resumed their steady pace.

David was riding alongside the driver on the near side of the wagon and asked him what he thought were the chances of the bushrangers striking again.

'I don't think they'd dare, so soon.'

'But if they did, the most likely place would be just before Elphinstone, behind that big rocky outcrop on the left. Don't y'agree?'

GOLD ESCORT

'Well, we never had no trouble there before,' the driver said doubtfully.

'That just it,' said David. 'If I was wanting to catch a coach or a wagon unawares I'd be up behind those rocks. You could see a wagon from up there as they approached and be on them in an instant.'

'Ye'could be right. Couldn't turn the wagon round there neither.'

'That's it! They'd have us. And, both previous robberies were in narrow parts of the road, don't ye recall?' David moved a little closer to the wagon. 'I don't want to get shot by any of those villains, and I'll wager you don't either. I think we should hold a council of war here and now and work out how to protect ourselves.'

It took David some time to persuade the other driver and the escorts of the merits of his proposal but in the end they all agreed that they would camp at Campbells Creek that night, with three watches in shifts, and when they and their horses were fresh in the morning, they would move on through Elphinstone. David had a further plan in mind for when they approached the narrow ravine but held his tongue for the moment.

The next morning as they decamped, David took the two drivers aside and said 'Before we get to the ravine, I want to take one of the other escorts and circle round behind that outcrop of rocks so that if there is anyone there we can come down on them from above before they attack the wagon.'

'But that'll leave us with only six men, plus the drivers.'

'I know. But it's the only place anyone could attack from, so if there's no one there, the wagon will get through alright anyway.'

'What if they come from the other side?' The driver asked, still not quite able to grasp the logic of David's plan.

'Well, we'll be pretty high, we should be able to see them before you do.'

'Well if this whole idea is a waste of time, I'll hold you responsible, Stavers.'

'And if there's no one there, then it's no loss. Agreed?' David looked at the drivers' faces, waiting for their nod of approval.

In spite of his convincing plan, David was apprehensive. Whatever made me think there might be an attack this time, he asked himself? He could find no answer beyond a gut feeling, perhaps some amalgam of knowledge he wasn't even aware of.

As the dawn grew into full morning David and one other escort split off from the main body of the caravan and began a slow ascent of the hills. They proceeded cautiously, alert and nervous, conscious of every sound, watching the wagon below as it moved slowly along the narrow road.

After about twenty minutes they slowed to a walk and when they reached the top of the ridgeline, dismounted and led their horses to the crest of the hill where they could look down. They had lost sight of the wagon for a while and were both feeling anxious. At first they saw nothing, then suddenly David thought he noticed a small movement off to the right of where they were looking.

'Look' he whispered urgently, 'to the right. I'm sure I saw movement down there.' He realised he'd pinned his reputation on this one idea and wondered had he imagined it. They waited several minutes before David started to say 'If I had a spy glass . . . ' he stopped, 'there they are! Behind the second largest boulder, on the right!'

'Got them!' replied his companion. 'What now?'

'We'll have to move fast, but we can't make any noise. I think we'd best lead the horses and get down there, just above them, as fast as we can.'

Quickly they secured their stirrups, pulled their carbines from their holsters and began to descend upon the rascals below.

In the event, it was over quite quickly. David and his companion had descended upon the band of robbers and when they got within range, they called. 'Hold Up. Drop your arms!'

The bushrangers turned and opened fire, but David and his companion fired back at them repeatedly, and were joined by shots from the wagon. Caught in crossfire, the villains withdrew still firing, but then quickly mounted and rode away into the dust, their plans in disarray.

David and his escort friend clapped each other on the back and quickly mounted and rode helter skelter down the hill to meet up with the wagon and the rest of the escort.

'We were ready for them. But they never fired a shot in this direction,' the driver informed them. 'They've headed west. We saw their dust.'

'Well done David. How did you know?'

'I just tried to think what I'd do if I was a bushranger!'

'Ohoh! Hark at him. He'll be the robber next!'

'I don't think they'll be worrying us again for a while.'

A few weeks later, the drivers and escorts of that particular consignment were each presented with an inscribed fob watch and David received a .38 Colt Revolver in a velvet lined rosewood case, in appreciation of his foresight and bravery and the fact that the consignment had been delivered without further incident.

After a few months working as escort David and Will established themselves at Amherst, with a small tent set up out on the flat, their cradle ready to rock by the creek and themselves busy up the gully with their picks and shovels.

'Watch out for spiders, Davey!' William flung a log aside revealing colonies of redbacks. 'These little divils can kill yeh, you know!'

David pulled back fearfully and realised once again how deceptive things were in this land. In his first weeks in Australia he had delighted in the spiders' webs in the mornings. Webs touched by frost and frozen droplets of water, glistening golden in the dawn light, draped from grassy stem to grassy stem, like curtains for a tiny stage behind which the day's play was waiting to be performed. They reminded him of home and ancient Celtic memories.

Now there was scant time for memories. Each day he and Will rose at dawn, and if they had not slept in their mud stiffened clothes, they pulled them on and emerged from their tent into the still air of early morning, yawning and scratching themselves into wakefulness. Then they would stir last night's coals, add a few branches and squat beside the slow, smoking fire, poking it and adding dry sticks until it burst into flame.

Each day was the same. Dig with pick and shovel for a few brutal hours, barrow the spoil from the gully to the creek, then, working in turns as a pair, shovel the gravel into the cradle, one rocking and one bucketting, and wash it with load after load of water. This they did during all their daylight hours, six days a week.

So it was not surprising that since leaving the ship David had grown more muscular and his Irish pallor had coloured to a ruddy countenance, and he was clean shaven now, in the manner of the honest digger. His hands, no longer smooth and uncalloused, were roughened and scarred, with rims of dirt beneath cracked and broken nails. He still wore rough bandages around them while the calluses formed. Each day he and Will worked to a steady rhythm, wordlessly taking turn about, shovelling, rocking the cradle and washing out the gold from the gravel.

Later they lifted out the pads which lay over the riddles at the bottom of the cradle and in the security of their tent, away from spying eyes, they would scrape and sift and shake out the golden remnants caught in the fibres. Then down to the creek for the final washing in the panning dish and the careful picking of the small seeds and beans and nuggets of gold for the day. Sometimes, after the long day's work, there was nothing to add to the pickle jar buried beneath Will's bed in the tent. Mostly they had a modest result. Rarely, a good-sized nugget to celebrate, before mutton and damper and falling asleep by the fire.

The only day that differed was Sunday. This was observed as a day of rest but in fact used by all the miners to wash their clothes, write letters, catch up with their chores, replace supplies.

David sat in the shade outside the tent and prepared to write to Eliza. It was December and hot. The wind was blowing lightly from the north where most of the horses were pastured and where the abandoned mine shafts were used as cess pits. The flies had come, drawn by the pervasive stench. At the back of his mind he could hear the constant barking of dogs, the voices of men, the thin note of a tin whistle. A distant voice singing 'Erin My Country, I Love Thy Green Bowers' brought a wave of nostalgia to him as he glanced up at the camp and its rough camaraderie of men. Before him he saw an expanse of dug up earth, heaped up beside each claim, with men moving in all directions. To David it looked like a giant ant colony with every individual going about his business.

He re-read Eliza's letter and leaned his elbows on his knees as he tried to picture her face. It seemed a thousand years since he had left Rureagh. Her letter said she had written many times but the letter in his hands was only the second he had received in six months. And lucky for that, he thought, if I hadn't been there when the bag arrived they might have just thrown it away with all the other unclaimed letters.

Flies crawled into the corners of his mouth and eyes and he brushed them away constantly. When he opened his ink bottle they settled in a ring around the top and flew from there to his face each time he dipped his pen. He wrote:

21 December, 1853.

My Dearest Eliza,

I am glad to tell you that Will and I are both well, and though we are not prospering as we might have hoped, have had sufficient success to encourage us. We have been mining now at Amherst for three months. This field is almost finished and we are moving tomorrow to Back Creek, several miles further north. We have had word of a new rush there and must make haste to be there early. I should tell you that Back Creek is over a hundred miles north west of Port Phillip.

Until today I have had but one letter from you, written in July, about the time we arrived in Port Phillip. There is no real post service and when you follow the diggings as Will and I do, it is very fortunate if a letter finds you, even though I go to the delivery point every week.

Being on the diggings is like being at war. Every time there is a new rush several thousand diggers arrive from other rushes. And following the diggers will come the hawkers and the sly grog tents, barber shops, dancing saloons and billiard rooms. Already several canvas hotels, stores, restaurants, skittle alleys and even a cigar shop have appeared.

Conditions are primitive but supplies soon follow any new strike and Will and I have decided to try our hand at selling hardware. We have determined to get a wagon and start a store selling picks and shovels. We have had enough luck of late to provide a bit of capital and if the Back Creek proves profitable we will set up a wagon or tent store and if our success continues, we shall build a more permanent building.

Will and I do not always agree about what we should sell. I am for selling only hardware but Will believes we should get a licence to sell Wine and Spirits because it is more profitable but I think it is not moral. He is not an easy man to work with and is much changed since he left home four years ago.

You would find me much changed also. The sun is very warm and has burned my face and arms to a ruddy colour. Also, I have shaved my beard so that I do not look like a Vandemonian. They are the convicts who have served their time and come now to Port Phillip to terrorise us honest men. Many of them are bushrangers who ambush travellers and they are always very rough looking and lawless fellows.

Two months ago I became a gold escort, riding as a guard with the gold consignment to Melbourne. Earlier a consignment of gold was held up by bushrangers at Heathcote and eight thousand pounds worth of gold taken. Two of the escort was shot. Recently we was almost attacked by a band of rascals but were able to outwit them. I do not know how long I will stay in the escort. Will says I am mad and will get shot but the pay is good.

So even though I long to be with you Eliza I would not wish you to be here. It is a lawless place and not likely to become less so in a short time. Now it is too harsh a place for a woman. Indeed those few women who are at the diggings are of a disreputable type who shame the good name of their sisters. Yet I hope in time that may change too, for this is a favourable place in which to prosper and a good life may be had with hard work.
Yours most affectionately,
David.

David folded his letter and addressed it. 'Will! Are you ready to go to the service?'

'Aye. You go on, I'll catch up.'

When Will joined him as they walked up the hill to Reverend Parslow's Sunday service under the large gum tree, David said. 'I think we would be gettin' along better if we had another couple of mates to work with us. What d'ye think?'

'I hope yeh're not thinkin' of askin' the new chums.'

'There's two lots. There are two yankees who look like they know how to work, or Jack Weir and Peter Patterson. I was talkin' to Jack last evening, he and Peter seem strong enough, and honest enough by my estimation. And not so raw as to be fools.'

'I don't want no yankees. I had enough of them in California. Only bring trouble, although those two seem decent enough,' Will conceded. 'I grant you Jack and Peter would be a more likely pair.'

David added, 'If we had two more in our band we could leave them in charge when we have to go to Melbourne. That way our gear would be safer, and we'd be safer too, travelling in pairs. I'll ask them if they want to join us. It'll be no loss if they say no.'

David found that the group of four worked even better than he had expected. While he and Jack were cradling, Peter and Will would be at the shaft, one digging the other hauling. From the shaft they could see the tent, and because it was close by they could take it in turn to be on duty cooking, washing, or keeping a lookout. Every week they swapped duties. They were all happy with the arrangement.

Jack proved to be a good friend for David and more and more they worked together over the four months they spent at Back Creek. During this time they also had good fortune with their gold and at the end of May, 1854, David and Will were planning a visit to the Oriental Bank at Melbourne to deposit their accumulated gold, and to renew their mining licences.

'The only way we'll make good money is if we have a grog licence.' Will said for the dozenth time.

'I can see the truth of that but I don't think its moral - trading on a man's weakness.' David protested.

112

'It's the only fair way. A licence each. It will work well for all of us.' Will reasoned.

Despite David's resistance, and unknown to him, Will was scheming to get a liquor licence whether David agreed or not. When they arrived in Melbourne Will begged a couple of hours to visit a friend. He was missing for most of the day and David was waiting somewhat anxiously for his return so that they could set off for Back Creek again. When Will walked in to Mrs Bentley's small kitchen he pulled a bundle of papers from his pocket.

'There! A merchant's licence for Jack. A mining licence for Peter. A grog licence for me and..' with a flourish Will played his winning card, 'a gold buyer's licence for you David!'

'A gold buyer's licence! Me, a gold buyer!' David laughed, 'How did you manage that Will?'

Will winked. 'You don't need to know about that Lad. It's a licence for you to make money, and it won't bother your tender conscience.'

'I'll not have anything to do with selling grog. You'll have to make your own arrangements about that.'

'Don't you worry yourself about the grog. I'll sell it outside the tent, you needn't do anything. Anyway you'll be too busy buying gold. Just send your diggers out the back when you've finished with them,' Will laughed. 'and I'll get their cash straight back off them!'

David smiled in spite of himself. A gold buying licence was a great advantage. How had Will managed to get that? One of his friends in the government office, no doubt.

'I must admit I've wanted one of these for a long time.' David said, his fingers resting on the gold buyer's licence. 'But I'll not accept it as a bribe. You must carry on your grog selling well away from my tent. The two don't marry well.'

'Aye, well. I'll make me own arrangements.'

And the two shook hands.

Despite David's misgivings, having four licences worked well for the four men and the group continued to work together with improved results for all of them.

As always, between him and Will, there was a tension, a struggle for leadership, so that in their day-to-day labours, David felt much more content working with Jack where there was no such strain. They seemed to approach a problem in the same way - standing back, working it out, then carefully trying out the possible alternatives until one way worked the best. Jack was of a cheerful disposition, with a nice appreciation of the humour their situation often cast them into. More and more David and Jack chose to work together while Will and Peter formed the other pair.

'Joe! Joe!'

David and Will heard the call and threw down their spades in exasperation.

'I'll not be abused by these wretched troopers for another day!' Will exclaimed.

'That's the second time this week.' David commented wearily as he climbed up out of their shaft and trudged off to their camp to get his Licence. The troopers walked their horses along behind and didn't even dismount at the tent. When David came out with the licences, the troopers gave them a quick glance then said.

'Tell your mates we're rounding up anyone without a licence. If a digger can't produce a proper licence he'll be chained to a tree till tomorrow and then he'll be fined and released.'

'And if he can't pay?'

'He'll be sentenced to a month's jail.'

'It's inhuman.' David expostulated. 'You charge us thirty shillings a month - most of us don't even make that much!'

'Suit yourself digger. Pay the licence or pay the fine - it's your choice.'

'It's no choice at all when we're breaking our backs digging every day and you troopers make us stop work to show our licences. Just on a whim most of the time. This is the second time this week for us. Come on Will, I've had enough of this. Let's get back to work, we've lost almost an hour already.'

The camp was restless that night with angry voices punctuating the air and disgruntled miners making speeches of rebellion as they gathered in groups at the grog shops and billiard halls.

'We're honest men breaking our backs to make a living and we have to pay thirty shillings a month for the privilege!'

'And what does Governor Latrobe do with it? Nothing that benefits the miners, that's certain.'

'We have to eat.'

'How can a man make an honest living when the government robs us?'

The babble of voices grew louder and angrier as each of the men expressed his concern at the unfairness of it all. Will and David felt no differently from all the rest. They were affronted that their honesty was doubted and indignant at the high impost. Life was hard enough without this extra burden that did nothing to help the diggers, or provide them with roads or bridges, but was used to build grand new buildings in Melbourne.

'I've heard there's talk of a petition,' Will said that night after they returned to their own campfire.

'Surely Latrobe can't expect this to continue. Thousands of diggers paying thirty shillings a month - that's the real gold for the Governor.'

'If enough diggers protest - he may reduce it.' David reached down for his tin of tobacco and took a thin plug from it and rubbed and rolled it in the palm of his hand before he filled the one pipe a day he allowed himself. He struck a Vesper on the sole of his boot then held it to his pipe and drew on it until it was it well alight then settled in front of the dying embers.

Will lit his own pipe, 'We'll start tomorrow - see if we can get signatures for a petition here as well.'

David rehearsed in his mind the words he would write on the pamphlet. There was such general approval of the idea that within days thousands of pamphlets and posters flooded the goldfields, spreading like a storm of paper across the district. The diggers were fired with indignation and every word brought forth a cheer of encouragement. Soon news came of a large meeting to be addressed by Peter Lalor and gradually, as the news spread, bands of miners gathered and determined to go to Peter Lalor's meeting in Ballaarat.

David and Will, bundling together the signatures they had collected, joined a small band and began the ride to Ballaarat.

Maggie never knew for sure what happened but soon after Mr Tarleton arrived back from England, the men went out one night on a hunting expedition. Maggie stood in the shadows beside the hut and watched as the men mounted their horses. She thought Mr Tarleton must have been hungering for fresh meat, a kangaroo or wallaby or perhaps a possum. Usually they carried only rifles but this time they had pistols too, she noticed. Their voices were low and their faces grim. At first Maggie thought little of it except to wonder at men's enthusiasm for hunting, but later in the darkest of the night, for a moment she thought she heard distantly the scream of a woman and she shivered in the warmth of her bed. She'd heard a sound like that before and Mr Wesley had told her it was a bird but Maggie didn't believe a bird could make such blood curdling sounds, like a woman screaming and sobbing for her life.

A day or two later when she was out looking for Bertie and Horrie, she found them whispering beside a heap of broken spears and boomerangs piled up with dried leaves and branches heaped over them, like a bonfire in preparation. Maggie told the boys to get back to the house and wash their hands and faces and after they had gone, she went over to the pile of discarded weapons. She leaned over and pulled one of the boomerangs from the heap then shuddered when she saw dried blood on it. A wave of suspicion swept over her as she remembered a scrap of conversation she had heard in the days just before Mr Tarleton returned. She had been standing on the verandah outside the big house, and heard Mrs Tarleton saying.

'The blacks are becoming a positive nuisance, you have to do something about it.'

Mr Wesley cleared his throat, 'What on earth do you expect me to do Bertha?'

'Can't you get rid of them? Give them a good lesson they won't forget in a hurry.'

'Really Bertha! It's not as if they're doing anything very damaging. Just a bit of pilfering here and there.'

'I don't like them around Horace and Bertrand. They're dirty and they're getting much too cheeky.'

'I'll tell them to move on.'

'You're too soft Wesley. Mr Tarleton wouldn't stand for it.'

ABORIGINAL WEAPONS

After the night of the hunting, Maggie did not see the blacks. At first she thought little of it, they often went off for a week or two at a time and Maggie gave little thought to their absence except to miss their cheeky laughter. She knew one day they would appear again, laughing and greeting her like an old friend. But this time they did not return. As the long weeks passed Maggie was haunted by the memory of the conversation she had overheard. And she never again walked past the place of the spears without a shudder and she never heard the sound of that strange screeching bird that Mr Wesley said was an owl, without dread in her heart.

As the spring warmed itself into summer, life settled into a pattern for the girls, their daily work, the passage of the seasons, their lessons in the evenings. The months passed and little changed except that Maggie could sense Mr Wesley's growing fondness.

One day Susannah said, 'I think Mr Wesley will soon be asking you to marry him Maggie.'

'But he's so old Susannah. He must be over fifty and I'm only twenty! Sure he's a kindly man but he's not the sort I'd like to spend me life with.'

'You're still thinkin' of that David Stavers, Maggie. You can forget him, for I'm sure he's forgotten you entirely.'

'Well, the thing is Susie, I'm not at all sure that I'll be marryin' anybody, for I've made a promise to meself that I won't marry until you and Lizzie are settled. So perhaps you'd better be lookin' at Mr Wesley yourself', she laughed, and Susie screwed up her nose.

When Maggie and her sisters first saw Mr Tarleton they were surprised. Maggie thought him more like Mrs Tarleton's's father than her husband, but despite his appearance, she had felt the strength of his grip when he shook her hand. Mrs Tarleton was forever fussing over him and Maggie and the girls had to run twice as fast and twice as far to satisfy his demands.

One autumn evening the girls were having their Saturday baths in the tub in front of the kitchen fire. It was Lizzie's turn to be first and in the soft glow from the fire, Susannah was bending and washing her back, squeezing the cloth out and running the soapy water over her shoulders. Lizzie's dark hair was pinned up, and tendrils curled around and framed her face. Maggie had gone to the privy and on her way back had gathered an armful of firewood. As she came round the corner she was shocked to find Mr Tarleton peering at the girls through a crack in the kitchen wall. When he heard her he straightened and pretended he was filling the gap with bark, blustering about the cold wind blowing in. From that moment on Maggie distrusted him and cautioned Susannah and Lizzie to be on guard.

But it was to be Maggie who was his mark. He caught her one still winter's day down behind the woodheap. He grasped her arm in his iron grip and forced her to her knees in the jagged chips. He struck her across the face. Maggie shook her head and twisted and struggled to free herself but he grasped her hair and wound it around his wrist and pulled her head back hard, and unbuttoned his trousers.

'Open your mouth, slut.' He held her nose until she gasped for breath then thrust his ugly knob into her mouth again and again. With each thrust Maggie gagged. She felt the rough serge of his trousers against her cheek, the smell of his mustiness in her throat as he groaned and grunted.

Afterwards he threw her down and pushed her away with his foot. He turned to walk away and as he buttoned his trews, he looked back and said, 'It's your sisters next, you slattern, if you breathe a word of this to anyone. D'ye hear?'

Maggie knelt in the woodchips and retched. She scrubbed at her face and mouth with the hem of her skirt. Coughing and spitting, brushing the chips from her scarified knees, she stumbled back to the kitchen hut where Susannah and Lizzie were roasting potatoes in the coals. Susannah glanced at Maggie.

'What've you done to your mouth, Maggie? Your lip's all swollen.'

Maggie hid her face and mumbled, 'I fell on me face in the woodheap.'

'Let me see.' Susannah rose quickly and went to Maggie. 'You've no splinters have you?'

Maggie turned away. 'Oh no. No splinters.' And burst into tears.

'What is it Maggie? What happened?' Susannah put her arms around her older sister but Maggie held her face down and said nothing. When Susannah went outside to get a pannikin of water Maggie rummaged about until she found the scissors and taking her dark, waving hair in her hand she cut it as close to her scalp as she could, hurling her dark curls into the fire, the smell of their acrid burning filling the hut. Lizzie crouched in the corner horrified. With each hank of hair hacked from her scalp Maggie shuddered and threw it from herself as if she could cast the memory of Tarleton into the fire with her hair.

'Maggie! What are you doin'? Your lovely hair?'

'I'll never grow me hair agen as long as I live!' Maggie stared at them, her pale face suddenly fragile on her slender neck, her ears sticking out from her ragged cap of thick black hair.

'You've never cut your hair. Ever!'

But Maggie remained grim and silent, determined to shelter her sisters from Tarleton. But no matter how many pannikins of water she gargled she could not remove the memory of him from her mouth. She scrubbed at her face and spat and gargled and spat again, but still the memory remained.

Mrs Tarleton was shocked when she saw Maggie. 'Whatever has happened? What have you done to your face?' She peered at Maggie carefully. 'Has someone struck you? Was it one of those dreadful blacks? Tell me what happened Maggie.'

'It was dark. I fell on me face in the woodheap.' Maggie repeated tonelessly.

'Oh dear me! And what has happened to your hair? Really you might have cut it a bit more carefully Maggie. Well if you are sure you are all right. You must wear a cap, until it grows again.'

After another week of backbreaking digging and cradling, David scrubbed a week's layer of sweat and dust from his body in readiness to attend Sunday service beneath the big gum tree. At the sound of a woman's voice he quickly grabbed for his shirt and put it on. He'd grown accustomed to the sounds of the day - the racket of the cradles, the scrape of shovel on gravel, men's voices, the barking of dogs, the clink of harness, the creak and groan of a windlass winding. But rarely the voice of a woman. At night the dogs barked from end to end of the field, and the sly grog shops boosted the voices and tempers of men living the harsh conditions of tent life. It was a world of men. Once again David reflected that living on the goldfields was like living in a war except that the diggers were free to come and go as they pleased and called no man sir or captain.

He looked curiously at this woman who was bold enough to venture into such an unwholesome place. She seemed decent enough, not one of the more disgraceful types he'd seen in Melbourne.

PASSING THROUGH

David nodded in her direction as she and her husband set about putting up their tent close by.

'I've not seen a woman on the diggings before. Not the place for a woman,' he murmured to Will.

'More fool him for bringing her here.' Will replied, shrugging on his jacket. 'You've a letter to be posted?'

'I've got one for Mother and Father, telling them we've left Back Creek digging's and we got enough gold there to set up a tent store here at Jones Creek. I'll be coming with you, there may be a letter for me. We'll just have time to call at the post tent before the service.'

David and Will walked away from the mail collection together and sat beneath a large tree. A letter hung from David's hand and Will in turn, had one hand on David's shoulder.

'Ye know Will, I never wanted to leave Ireland.' David held his hand over his eyes for a few moments. 'I've always regretted that I did not farewell her more fondly. Or give her some sign of my affection. Our sisters will miss her sorely.'

'I pity our poor sisters, having no mother.'

'I don't know how they'll be managing. Father can be a hard man.'

'I knew she was ill but I little thought she would be called home so soon. Poor Mother. I hope it was not too bad an end for her.'

'She was a good mother to us.'

'Aye, that she was.' Will said. Suddenly he kicked the tree trunk. 'Why wasn't it him to go? Instead of poor Mam.'

David rose to his feet. He took off his hat and swept his face and hair with his hand and tried to disguise the tears sitting at the corners of his eyes. 'At least she'll not be having any more pain now the dear soul. Even when I left she wasn't able to do much. The twins was doing almost everything then.'

'How old are they now?'

'They must be twelve by now. 'Tis hard to believe she's been gone these three months. Might be we could send some money for them to come here.'

'Yes. We'll be doing that. Come on now, Davey m'boy. We must to the service and offer a prayer.'

As Will walked briskly on, David looked at his back and wondered how it was that he seemed to absorb loss so easily. As if it was of no account beyond the moment. Was he really so hard? Didn't he remember her arm around his shoulders? Her soft encouragement when Father was at his angriest? The way she brushed the flour from her hands on her apron before she patted his head or gave him some morsel to eat? Perhaps its not that he's strong, but I am weak, David thought to himself. Yet she was our mother and I cannot feel her death lightly.

That afternoon when they returned to their tent Mr and Mrs Armand, the couple they had seen arrive that morning, came to their tent and introduced themselves.

'Bill Armand, and this is my wife, Alice. We're from Antrim, just a few miles north of Belfast. Where are you from?'

'David Stavers, and m'brother Will. We're from Rureagh, not so far from Belfast either. But south. How long since you left home? Are things any easier?'

'Ah, 'tis still the same. Our people are still leavin' the country. 'Tis a wicked evil thing.' Bill Armand's voice was bitter and angry, his eyes haunted. 'The English drove the cotters from their homes like cattle, then burnt their homes before their very eyes. I saw a dead mother laying with her half dead child sucking at her cold breast. I thank God we were able to leave.'

Alice touched her husband's arm. 'We're here now Bill. You must put all that from your mind.'

When Alice heard of the death of David and Will's mother, she offered to pray for their mother. Indeed, her presence seemed to have a civilising influence on the field, for when she was near, the diggers refrained from cursing, and doffed their Jim Crow hats to her.

During the months of August and September in the year of 1854, David, Will, Jack and Peter were still working their claims at Back Creek. Over the eighteen months they had been together they had found that David and Jack worked well together, and Will and Peter seemed to combine agreeably for the most part. As well as digging and cradling, they all shared the chores of cooking, fetching wood and water, keeping the tent weatherproof and obtaining supplies of meat and flour. The tent was a few hundred metres from their claim and as experienced diggers, they had learned to cover it with bark and leaves to improve its weather proofing, and to seal its gaps with bright red sealant. Like most diggers, David and his mates distinguished their tent from all the others around it by nailing a flag to its ridgepole. Theirs was a blue colour, divided into four with an initial in each quarter - D, W, P, J. This flag David had made, cutting the body of the flag from the tail of a worn shirt, and the letters from flour bags and stitching it together one Sunday afternoon in the early spring.

Working together each day as they did, David and Jack had become good mates. They found a similar rhythm in their working, and in their aspirations. As they walked back to the tent each evening they spoke of their hopes for the future, for the time when they would no longer have to dig for a living.

On this particular Sunday, David and Will were once more grumbling about the Joes, and their brutal treatment of the miners in their constant search for licences.

'Did you see that party of troopers yesterday? Jack and I saw them. Chased old Barney down they did. He never did no one no harm and his licence was only two days over and they still locked him up. It's terrible unjust what they do. Thirty shillings a month is a lot to find if you don't have any luck digging. Where's Jack this mornin'?' David asked.

'Gone to the butchers to get fresh meat.' Will mumbled as he tapped his pipe out on a stump.

'I'll see if there's any mail, on the way to service, might be a letter's come from Eliza.'

'Ah, she's forgotten you, Lad. Don't waste yeh time.' Will picked up the water bucket and filled the kettle, then stood the bucket upside down on a tent peg to drain. 'I'll fetch some more water this morning, the creek's running clear just now.'

'You should come to service too, Will. For the good of your soul. Mr Parslow is not such a bad preacher.'

'I've no heart for it, Davey. It never did me no good.'

'No more did brandy.'

'Mind yeh business.'

David walked up to the Commissioner's tent where the mail was being distributed. He waited to be called and his heart pounded when the trooper who was sorting the mail recognised him and tossed him a tiny letter. He took the small letter and let out a sigh of disappointment when he saw that it was for Jack. He looked around for his friend but could not see him amongst the assembled diggers, so put the letter in his pocket and headed for the service.

When he got back to the tent David asked Will, 'Any sign of Jack? I've got a letter for him.'

'Haven't seen hair nor hide of him this last two hours. Nor Peter.' Will had set out the tin plates and pannikins on the rough table in readiness and they sat down to their meal with a bit more formality than their usual crouch by the fire. David appreciated the way Will always kept an orderly camp and tried to maintain some standards, especially on Sundays.

Suddenly they heard a volley of shots and shouts. 'Likely some-one's lost his temper. And on the Sabbath too.' David stared disap-

MINERS CAMP

125

provingly towards the commotion as Peter came running down to them.

'Quick! Quick! They've shot Jack!'

David stared at Peter, uncomprehending. 'What d'ye mean? Who's shot him?'

'I think he's mortal wounded.'

David jumped to his feet and was pulling at Peter's jacket. 'Why would anyone be shooting at Jack?'

'I don't know! He was up at McCafferty's shop when a fight broke out. I think he tried to stop them from murderin' each other and got in the way.'

'God save us! Doesn't he know enough to mind his business!'

They ran to the place where Jack had been shot and found where they had laid him in the shade of a tree. Someone was fanning the flies from his wound. David knelt beside Jack's head, and taking off his jacket, folded it into a pillow for him. 'Is there a doctor? Can no one get a doctor here?' Jack's face was pale and damp with sweat. He breathed raspingly and groaned.

'D'ye have much pain?' David asked gently as Jack's body spasmed. David grasped his friend's hand and held it firmly, afraid to look at the wound in his chest.

At the sound of David's voice Jack turned his head slowly towards David's face. His eyelids closed, then slowly opened again. David thought how young he looked. He touched Jack's face, 'God help you, my friend,' and signed a cross in the air above his head. Jack coughed and David stared down as blood welled in Jack's mouth and spilled down the side of his face. With the tenderness he might have given to an infant son, David wiped his friend's mouth, then reached into his pocket so that he might read to Jack the letter from his mother. David had read but two lines when Jack gurgled 'Ma . . . ' and his body fell limp.

'What's the sense of it, Will? Jack never hurt anybody.'

'Davey, m'boy, that's the way it is here. You know that.'

'Sure, he was hot headed and didn't know when to hold his tongue. But they shouldn't have shot him for that.'

Will spread his hands in the air. 'It's a mad, lawless place we live in.'

David swallowed and his eyes welled with tears as he thought tenderly of his friend. 'He was only twenty.' David sighed. 'I'll have to write to his mother. What can I say? I can't tell her that he's been murdered. That would be too terrible, but murder it is. No one will be held to account. Those cursed troopers are here aplenty to gather gold licenses, but not to be found when an innocent body's murdered.'

That night, by the light of his tallow candle David sat and agonised over his letter to Jack's mother. At length he wrote.

Dear Mrs Weir,

My name is David Stavers and for the past fourteen months your son Jack and I have been working together as mining partners. I'm sure he would have told you about me in his letters.

It is my melancholy duty to tell you that your son has been killed in a most unfortunate accident. In attempting to break up a fight between two villains, an action which all who knew him would realise was second nature to him; he was caught in the crossfire and sustained mortal wounds. I was with him in his last moments . . .

David pushed the pen away from himself and held his head in his hands. After a time he took a deep shuddering breath, picked up his pen again, dipped it into his ink bottle and continued.

. . . and I can tell you that his last word, his last thought, was of you.

I had intended to write more to you but just now I cannot. He was the greatest of friends to me and his loss is almost more than I can bear.

David Stavers

After he had sealed up the letter, David blew out the candle and lay back on his stretcher bed thinking about Jack. It did not seem possible it was less than two years since they had met. It felt more as if they'd been friends all their lives. He remembered vividly his first sight of Jack with his flaming red hair, round a face richly freckled by the sun. The way he laughed off his blistered hands in the first days of his digging. How he had laughed off everything. How could a man as laughing and alive as Jack be not living? David tried to laugh at Jack's death, but his throat tightened and his false laughter turned to sobs.

They buried him next day in an abandoned claim, their chests aching as they plied their shovels in a familiar rhythm. No nugget in this claim. No count at the end of this shift, nothing to recall except their sorrow as the dull gravel fell on his canvas-shrouded body.

David and Will demanded an inquest into their friend's death but witnesses were few and the two men who had been fighting vanished within hours and were nowhere to be found. The finding was that Jack was accidentally shot by an unknown person.

After that, after his mother's death, followed so soon by Jack's murder, David changed. The softness was gone from him and he was tougher in his dealings with others. Those who knew him well, later said he became more like his brother Will. Taciturn and off hand. Harder to get close to. And not long after that when Eliza wrote to say that she was no longer willing to wait for him and would marry Edgar Farley the next spring, David no longer hurried eagerly to the post each week but turned his thoughts only to digging and gold, and as time went by, billiards and brandy.

On a hot north wind day, early in the summer of 1854, David and Will were trotting smartly along on their way to Ballaarat to attend a meeting called by Peter Lalor. Many weeks previously they had added their signatures to the 40 yards long document, petitioning the Governor to reduce Gold Licence fees. As they rode that day, they met several travellers who told them that the diggers were gathered in an encampment at Eureka. There was a scent of dust in the dry air and as they came over a low rise they could see in the distance a structure of fallen trees and barricades with guards set and lookouts. And a troop of soldiers gathered some little distance away.

'Looks like they've fortified themselves. They must be expecting a fiery meeting.' Will's experience on the gold-fields of America had accustomed him to clashes between diggers and authorities.

EUREKA STOCKADE

'Looks like there's no gap in the fortifications on the west. We'll have to ride round and come in from the east if we want to get in.' In the soft light of early morning, they began to circle their horses a little to the right and headed for a break in the enclosure where two diggers stood on guard.

They heard a single shot.

David stood in his stirrups and shaded his eyes while he tried to see where the shot had come from. Then there was another. 'It looks like the troops are falling in.'

David and Will spurred their mounts on in haste to reach the opening when suddenly they heard the call 'Charge!' followed by a volley of shots.

'My God! The troopers are shooting at them!' David reined in and wheeled his horse towards a small copse where he and Will dismounted and crouched behind some trees, their minds occupied by images of the defenceless men within the stockade.

'They're shooting their own countrymen!'

'Dear God! They're killing them!' An image of Jack's shattered chest filled David's mind. He and Will crouched low while volley after volley was fired into the stockade, their hearts thumping, their horses rearing and whinnying. Digger after digger fell to the murderous firing. Men filled their places and fired back, but the troopers' superior equipment and discipline overwhelmed them. David glimpsed men writhing on the ground, and heard the screams of both men and women between volleys. Even a child crying.

The air was full of dust from the troopers' charge and was thickening and drifting across the open ground before them. A trooper went down with his wounded horse. David watched as the animal tried again and again to rise, its broken leg crumpling beneath it every time. He wanted to do something. Shoot the horse for God's sake - stop it screaming. Aye, and stop the men screaming too he thought. Dear God . . .

For a moment there was a lull in the firing. 'Come on Will, let's try to get out of range.' As they ran, a couple of bullets kicked dust behind their horses making them panic. David stumbled and was pulled off balance when his horse reared and dragged him a few yards but was able to hang on until he regained his footing. Will struggled to control his mare and slapped his reins across her neck, jerked her head down. When they reached some larger trees they pulled the horses in behind them and tried to soothe them and see what was happening. A small group of troopers swept past, their pennant waving and the trumpets sounding the 'To Arms'. David turned, drew his pistol and was about to fire when Will put out his hand and stopped him. 'There's another troop coming up on the left.' He yelled. 'Lay low.' David saw a puff of smoke and recoiled from the zing of a bullet as it ricochetted off a stump. 'Get down! Get down!' David's hands trembled in fear and rage.

They stayed behind the shrubs for some minutes. 'I daren't fire. I can't tell one side from the other in this dust.' David tried to make himself heard above the sounds of battle.

'Hold. Hold David!' Will put his hand out and stayed David's firing arm. 'They're sounding the retreat. The troopers are regrouping.'

For a time there was silence as their ears thrummed to the echoes of gunshots, then slowly the silence became wails and moans and shouts. A lone voice screamed, 'Murderers!'

Maggie held the address in her pocket tightly as she climbed down off the cart in Fitzroy and pulled her shawl close about her as she entered the public house.

A man who was wiping down the rough tables, glanced at her without interest and went on with his cleaning.

'Would you tell me if a Mr Staver's been livin' in these parts at all?' Maggie asked firmly.

'And what would you be wantin' with Mr Stavers, eh? A small matter of some urgency, I'll warrant,' he leered.

'Wouldn't you think now, you could just mind your own business and tell me which house he was livin' in.' Maggie retorted, blushing furiously at this slur on her character.

'Well now. There was a young man here last week it seems to me but I'd say he's headed off back to the goldfields, Miss. Mother Bellamy on t'other side of the road, she might be knowin' where he was headed. Then agen, might be she don't.' The man leaned on the table, stared at her with mingy eyes.

Maggie shook her shawl to rid herself of his looks, as she hurried over the road to some small timber dwellings and hesitated, not knowing which one to try. One of them had cabbages growing, dull green beyond a low fence, and she recalled David's words as her landlady had read them to her. '. . . cabbage every night for dinner.' She hurried round to the back of the cottage. Surely if this was the right house, she would see some sign of his being here. Maggie knocked and waited. She heard no step or voice. I'll not go back without knowin' if he's been here. She knocked again and when there was no response, at length she tried the door. It creaked as she pushed it open and walked into a small room with an open fireplace and rough table and chairs.

There were three doors opening off this. Maggie's heart was thumping as she crept across the room. What am I doing? What if I am in the wrong house? She looked into each room. In the first she saw a skirt and a bonnet hanging on a hook and a shawl over the back of a chair beside a bed. She opened the second door, then quickly closed it again as she saw it was stacked with boxes and fur-

131

niture. The third room was also closed. She knocked, waited again, then quietly opened the door.

Was this David's room? She saw only unfamiliar objects, a small wrought iron bed, a palliasse folded back, a chair, a small rickety table. There was no sign of an occupant, nothing to indicate that David or anyone else might have used this room. Despondently she sat at the table, bent her head to her folded arms and fought to hold back tears of disappointment. She told herself not to give in to despair. Of course he would not have left anything behind.

Perhaps he had sat in this very chair. Without lifting her head Maggie opened her eyes - so close to the tabletop she could see the timber grain rippled like sand on a beach when the tide has run down. There was a dark stain. What was it? Ink? Maggie lifted her head and stared at the stain and its margins where it spread into the grain of the wood. Had David made that mark? She sniffed it, ran her hands over the table, put her fingers where his might have lain, stroked softly and turned to stare at the folded mattress. Slowly she rose and stepped to the bedside. She reached out and flipped the mattress out flat and stood there beside the bed, not moving, for a long time before she lay upon it, her face flushing, her breath coming quickly. She imagined the shape of his body where she lay. Felt her body sink into his form. The hollow of his hip, his shoulder, his head. Maggie looked where David might have looked had he lain on this bed and opened his eyes on a clear winter's morning. She saw a timber wall, and window full of clear blue sky, the edge of the table, and coming closer, the mattress. Her eyes opened wider as she saw on the edge of the mattress, a strand of linen. The same colour as David's coat. He had been here!

Holding the strand of linen in her hand, filled with new hope, Maggie quickly rose, went out of the room, and into the garden to wait for the landlady's return. She paced quickly round the garden's paths, looking up and down the street with each turn. Surely she would not be long.

Mrs Bellamy was a huge and garrulous woman, only too willing to tell Maggie that David had indeed been her boarder from time to time, and yes, he had stayed with her only days previously and as far as Mrs Bellamy knew, after he had concluded his purchases of stock for their new store, he was on his way to meet with his brother at Jones Creek. While she was telling Maggie this, Mrs Bellamy heaved round the room and got a chair for Maggie, put some more firewood on the coals and swung the kettle on its hook over the hottest part of the fire then plumped into a chair herself.

'And that's all I'm knowin' Miss.' she gasped. 'That, an' he'll be back for sure, for he always stays with me when he comes to Melbourne town.'

'Mrs Bellamy, me and me sisters . . .' Maggie began, but Mrs Bellamy was so kindly in just the way that Maggie's Mam had been kindly, that her tears began to flow.

'There, there dearie. What is it that's troublin' you?' Mrs Bellamy put a plump arm round Maggie and patted her shoulder. 'Now it can't be that bad, for can't I see you sittin' in front of me and lookin' pretty as can be, even though your hair is a bit ragged.' and Mrs Bellamy gently ruffled Maggie's roughly shorn head. It was the first time since her Ma had died that anyone but her two younger sisters had given Maggie any sign of affection and it was almost too much for her.

Maggie sniffed and smiled wetly.

'Mr Tarleton. He's the master, Mrs Tarleton's husband. She's a good mistress, but he's . . . he's horrible. He's been away, but then he came back and he did something horrible to me and he said if I told anyone he'd do it to me sisters and I can't tell anyone and you mustn't tell anyone either and I don't know what to do for I can't bear to stay there, and there's no one but meself to look after me and me sisters, for me Da died and Hugh's gone back to Ireland.'

Mrs Bellamy rocked Maggie in her arms, 'There, there my poor bairn. Are you with child?' she asked gently.

'No. No.' Maggie sniffed and shuddered at the thought, 'But I am afeared of him for meself and for me sisters too. And he's so strong, and he lurks about the place and spies on us and I'm never knowin' when he's goin' to come at me agen.' And Maggie poured out the whole tale of what had happened over the past few months and how she had cut her hair, and couldn't tell Mrs Tarleton, and even if she could, how could she say what Mr Tarleton had done to her for it was too horrible to tell and she was ashamed that such a thing had happened to her.

Mrs Bellamy poured boiling water into a teapot and handed a steaming cup to Maggie. She sat down beside her, cradling her own cup, and leaned forward.

'Well it seems to me there's nothin' in all this for you to be ashamed about. What happened is no more your fault than the angels. I'd be likin' it better if you was feelin' angry with him for that's what he deserves, the beast that he is. Now, I'm not knowin' David's address, but you can be sure next time he comes down that I'll be tellin' him you need his help.'

'But please don't tell him what happened' Maggie begged, 'For here's meself thinkin' I couldn't look at him at all if I thought he knew.' Maggie blushed and looked down, 'David . . . Mr Stavers . . . he's such a gentleman.'

'I know, dearie. I'll not be tellin' him anything, but I will let him know you cannot be stayin' at Plenty. He comes every few weeks so it shouldn't be too long before I see him. And there's one more thing. If you're havin' any more trouble with that horrible man, you must tell Mrs Tarleton.'

Maggie trembled. 'But he'll hurt me sisters.'

'I don't think so. Don't let him doubt for a single minute that you will tell her. That man is a coward and wouldn't want to be shamed before his wife.' Mrs Bellamy did not say that Mrs Tarleton might not believe her, she just said 'You've got nothing to lose for you want to be gone from there in any case.' And Mrs Bellamy patted Maggie's shoulder reassuringly then insisted that Maggie could not set out for Plenty that afternoon and must take supper and stay that night with her.

The next morning, before Maggie set out, the older woman took her out to the garden and cut a fresh cabbage for her to take home before waving her goodbye and Maggie smiled to herself to think of the meal she had eaten the evening before.

As Maggie rocked along in the cart on her way back to Plenty she thought about Mrs Bellamy and how kind she was, and how like her

Mam. The memory of her mother seemed far away, like a story of someone else, of someone she once knew. Someone who, through all the cold and hunger, had shared her childish happiness.

Each week when the cart came with the mail Maggie waited near-by, hoping for a letter from David Stavers. She was to wait for many weeks before it came, but when it did, she was able to read it for herself. She took it to the kitchen and sitting at the rough table, spread it out and read.

> *Dear Miss McFaden,*
>
> *Mrs Bellamy has told me you are not happy at Plenty. I am very busy in the store at this time but can tell you that Mr and Mrs Bentley at Ararat will be glad to offer you employment. The Bentleys are a family I met while travelling some months ago and I can assure you they are of the utmost reliability. I have enclosed a bank note for two pounds and a letter of introduction to the Bentleys. I hope that this will help you in moving to Ararat. It is rather far away - our store is at Jones Creek, but in time perhaps we will meet again.*
>
> *Yours in haste, David Stavers.*

Maggie leaned back in her chair and looked at Susannah and Lizzie, 'Mr Stavers has sent us a banknote for two pounds. And he's sent me an introduction to a family at Ararat. He's says they are looking for a housekeeper.'

'What about us? Does that mean we'll be livin' at Ararat too?' Susannah asked. 'I like it here. Mrs Tarleton's a good mistress.'

'Who'll be lookin' after Bertie and Horrie?' Lizzie wanted to know.

'I think you and Lizzie will have to live in Bunninyong near MaryAnn. We've been here near two years and it's time we was closer to the rest of the family. I don't want to live with MaryAnn and James, but to be closer would be better. And you'll be livin' in a town, not out in the bush like we are here. I'll be a bit further away at the Bentleys but I'm thinkin' I'd rather be by meself for a while.'

135

Susannah and Lizzie were shocked at the suddenness of Maggie's news but soon the excitement of going to a new place replaced their disappointment. They watched while Maggie wrote to MaryAnn, each helping with the spelling.

> *Deer MaryAnn,*
> *Susannah and Lizzie and i are leeving Plenty in too weeks and will be coming to Bunninyong i have a posison with a family called Bentley at Ararat and will be living with them can you find work for Susannah and Lizzie, do you not think we have been too long without family? and i think it wold be better for the girls if they was close by each other*
>
> *Maggie, Susannah and Lizzie.*

That very afternoon Maggie went to Mrs Tarleton.

'Mrs Tarleton, Excuse me Mam, but me and me sisters . . . '

''*My sisters and I,*' Maggie.'

'My sisters and I' Maggie got all flustered and forgot what she had practised to say. 'My sisters and I . . . we want to leave.'

'Maggie! What can you be thinking of?' Suddenly Mrs Tarleton looked sharply at Maggie. 'What has happened Maggie? Has . . . has anyone upset you in any way?'

Maggie's fingers were busy twisting and untwisting the edge of her pinny. Maggie wavered, but could not bear to tell. 'We've been very happy here with you Missis,' she hesitated and then her words came out in a rush, 'but we're missin' our family and want to be nearby them.'

LEVIATHAN COACH

'I've paid you well, have I not? You have your own room.'

'I'm very sorry Missis, it's not you, but it's almost two years we've been here, and . . . and . . . it's very lonely out here.' And Maggie began to cry a little, and wiped her nose on her sleeve

'Here you are girl,' and Mrs Tarleton handed Maggie her hand-kerchief, 'do stop crying. I thought you were happy here, and the boys are certainly very happy with you.'

'And we's fond of them too Missis, but . . . '

'Mrs Tarleton, please. Oh dear. And it's so difficult to get good girls. I suppose I shall have to begin all over again. Perhaps if I paid you a little more?' Mrs Tarleton offered.

'No Missis. I mean, Mrs Tarleton. Our minds is made up. We are goin' to our sister at Bunninyong.'

'Very well then Maggie, if I cannot change your mind, I shall arrange for your payment to be ready when you leave and I really don't know what I shall do. I must say I shall be sorry to see you go.'

When the Cobb coach pulled up in Bunninyong in December, 1855, after a bone jarring journey of several hours, Maggie, Susannah and Lizzie stepped into their first real experience of a Victorian gold rush town.

The last three hours of the journey had been stiflingly hot and there was a hint of a change in the wind. It swirled down the dusty street and caught at the girls' skirts as they clambered down from the coach and waited for their baskets and bags to be handed down from the roof.

The two years since their arrival in Port Phillip had changed the sisters. With good food, their bodies had filled out and their eyes were clear. Although they always wore bonnets when they went outside, their arms and faces were no longer pallid, but honey coloured. Maggie was barely five feet tall, but she was nicely made with a full bosom and small waist about which she was a little vain. She no longer had the pinched look she had on the ship and her even features suggested firmness and intelligence rather than prettiness. She gazed out from beneath her dark brows with green eyes so penetrating that those who did not know her, would look away, fearing she might read their thoughts.

Susannah was taller than Maggie now and still slim. Everything about Susannah suggested slenderness. Her face, her body, her limbs, even her hair was straight and her fingers long and slender. She bemoaned her lack of bosom to Maggie and secretly prayed at night that her breasts would grow.

'Look at all the shops Maggie.' Lizzie said, thinking of the things she might buy with the money Mrs Tarleton had given them when they left Plenty.

Maggie and Susannah watched Lizzie's boyish figure as she ran from shop to shop entranced by the clothes and boots and bonnets and ribbons for sale.

'What would you want to be spending your money on Lizzie? You best think about eating, before ribbons and combs.' Maggie laughed and picked up her bags and turned to walk along the dusty road. 'Let's walk up to the public house and wait there.' Just like MaryAnn to forget us she thought. No sight nor word from her for two years and now there's nobody here to meet us. Wasn't I feeling she wouldn't want us, and now I'm not at all sure that being here is what I want to be doing meself. 'We must just make the best of it.' she said aloud. 'The sooner we can find places with someone else, the better, although we won't be lucky enough to be all together like we was with Mrs Tarleton.'

At that moment Lizzie came back and joined in. 'I can be doin' most everything you can do Maggie. I can be a housemaid,' she volunteered, then added a little doubtfully, 'As long as we are in the same town.' She pulled at Maggie's sleeve, 'There's shop over there that's got pink ribbons with the prettiest roses on them, come and see.'

'Oh surely you can Lizzie. And we'll always be close by each other. I'll always be looking after you. You and Susannah and me, we're like peas in a pod. Now show me these lovely ribbons.'

Suddenly Susannah said, 'There's James. Along the road there in the pony cart.'

Lizzie hung back, reluctant to leave the abundance of good things spread out before her. There had been no shops at all at Plenty and since their arrival, the girls had had little opportunity to indulge themselves. At twelve Lizzie was at that point of girlhood where she might stop growing soon and be like Maggie, or suddenly shoot up and become like Susannah. She was just beginning to practise putting her hair up, although she still wore it down when away from home.

'Come along Lizzie,' Maggie called as James drew closer.

He waved his hat and trotted the pony round until the cart was beside them, then jumped down and embraced them each in turn.

'Oh James, 'tis good to see you. We've been so long without family; I was beginnin' to think I never had any. How's MaryAnn and little Eleanor?' Maggie asked.

'They're thriving. Ellie's not so little any more, runnin' around like a puppy and full of mischief.'

Lizzie was prancing about and telling him all about their journey while Maggie and Susannah settled their baskets in the cart and they climbed in.

As they trotted along James said, 'We've done well since comin' here. I was lucky on the diggin's and only a twelvemonth after we arrived I selected 20 acres on McCallum's Creek. It's good land but we'll be needin' more before long. Most likely MaryAnn will be adding to our family soon.' James flicked the reins and the pony trotted on.

A shiver of the old dread spread over Maggie as she thought of MaryAnn and she determined to make her stay as short as possible in spite of James' warm welcome.

Motherhood, and the demands of life in a new land had changed MaryAnn somewhat so that she and Maggie, both guarded at first, soon established a respectful regard, each for the other. There was much for them to talk over. Their father's death, Hugh's departure for Ireland almost immediately, then later their experiences in the two years since arriving in Melbourne.

Although Maggie was surprised at the ease with which she and MaryAnn settled into their new relationship, she was not so easy

139

that she could tell her older sister about the horrible Mr Tarleton. Somehow that was a secret that she could never tell. But there remained much that they could share and the next few days passed quickly with much chatter between them all. Maggie's concerns about staying too long were soon allayed as MaryAnn had arranged a position for Susannah with her neighbours who had a store in the main road, and confirmed that Maggie was to be housekeeper for the Bentley family at Ararat. Lizzie was to stay and help MaryAnn. Maggie was glad Susannah and Lizzie were to be reasonably close to each other, but concerned that she would be further away with the Bentleys. 'What's Mrs Bentley like? And Mr Bentley? Are they decent folk?'

'I think you'll find them fair enough to work for. They's English but still decent enough. They selected here almost ten years ago so they's well settled, with a lot of sheep and they keep a cow and have an orchard and a garden. There's two men who help on the farm so there'll be five people to cook for as well as their three children.'

'I'll not be able to see Susannah and Lizzie so often,' Maggie said doubtfully.

'Mrs Bentley said you'd be having a half day off every week. You can likely visit then.'

'Do you think Susannah will be safe from temptations, livin' at the store?'

'She'll only be there durin' the week. Saturday she'll come back here and come to church with us on the Sabbath.'

'MaryAnn, I've not been to a church since before we left Ireland!' Maggie muttered and turned away. 'And I don't know that it would have improved me life if I had.'

'Maggie! You've become a heathen! How can you say such a thing?'

'I never missed it much all the time I was at Plenty and it never stopped me prayin' or helpin' people or bein' honest.'

MaryAnn had never thought that it might be possible to live a good life without going to church and though shocked, she was amazed at her younger sister's independence of thought. 'How old are you Maggie?'

'I don't know. I think I'm twenty. I don't know when me birthday is exactly.'

'I was about eight when you was born. 1835 I think it was. I think you was born on the twelfth day in September so you must be twenty. The first time I saw you I thought you looked like a plucked chicken but our Mam thought you was beautiful for some such reason.'

'I was altogether thinkin' you didn't like me.' Maggie said tentatively.

'Our Mam was always sick. I was the oldest and big enough to help. 'Tis bad enough tryin' to manage when you're feelin' well, but I can see now our Mam was almost always sick. She depended on me. I don't remember a single day that I didn't fall into me bed at night, with not a bit of strength left in me limbs. Even when I was only three or four years old I had to help her. I never had no strength left for likin' or not likin'. Now I've got my own babby I know how much a mother needs that help. And likely we'll be havin' another soon enough. That's why I want Lizzie to stay here.'

Maggie began to understand that perhaps MaryAnn's life might have been even harder than her own and that being the oldest of ten children was a heavy burden. 'Well, you'll not be too hard on her will you MaryAnn? She's only twelve and she's known nothin' but work all her short life.'

'Well then, she's no different to any of us, is she?' MaryAnn said as she briskly cleared the cups from the table and carried them out to the scullery.

That night as she got into her bed, Maggie held her mother's stone in her hand and for the first time in two years, allowed herself to think about her mother and the life she had left behind in Ireland. She remembered all too well the year her mother died. That terrible autumn when the crops failed, the hunger and the dying days of winter when all they had to fill their hollow bellies was a spoonful of corn meal in a pot of boiled weeds. A whole winter scrabbling in the frozen earth for a few straggling bits of weeds. Seeing the dead being eaten by scavenging dogs and rats because the living had no strength nor money to bury them. And the landlords driving people out and burning their houses. And the stench of death everywhere. Now that she was here, well fed and healthy, Maggie could hardly believe she had lived through such agony. I'll not think of it ever again she said to herself. 'Tis altogether too terrible.

But there were small, distant memories of a time before the famine. Of the lake and the mountains beyond, and the sweet smell of a peat fire. Her mother's arm around her shoulders. Her sisters' laughter. And in Ballyeasboro she knew everybody in every cottage for a mile around. My belly is full now she thought, but somehow the rest of me feels empty. As if there's no real place for me here. No place that feels like home - just all those miles of eucalyptus trees and the hot sun, and flies and spiders and snakes and everything I'm afraid of. Will I ever be easy here?

As soon as Maggie was settled with her new family she wrote to Sarah.

> *Deer Sarah,*
> *i have been now over two yeers in Port Phillip and i must tell you that i have had meny tryals in this time not three months after we landed our Father dyed and our brother left us and saled back to Ireland i was left with Susie and Lizzie to look after and MaryAnn was far away with her one famile and not concerned with us Our first mistress was a good woman but her husband was an evil man who i hop i will never meet agen now i am in the employ of Mr and Mrs Bentley at Ararat and they are good peeple but I am much alone as Susie and Lizzie are working elswere but I am happy enuff with that for now plees rite to me as soon as you get this as I am lonly for a word from home*
> *your loving Maggie Mr Wesley at our first employ taut us to reed and rite.*

As Maggie wrote Sarah's name on the envelope and sealed it, it was as if she placed a tiny part of her heart in the envelope with her letter. She tried to imagine its long journey. First the coach to

Melbourne, then the ship sailing across the sea, and if it did not sink, and if the mail was not rotted by the water in the hold, perhaps in a few months time it might reach her friend. And she patted it and pressed it to her lips and prayed as she put it in with the other letters from the household, that it would reach its destination. Maggie then walked down the dusty street to the little store, and handed her bundle of letters into the hands of the postmaster.

One evening during the time David and Will had their wagon store, they sat down to their usual meal of mutton, damper and tea. Will tapped the ash off the damper and broke it into pieces while David pulled the meat bag down from the tree and shook out a haunch of cooked mutton.

He exhaled a deep breath when he saw the meat, and flicked maggots off with his penknife before cutting some slices from it. As they sat down to eat in the firelight, David said, 'I heard some of the men grumbling about the Chinese again.'

'Well, the Chinks're heathens aren't they? They send all their gold back to China to build idols, or even worse, to bring more of their hundreds out here.' Will picked at his meat with some distaste.

'They buy a lot of our picks and shovels. They're good customers.' David conceded. 'But just the same, I think there's too many of them. They're dirty and live like dogs. They only work the deserted claims. They're heathens, and if they keep breeding up they'll run us over.'

Will stood up and went to the fire and poured a pannikin of tea for each of them, 'Davey m'boy. You've a lot to learn up here. Keep out of other people's troubles. You've got enough of your own.'

'But Will, don't you want to stand up for our rights? If everyone was like you and did nothing, who knows what would happen. We want to make an honest living. We don't want to have the Celestials sneaking round and filching good dirt from people's claims. Anyway, tonight there's a meeting at Finnegan's Hill. I'm going.'

'As you will. I'm for sleep. You'll close up?'

The frogs' song made a throbbing in David's head as he rolled down the canvas sides on the wagon. The latest arrival of Chinese from Port Adelaide had cleaned them out down to the last pick and shovel and although it meant yet another trip to Melbourne to replenish stock, David wasn't about to complain about that. The Jones Creek rush had been good for business.

He climbed into the back of the wagon and in the darkness, felt along its floor next to the side till he came to a slight ridge. He slipped the tip of his penknife into the gap and prised open the top of a small sliding drawer and quickly and quietly packed into it the gold he had received in payment that day. The lid slid heavily back into place leaving no hint of the drawer's presence. Before reaching outside for his lamp, David divided the coins about his person, placing some in each pocket and patted them with satisfaction. If the present rush continued he and Will would soon be able to sell the canvas topped wagon and build a more permanent store.

David pushed his revolver into his holster before mounting his horse and riding to Finnegan's Hill. It was a clear cold night and as he rode he looked at the stars glittering between the branches of the eucalyptus trees and wondered that those celestial bodies should have given their name to such low creatures as the Chinese.

When he arrived at the meeting there was much shouting and agitation. Dan Dorrow was speaking and inciting the crowd to vengeance although David wasn't altogether clear as to what they were avengeing. He saw many men he knew, men with whom he'd shared a drink, who had bought goods from him.

Suddenly, above the speakers, a voice called, 'Let's get the Coolies!' It was repeated once or twice, then it began to beat like an evil heart, 'Get the coolies! Get the coolies!' The chant began to rise. Leaderless but with one mind, the crowd's mood changed and they became a mob, filled with the intention of scalping and robbing the Chinese in the hope of driving them away. Grabbing flares and burning branches, they swept down the Finnegan's Hill towards the Chinese encampment.

'Get the coolies! Get the coolies!'

David unholstered his revolver and swung his mare into the mob. They rode at a canter, gathering more and more men as they swept down the hill and across the flat to the lowest part of the diggings where the Chinese were encamped. Ahead of  him men flashed knives or shot their firearms into the air as they rode helter skelter down the hill.

As the mob spilled into the camp the riders jammed up against one another, pushing their horses forward, cutting the tent guys. The terrified Chinese spilled from their meagre homes.

David shot into the air once or twice and spurred his little mare on, taking pot shots at anything that moved. Ahead of him a Chinaman cowered before his tent and David raised his left arm and rested the barrel of his revolver on his forearm and took aim. Just at that moment another rider cut across in front of him and leaned down and grasped the man by his cue. He held him head-hard against his saddle, and hacked with his knife at the Chinaman's scalp until his victim fell to the ground, and the rider wheeled away, waving his grisly trophy.

David's revolver hand fell to his side as he looked down at the bloodied Chinese. He gagged and shuddered, feeling suddenly cold and trembling, appalled at the violence he was embroiled in.

The Chinaman lay at his feet moaning while the blood poured down his face. David heard a cry behind him and he turned and bawled 'Stop! Stop it!' as four men tore another coolie from his tent and began beating the cowering man.

'Let's get rid of the filthy hordes!' they screamed, 'Brain him! Get rid of them!'

'Stop! You must stop! This is murder! You must stop!' David

leapt from his horse and scrambled between the man and his tormentors and stood facing the marauders. He pointed his revolver at them, and then fired a shot over their heads. A flicker of recognition made them hesitate for a moment. 'Come on boys! After the Chinks!' And the mob pushed him aside and struck him across the shoulders as they passed, turning their fury towards other victims.

Flames leapt all around as the mob rode on and fired tent after tent, cheering as each new flare lightened the hideous scene. They surged on, rounding up the terrified Chinese like a flock of sheep and beat them with pick handles, or stabbed them, whipped them and bludgeoned them. Then without shame, robbed their victims of their meagre possessions.

David bent and put his hand on the Chinaman's shoulder for a moment. All the time gazing at the man's bloodied head, David slowly pulled his shirt out and tore a strip from it and knelt and bound it round the Chinaman's head. Then silently, he turned and led his mare away from the melee.

It was reported in the newssheets that 'a few' Chinese had been injured. But the murmurings around the diggings were that the numbers were far greater. It was even whispered that the marauders had been joined by women and children in the robbing of the Chinese. David and Will were silent when they saw the abundant evidence of the violence. In the following days there were many Chinese men with bound and bloodied heads hiding round the permimeter of the field.

David was consumed by shame for his part in that dreadful night and the next evening he said to Will, 'I don't think I can stay here any longer.'

Will looked up from his contemplation of the fire, 'What happened?'

'I don't want to talk about it. It was an evil night and one which I will not soon put from my mind.'

Will considered for a few moments before spitting into the fire. 'Then it's time for us to move on. We've made enough profit here. Such evil leaves a bad taste in the mouth.'

146

But it was not so easy to ride away from the memory of that night.

A day or two later David asked 'Is there any talk of new rushes? We want a place where the gold will last for more than a few weeks.'

'If I knew that I'd be a rich man, Davey. But I did hear about a place called Pleasant Creek. That might prove to be good diggings. What do you think?'

'If it's good digging its good business. I vote we go there.' and with that the brothers began to pack and move on.

Winter in June of 1856 was cold and wet. It rained day after day and Maggie was hard pressed to keep up with the mud that was constantly walked through the Bentley's house, with getting the washing dry, and stopping the water where it dripped and trickled through the roof. The chickens sat in their pen, bedraggled and morose and Maggie was feeling pretty much the same when Mrs Bentley came out to the kitchen one Tuesday morning and said 'Richard Watford, a friend of the family, will be coming next week from the Ovens. He'll be staying here for the next couple of months probably. Would you fix a bed for him on the verandah? I'll get Charlie to nail up a canvas to keep the rain off and if you could make up a bed down at the end, near the kitchen window. I think he'll be dry enough there.'

As Maggie made up the bed with fresh sheets and a possum skin rug, she wondered about Richard Watford. Mrs Bentley had said he had had some good fortune up at the Ovens and was thinking of farming and wanted to learn from the Bentley family and their successful enterprise.

Maggie was surprised when Richard arrived. Mrs Bentley was in her forties and Mr Bentley looked even older; that they should have a friend who appeared to be under thirty was unexpected. And his easy manner made her feel comfortable too, for when he spoke to her it was as if she was not a servant. Soon Maggie found herself hoping Richard Watford would stop by when she was feeding the chickens or gathering vegetables from the kitchen garden.

Richard bent his tall frame to Maggie when they spoke and kept his brown eyes on hers as if there was no one else in the world he wanted to talk to.

'Tell me about yourself, Maggie. How long have you been here?'

For a moment Maggie was speechless. Rarely had anyone shown interest in her, mostly they were more eager to tell her about themselves. All the unexpressed thoughts that continually occupied her mind jostled for voice and she hardly knew where to begin. Richard leaned towards her, looking and waiting.

'I've been in Port Phillip for three years and here with Mr and Mrs Bentley for an eighteen month or thereabouts. And a very pleasant place it's turned out to be Mr Watford.'

Richard was enjoying Maggie's formality, her slight agitation, 'Please call me Richard,' and watched as a flush washed over her face. 'They really are the most honest and good people, aren't they? I've known them ever since my parents died. They helped me at a time when I needed someone generous and understanding.'

'You're lucky then, I could wish I'd had such a help when me own Da died and me brother went back to Ireland.'

'When was that Maggie?'

'Only three months after we arrived here.'

'And your mother?'

Maggie's hand wandered into her pocket and held her small stone. 'She died when I was twelve. So, there I was with me two sisters to look after, and me only eighteen.'

'It must have been very lonely. Frightening too.'

'I think it was the unhappiest time of me short life. Being by meself, I don't mean livin' by meself, but not havin' any family, it made me think how everyone needs a place, and familiar bodies around them. The first family we was with, the Missus was a good woman but when the master came back from England, well, I wasn't likin' him at all.'

Richard wondered what lay behind Maggie's words. 'Was that why you left there?'

148

Maggie slipped back into prevarication. 'That, and wantin' to be closer to me oldest sister.' Not wanting to be drawn further on the Tarletons, she added, 'Sometimes I look at the black people here and I wonder how they live. I think they're like we was back in Ireland. Pushed out of their place altogether, treated no better than animals.'

'I've often thought that myself. But aren't you a little afraid of them?'

'Once I was. But when I first came here I was lost in the bush one day and they was kind to me and showed me how to get back. And then later . . . ' She hesitated.

'Later? What happened later, Maggie?' Richard prompted.

Maggie wavered for long seconds then turned and walked to the seat on the verandah. She sat down and took her hand from her pocket. 'When I left Ireland I brought this stone with me.' And she held out her hand and showed it to Richard. 'It's not a very special lookin' stone at all. But it is special to me because it came to me from me Mam.'

'Did she give it to you?'

'No, she didn't exactly give it to me, but that's not what I'm after tellin' you now. When I first saw the savages, the ones who used to come to the homestead at Plenty, they was always laughing and kind. They stole a few things, but nothing big it seems to me. The mysterious thing is that since I've been here with the Bentleys, every now and then I meet this black girl. I give her some bread, or a bit of meat and sometimes she shows me things. Once she brought me a fish and I gave her some cheese but she didn't seem to like it. And I've got a necklace she gave me, made of teeth, but I don't think I'd ever be wearin' it for it looks so savage.'

'You must show it to me one day.'

'Sure and I will. I think she's the same age as meself, but then I think she's older too, for now she's got a babby and another one comin'. But it's more than that. She's older in a different way.' Maggie paused. 'And she's got a stone too. And she holds it in her hand and polishes it with her fingers and when she's carryin' the babby she wraps the stone in a piece of bark and carries it in her

149

hair. And somehow it's bringin' me closer to her, knowin' she's got a stone. It's as if we's the same.' Suddenly Maggie realised what she'd been saying, for she jumped up and put the stone back in her pocket. 'I'm sorry to be worryin' you with my fancies Mr Richard, I'd best be goin' on with my work.'

Richard put his hand on Maggie's arm 'I have a friend amongst the blacks. I think I know what you mean when you say the stone has special meaning. Wongarra had a way of calling a tree or a stone 'he'. Perhaps it is a way they have with the world that we have forgotten. I have also found him to be one of the most happy and generous men I have ever met.'

Maggie came away from this encounter with a deep feeling of understanding and connection with Richard. They never spoke directly of it, but Maggie was sure Richard felt the same.

One day when she had just washed her hair and was brushing it out in the sunshine to dry, Richard came and sat beside her on the edge of the verandah. Ever since Plenty, though Maggie had eventually grown her hair again, it was seldom allowed out of its bun on the nape of her neck and Maggie was embarrassed to be found in such disarray. 'I'll just be windin' it up so I can see you.' she laughed.

'It's beautiful. Don't put it away. Let me brush it for you?'

Suddenly Maggie felt sick and pulled her hair away. 'It's such a mop Mr Richard. It's not at all worth it.'

'Oh but it is Maggie! I used to brush my wife's hair, I know how to do it gently. I promise I'll not hurt you.'

A wife? He had not mentioned this before. 'Won't you now?' Maggie said wistfully, still reluctant to let another hand touch her hair. 'I can't Mr Richard. I'm sorry, I just can't bear it, anyone touchin' me hair.' She drew away. 'Where's your wife then?'

'She died with our first child. Four years since.'

'That's sad. That's sad, that is.'

'You should never wind your hair up. It's like a cloak waving down your back.'

'Well, I don't see me hair from the back do I?' Maggie laughed, turning and trying to look over her shoulder. Richard leaned forward to take in the fresh clean scent of her and his hand covered hers and slowly they began to brush together. Maggie could smell Richard's nearness; taste his nearness in her mouth.

On his next visit he brought her a gift. 'I made it so you can see how beautiful your hair is.'

'A mirror! You've made it for me?' Maggie ran her fingers over its surface, and her eyes took in the delicate engravings on the back. 'Tis beautiful Richard. I don't ever remember havin' a gift made special for me at all, at all. How can I thank you.' And she looked down to hide the tears that had sprung to her eyes.

Richard thought her actions thanks enough. 'The decorations on the handle are from the mother of pearl shell. I thought you would like it - it has so much colour in it, like rainbows. And the black line around the mirror is to remind you how your hair frames your face.'

Maggie held the mirror in her hands and ran her fingers round its rim, feeling its smoothness. She held it up and admired her reflection, then met Richard's eyes in the glass and in that moment of surrender would have allowed him any liberty with her hair at all.

They walked to the lagoon one still autumn evening and sat on a fallen tree, watching the stars appear on the surface of the water, trying to find the constellations in the shimmering reflections. When Richard took her hand, Maggie let it stay, folded in his. There was about them a stillness, deep as the sky mirrored in the water. Maggie leaned her head on Richards shoulder and relaxed into the curve of his arm. They breathed each other's breath gently.

'Will you trust me Maggie?'

'I do.'

'Will you marry me?'

'I will.'

They stood and held their bodies together, then joined their hands and leaned back, each leaning into space, trusting the other to hold. Richard balancing his greater weight against Maggie's lightness as they stood in their triangle of love.

'I will hold you Maggie.'

'And I will hold you and trust you Richard.'

As they walked back to the homestead that night, Richard put his hand at the nape of Maggie's neck and loosened her hair, caressed her head. She leaned her head into his hand, then turned and kissed his fingers. He put his hand under her chin and lifted her face, tracing her eyes and nose with his fingers, touching her lips, then bent and kissed them, small nibbling kisses so that she responded and began to enjoy the play of it and when Richard's tongue probed into her mouth she did not remember her fears and reached up so that she might return his caress.

'I think we best marry soon Richard.' Maggie whispered.

'Tomorrow?'

Maggie laughed, 'As soon as we can get the banns.'

One morning a few weeks later, Maggie was kneading the bread and listening to the sound of Richard's axe as he cut a load of firewood. In her mind Maggie could see him stretching high, the pale sun lighting his arms and she heard the steady tock, tock each time the axe came down. Suddenly she heard a cry and the tocking stopped. Maggie went to the door cleaning her hands on her apron and saw Richard bent over, holding his head. She grabbed a towel and ran to him. He was moaning, 'My eye! It's in my eye! Get it out! Get it out!'

'What is it? Quick, lay down, Richard.' Maggie squatted, with his head held tight between her knees and peered into his blood filled eye socket. She spread the lids with her fingers then leaned down and tongued his eye where the blood oozed out. She felt a sharp cold spike. 'Hold fast. I can feel it with my tongue.' She tried to grasp it. 'Hold still. Hold still. I can get it with my teeth.' She tried again, feeling with her tongue, pressing her teeth close while Richard writhed and groaned, his back arched, his arms uselessly flailing the air.

'Keep still!' Once more Maggie bent and felt with her tongue then gripped her teeth on cold metal and pulled. Out came a sliver of steel, streaked with blood.

Maggie could taste Richard's blood as they held each other and stumbled to the house. 'Can you ride, d'ye think?'

Richard's body was shaking. Maggie felt a faint veil of sweat at his temple and his face was pale.

'Sit here. I'll get the horse.'

Maggie could never remember how she caught the horse or how they trotted the eight miles to Ararat and the doctor. All she could recall was that she had one hand on the reins and another behind her holding Richard. And the image of Richard's eye and the feel of his body shaking beneath her hand.

'I don't think I can save his eye.' The doctor said. 'It's badly damaged. I'll have to put some stitches in the side there. Here, drink this.' He handed Richard half a tumbler of whiskey. They waited a few minutes for the alcohol to take effect then bound him to the table and called the butcher from over the road to help hold his head still while the doctor cut and stitched at his eye.

Later, Richard looked at Maggie with his other eye.

'It's all right.' Maggie put one hand to the side of his face. 'Your eye's hurt, but you'll be better altogether in a few days. The doctor had to take your eye out. He said it should heal quickly.' Maggie didn't tell Richard that the doctor hoped the spike had not penetrated Richard's brain.

'Hold me Maggie.'

'I will, always, me darlin'.'

After the journey home Richard fell into a deep sleep and they waited for his body to heal itself. Maggie was constantly by his side, barely eating, sleeping with her hand holding his, awake at his smallest movement. When he did not wake by the second day, they began to be alarmed and sent for the doctor again. Richard had begun to beat with his hands at his head and face.

'There's no fever. That's a good sign. But he seems to be in pain. I'll put some leeches to his temple to draw away the bad blood.'

By the fourth day he seemed calmer and in less pain but still had not regained consciousness.

Maggie sat beside his silent body and told him of their lives to come. 'We will be married Richard. You with your one eye and me with me hair hangin' down me back. And I will love you and hold you and at the end of the day we'll smile at each other and wherever we are and whatever happens, we'll be together. And we'll make sons and daughters to fill our days and we'll be altogether happy.'

Maggie gently pressed her fingers into the corners of Richard's mouth to make a smile. His jaw fell open a little and she put the tip of her finger in his mouth. With all the longing of her heart she whispered, 'Can you hear me Richard?' She felt the faintest movement of his jaw. Ah! He knows, he knows. And she laid her head beside his on the pillow and imagined waking up every morning for the rest of her life with that view of him; his hair, his ear, his jaw, his face, his mouth, his damaged eye.

Before first light the next morning, the day of their planned wedding, Maggie was beside him when he woke. His eye fastened on her face for a moment and his hand reached out to her briefly. Her heart throbbed in her throat as she saw his eye staring at her, heard his groan, and felt the long, last breath as it fluttered from his body.

'Richard! Ah, don't be leavin me, Anam Cara. Please stay! Oh! Please Dear God, let him stay. Let him stay.'

As Maggie covered Richard's face with kisses she cried over and over Anam Cara! Anam Cara!

Then taking her stone she pressed it to Richard's lips, and to her own. And Maggie held her small, cold stone to her heart and laid her head on Richard's still breast.

For a time after the funeral Maggie stayed with MaryAnn, but she was restless and distracted and after a few weeks she announced 'I'll be goin' home to Ararat tomorrow MaryAnn. I can't seem to settle.'

'James and I want you to stay as long as you wish Maggie.' MaryAnn could only offer prayers, but suspected they were meaningless in the face of Maggie's grief, and gave up trying to persuade her otherwise.

When Maggie got back to her tiny room at Ararat, she sat on her bed for a long time. She was very still. Going back in her mind to that other time. Her time with Richard. At last she picked up the mirror and ran her fingers around its rim, then held the cold glass to her cheek. Her breath misted the glass and when she looked into it, she fancied she could see Richard's eyes, gazing back at her from her own reflection. That's how it was, she thought. Looking into Richard's eyes and seeing meself. Like looking at meself for the first time, fresh and innocent, as Eve might have looked at Adam, before the Fall. He is not dead she told herself, for always I'll have the memory of him. But I saw him die. And would have died meself too if only I could have. I held him with every scrap of me love. But I saw him die. No matter how hard I held him, he died. And I'll have to be dying meself to be with him again. All I have is me mirror.

Maggie undid her hair and spread it over her shoulders like a cloak and curled up on her bed with her mirror held tight to her breast.

In the year since Richard's death Maggie had not seen any of her family. Her sisters had written to her each week as always but still no word came from Maggie. She had withdrawn from life and even Mrs Bentley seemed unable to interest her in anything. In desperation she and MaryAnn contrived for her to pay a visit to Pleasant Creek to see Susannah who was then working in David Staver's store. It was only after much cajoling that she agreed to go.

As the coach arrived at Pleasant Creek she was surprised to find a town that was quite well developed with many shops and even one or two brick buildings. Maggie stepped down from the coach and looked about for the Live and Let Live Hotel. Soon she saw its sign and across the road, a small timber and canvas store with the name Stavers painted across the top of the timber framed door. Habit led her to pat her hair into place and straighten her skirts before open-ing the door. Its bell jangled and as she entered she saw David Stavers emerge from behind a partition at the back of the shop. He wiped his hands on a cloth and proceeded to wipe down the counter as well. 'Yes Miss?' He looked up. Framed against the soft light of the canvas walls, he saw a young woman, neatly dressed, with thick hair coiled beneath a pert little bonnet. He noticed her clear eyes, her dark brows and a certain flush to her cheeks that he found rather attractive, in spite of his usual guardedness with women.

Maggie had not seen David since they left the ship five years previously. His face was thinner, clean-shaven and looked noticeably older. She saw that lines were beginning to form at the sides of his mouth, his eyes were scowling and his manner abrupt. She was in some faint way pleased to see that he was wearing the linen jacket he had made on the ship even though it sagged a little and was wrinkled at the elbows. But in spite of these nostalgic thoughts, as she looked at David, she could see only a stranger. As she waited for his greeting she saw there were changes in his eyes too - they were not so eager, nor so clear as before and he did not look at her directly - and she wondered what sadness and trouble had happened in his life.

'Good morning Miss. What can I get for you this morning?'

Not being recognised, Maggie pretended unrecognition herself. 'Is this the store that Susannah McFaden is workin' in? Would you think she is somewhere about at all?'

'Why yes, Miss McFaden does work here. She is out on an errand just now.'

'She'll be back soon?'

Something about her voice made him look again. This could hardly be Margaret McFaden from the Miles Barton; she who was so thin and unkempt. This young woman was well dressed and plump of face and body and she had a certain air of confidence about her that the other Margaret had certainly not possessed.

'Miss McFaden? Margaret?'

'Yes. It is altogether. 'Tis good indeed to be seein' you again Mr Stavers. I've come to visit Susannah but since you're here, I believe I owe you more than thanks for introducin' me to the Bentleys. I've altogether regretted not writin' you a better thank you, because I do find myself settled in a most agreeable position with them.'

'It was but a small service I could provide.' David came from behind the counter and shook hands with Maggie warmly. 'I was confident in recommending you and felt sure it would work out well. Do you know, I'd not seen another soul from the ship these last five years till your sister came to work for me.'

156

Maggie found herself wondering what might have happened if her girlish feelings for David had had the chance to become something more permanent after they left the ship. Perhaps by now we would have had a family, a home. Would we have been happy she wondered? It was all she'd ever wanted, her own home, and a family. But Tarleton had made her fearful of all men, until she met Richard.

Just then Susannah came back from her errand. 'Maggie!' The girls laughed and embraced. 'Oh! 'Tis good to see you, Sister Dear. When I got your letter I was so excited to think I'd be seein' your face again.'

'The Bentleys seem to think I need to have some time visitin'. They're such good people. I've been gettin' along.' Maggie turned and looked about her, 'I can see you have a good place here Susannah.'

David interjected 'Since we are not busy, perhaps you would like to go and have a pot of tea together. I can spare you for half an hour,' he said, looking at Susannah. He held the door open for them as they thanked him with a grateful glance, linked arms and hurried along the street. He stood in the doorway and watched them, and briefly imagined himself walking between them, a hand on each waist.

The girls hugged each other as they walked along.

'Maggie, I've so much to tell you, and I want to know what's been happening to you too.'

'Susie, you've lost a tooth!'

'I know.' Susannah put her hand up to her mouth 'I was helpin' a cow get its leg out of a fence and the beast kicked me for my trouble. You should have seen me. When I looked in the mirror I near fainted. Me nose was all bloodied and squashed and me lips was swollen like that time you fell in the woodheap, remember?'

Maggie remembered all too well, but would rather not.

'Me face got better but now I've got a big gap in me mouth and I've stopped smilin'.'

'Oh Susie. You mustn't stop smilin' for it lights up your lovely face.'

'That may be, but I'd be thinkin' twice before lookin' at meself in a mirror!' Susie laughed. And the girls hugged each other yet again.

'Are you happy with the Bentley's Maggie?'

'Happy enough. They really are the best people to work for, kindly and good-natured. I don't need any other friends.'

'Do you never go out then?'

'I don't go to any of the fairs and fetes at all so I don't see anyone else. Only a black friend who visits now and then. Now tell me, how do you like workin' for David Stavers?'

'Well Maggie, he's good tempered enough generally, but he don't tolerate my makin' any mistakes and some days he's cross as can be.'.

'Is it better than Tarleton's, at Bentleys?'

'It's much better Susie, although there's a lot more to cook for, six adults and three children, but they've got a nursemaid for the children so I don't have to look after them. I mostly cook and clean and there's a woman comes and does the washin' sometimes.'

'Remember the day Mrs T's drawers got caught on the cow's horns and she galloped right up to the big house with them swingin' and spooking her all the way!'

'And Mrs Tarleton and that Captain Bridge was there and he never realised what he grabbed until he handed them to Mrs T. I thought she'd explode, she was so red in the face!'

'Mrs T saw more of the washing than she wanted to that day!'

'But she was fussy enough about it. Remember how if I even had one wrinkle in her dresses when I ironed her them, she'd drop them in the tub and make me do them again.'

'She was certainly most exactin'.'

'Oh Susie. I miss havin' a laugh with you. Mrs Bentley is the most agreeable woman. Altogether kinder than Mrs Tarleton and the kitchen is better, and they've got tank water, so there's no carry-in'of it. But I do miss you and Lizzie. Have you seen her?'

'I had a letter from her just last week. She said she's grown tall and is putting her hair up now. Has yours grown again? I could never understand why you cut it that time Maggie.'

Maggie patted the coil at the back of her head. 'Well, it's grown again now, much good it will be doin' me.'

'Whatever's the matter Maggie that you're soundin' so gloomy? Are you still pinin' for that Richard Watford? Surely there's plenty of bachelors hereabouts.'

'Ah well. I'm too old for that now Susie. Come, let's have that pot of tea!'

As Maggie jogged along in the trap on the way back to Bentleys that night she thought about David Stavers. It had been good to see him again even though he seemed different from the David she remembered on the ship. Older, certainly. As she was. But there was an edge of bitterness to him now that was not there before. I wonder what has happened to make him so? Susannah did not seem to know, but then she was not attracted to him as I was. It's strange that he has not married. Has he not found a woman he loves? Many men don't marry until they have a home to take their wives to. He'd be like that.

Maggie visited Pleasant Creek many times over the next few months as she slowly came back into the world of friends and family. During her weekly visits she and David often met at James and MaryAnn's, or walked together while they discussed the progress of David's business or perhaps the next quadrille assembly.

David and William had formed a group that met monthly in the Pleasant Creek Presbyterian Church Hall for the purpose of dancing the quadrille. They had strict rules of membership so that only the most respectable ladies and gentlemen could attend. Once a month they would decorate the hall with branches of eucalypt leaves and prepare the floor by scattering shaved candle wax across it. They would place a large rock in a sturdy box with a carpeted bottom and if the boys in the town dragged it round for an hour or so until the floor was shiny and 'fast' and ready for dancing, they would be allowed to slide up and down as their reward. A fiddler and an accordianist supplied music for this delightful enterprise. But though Maggie and David danced together and often met at MaryAnn's, there was no romance between them.

One spring night in 1859 Maggie and David had dinner with

MaryAnn and James followed by several games of draughts. Having won all three, David was feeling in a benign mood and as Maggie replaced the black and white counters and closed the box he asked, 'Will you walk with me, Maggie?'

As they strolled along the main street past the bowling alley, David announced, 'Will and I have bought a block of land just down here.'

'And what are you're proposin' to do with this block of land?' Maggie flushed when she realised she had used the word proposing, not eager to wake the thought in his mind.

'We're going to build a timber store and dwelling house. There's to be double entrance doors in the middle, with windows on either side for displaying our goods. Two rooms at the back, one for living and one to lock up for storage, with a kitchen lean-to outside.'

'I'm altogether glad you're prosperin' David, it sounds very grand.'

'It'll be more permanent, more solid. I've never been happy selling wine and spirits, especially from the tent store, but I must admit without it, we would have gone out of business. A timber building will be more secure for the grog.'

''Tis much of a temptation to any man, I wonder you haven't tried it yourself.' Maggie probed, smiling.

David dropped his face to hide his guilt, for he had tried to keep his drinking secret and separate from Maggie and her family who had been such staunch friends to him.

Ever since Jack had died, although David knew something had gone out of his life, he did not know what it was. He had tried drinking, at first just a tot at night before sleep. It didn't help much really, just made him feel drowsy at the end of the day. But in the five years since Jack's death, his dependence on drink had grown until now he could hardly get through the day without a few tots.

Lately he had found that visiting his friend Maggie gave him much pleasure, and knew that for the first time since Jack was shot,

160

he felt a comfort that was absent in the rest of his life, and a trust that Maggie would support him whatever happened.

He was about to confess to his drinking when Maggie said. 'If I was thinkin' of marryin', it would never be to a man who was a drunkard. Men seem to have no care for their wives and children when they drink. I've no desire to live a life like that.'

'Indeed not. And I would not wish to see you do so either.' David's thoughts quickly turned to other matters. 'By the way, I was down in Melbourne last week. All the streets are lit by gaslight now. In the evenings it is as bright as twilight and respectable people can walk the streets safely.'

'I read in The Clarion that the Public Library will soon be opened. They say it will hold thousands of books.'

'That's right. The building plan is most ambitious. Just think, it would take a lifetime to read so many books. I think I could spend the rest of my life there. And did you know, you can telegraph from the post office in Melbourne to the post office in Sydney now and a message will get there instantly. And an answer can come back within the hour!'

'How can they do such a thing?'

'There's a wire strung along posts all the way from Melbourne to Sydney and they send electrical impulses along it with a musical key in a sort of code. It sounds like ditditdah, ditditdah. And they read it out at the other end. This invention will change our lives Maggie. Can you imagine how quickly we will be able to carry out commerce?'

'Well I can see that you can get an order really quickly, but I don't suppose you can send a barrel of salt fish on your ditditdah!'

As David rode the long journey from Melbourne to Pleasant Creek for the third time in the September of 1859, he looked for a suitable place to plant the pear cuttings he had been given. Spring's earth was soft and fragrant from the rains and would make a good bed for his pear trees. Already plums and apples planted by earlier travellers were in flower and would be ready to pick in the autumn. It was pleasant as he rode along to be able to pluck a fresh pear or an apple and David remembered with gratitude the first settlers who had planted these trees in earlier times. In a few years others would feel the same gratitude to him he thought, as he looked for the best place to plant the cuttings.

David chose the north bank of a small creek, where they would get plenty of sun and some runoff from the rain. He watered them in, then lay on the bank in the thin sunshine and relaxed for a few minutes before continuing his journey.

He closed his eyes and imagined his trees, grown and burdened with ripening fruit and fancied he heard the laughter of young women as they rode up to the tree, then the creak of leather as they dismounted. He saw that Eliza was there and watched as she plucked a ripe pear and sank her teeth into the sweet flesh, licking the juice from her fingers and lips as it ran down. David picked a pear himself and he too bit into its flesh, then pressed the fruit to her lips, leaning down and licking the juice as it ran from the corners of her mouth, cupping her breasts in his hands to catch the flow.

He stirred and rolled onto his side, glad there was no one there to observe his erection. He was ready for a wife, he knew. And it must be a wife, for he could not be like Will with his many paramours, his widows and the lively single women engaged by his easy charm. He never even seemed to contemplate marriage, while for David it was a lifetime commitment.

Wherever David looked he saw creatures making partnership, the birds, the kangaroos, the lonely cow calling the bull, even the kookaburras were tumbling through the air together. He felt no joy at the prospect of arriving home. He would be comforted to sleep in his own bed this night and satisfaction at what he and Will had achieved, but there was no warmth, no real sense of homecoming. Just two work weary bachelors who had lived together the past six years with little respite from their labours. He sighed. What was the point of it all?

Despite Eliza's betrayal she still filled his imaginings as an ideal wife. He could not have told another of the depth of his pain in that rejection but it was there to be seen in his suspicion of women, his lack of trust, his bitter expectations.

He thought of the single women he knew and tried to imagine married life with them. There was that red haired Foley girl but she was probably Catholic, he'd certainly never seen her at church. Or perhaps Mrs Benson's niece whom he'd met once or twice. But she was dull and he could not abide doltish people. And the McFaden girls. Now they were all good solid citizens and he'd always valued highly his friendship with them, but it was mostly business. Susannah was a reliable and hard worker in the store, and Lizzie at fourteen was hardly more than a child. He counted Maggie as near to a friend as Jack had been, trustworthy and dependable, the one he turned to when he was troubled, and the one who offered wise counsel. But she did not fit his inner image of a wife.

As the year grew to its end, life settled for David, business was good and in a short time he and Will would complete the new store. Then one day, as he walked down the street in Pleasant Creek he saw Maggie walking with a stranger.

David crossed the road and deliberately walked towards them. 'Tis a beautiful morning, is it not Maggie? I did not know you were visiting so early in the week.' He paused and waited for her to introduce her companion.

'Oh David. Good mornin'. This is Robert Ennis, James' brother. Robert, this is the David Stavers I mentioned to you before,' she turned to David, 'the Bentleys are away again for three weeks and I am takin' the chance to visit me sisters.'

Several questions sprang into David's mind. Why was Maggie speaking to this man about himself? And what was James Ennis' brother doing here, and more importantly, what was his interest in Maggie?

'And what brings you to Pleasant Creek Mr Ennis?' he asked rather brusquely.

'I'm thinking of taking up some land in the district and Maggie has told me there are some good acres to be sold soon out by Hunters Creek.'

'Are you speculating or do you intend to live here?'

'Well, the area seems promising. As good as any other I've seen.'

'We all think it would be best if he was to buy in this district.' Maggie added with the air of one who knew all.

'Well I wish you and your family well in your enterprise.'

'I've no family as yet Mr Stavers. But I live in hopes.' Robert smiled.

'And I too' replied David and he turned to his friend, 'Maggie, perhaps we may share a pot of tea later today?'

'Oh David. I'm sorry, but I'll not be able this day.' Maggie made no future promises and a deeply troubled David said his good byes, lifted his hat and continued on his way.

That night as David was preparing some gold samples to take to Melbourne, he came across a parcel of nuggets he had bought a few days previously. They were a particularly beautiful pinkish gold and as he handled them he decided to take them to a jeweller. Too attractive to be melted down to ingots he thought, and in his mind saw an oval locket gleaming with warm light. And a chain of the same gold. And saw himself clasping that slender chain round a young woman's neck.

With a small shock he realised the young woman he was imagining was not Eliza but Maggie. He stared out of the window, unseeing, his mind a tumult, astonished that he had not realised before. Of course. Maggie. His faithful friend. His constant source of wise counsel. He set off for Melbourne the very next morning in a buoyant mood and with his mind made up. As he rode he imagined the design of a locket. At first he thought a decoration of vines and leaves, but then he thought of Maggie and it seemed a perfectly plain design would be best. But it must be beautifully made, good craftsmanship, pure and lasting. Immediately on his return he would give it to Maggie and ask her to marry him.

David returned to Pleasant Creek some days later with the precious locket secure in his saddlebag. As he unsaddled his horse and was rubbing him down, Will strolled into the yard.

'That friend of yours, Maggie McFaden, she's been driving round the town with Robert Ennis I hear. Seems he's settled on a property. Somewhere near Hunter's Creek. I'll warrant she's going to marry him.'

David looked up and his arms dropped to his sides. 'But she can't! I've just decided to ask her to marry me.'

'Well, looks like you might have missed your opportunity lad.' Will chivvied him and poked him in the chest.

David turned away, but Will could see the droop of his shoulders and the small frown as he turned back to say, 'I thought there might be something going on between them. Is she talking of marrying him? Or is it just gossip?'

'All I know is she's been spending a lot of time with him. I did hear some mention of him looking for a home paddock. Can't remember who said it though.' Will smiled.

David's first thought was to see Maggie immediately. But it was nine pm. Too late to call now. But despite the lateness, he saddled up again and rode round to the Ennis house where she was staying. It was in total darkness. He dismounted and crept around the back to see if Robert's horse and gig was there but the dog began to bark and was soon answered by another and another, so before anyone came out, he quickly remounted and rode home again to spend a sleepless night haunted by visions of Maggie, walking arm in arm down the street with Robert Ennis.

The next morning David rode to the Ennis house as early as common decency allowed, Maggie had already left, MaryAnn told him. 'Yes, to Hunter's Creek with Robert.' And in response to his question, 'No. I don't know when they'll be back.'

Immediately he determined to ride to Hunters Creek. He cantered back to the store, grabbed a saddlebag and quickly prepared some food and a flask of water. Making sure the locket was safely tucked into his pocket, he set off.

Maggie was very surprised to see him when he cantered up to where she and Robert were strolling along the boundary of a roughly fenced piece of land.

'Good morning Maggie.'

'Good morning David' she smiled. 'What are you doing here?'

David fervently wished Robert in some distant place.

He leaned down from his mare. 'I must speak to you Maggie. It's very important. Immediately.' His voice was low and urgent.

'Well, meself is entirely here, David.' Maggie teased.

'No. No.' he muttered and averted his face as he dismounted. 'In private.' he said in a rough whisper, and turned, the reins in his hand and walked a little way, saw how clumsy he had been, then turned again to take Maggie's arm.

Maggie rustled her skirts into place and said, 'Will you be after excusin' us Robert?' and asked, 'What ever is the matter? You're so agitated.' And as they walked away she called over her shoulder 'We'll not be more than a few minutes Robert.'

David dropped the reins over a fence post then turned suddenly to Maggie. He had no idea where to begin. For seven long years he had dreamed only of Eliza, holding himself back from any other relationship. Unlike Will, he had no fine airs, or practice at charming the ladies.

'I want you to marry me Maggie.' David burst out. 'I'm not a ladies' man, but I'm honest and I've got a good business going now.'

Maggie put her hand to her face to hide her amusement at this unexpected and clumsy proposal. She looked down, 'I don't know what to say at all.'

'You're the best friend a man could have and I've just realised it.'

Maggie was truly surprised by her friend's impetuous offer and felt a wash of anguish at the thought of what she had lost when Richard died. David is a good man, she thought, I don't want to be hurtin' him, but here's meself not even knowin' how I feel at all. 'You take me by surprise David. Wouldn't you think now, you'd be choosin' a more . . . a more romantic settin' to make such a serious proposal? What has made this so sudden important?'

'I hardly understand myself, Maggie, but I am sincere in my proposal, even though it may seem impulsive to you. I don't expect you to answer immediately but I hope and pray you'll consider it carefully.'

'I am 25 years old David. You know I've been altogether responsible for me sisters these last seven years. I vowed I wouldn't marry 'til they was settled.'

'Susannah's almost engaged, and I'm sure Lizzie will soon find a husband.' David offered hopefully.

'Yes. Well, they's older now and better able to care for themselves.' And there's been many times when I thought I would not be marryin' at all, she thought. 'It's not a thing I would be enterin' into lightly David, and nor would you.'

'Then can I at least hope?'

'I'm thinkin' that it's all a bit rushed. Perhaps it would be better if we both go home and think on it. And this does not seem to be the best time and place. Perhaps in a day or two? Say tomorrow evenin' after we have both had a little quiet time.'

'Will you accept this as a token of my sincerity?' His hands shook a little as he took the package from his pocket and pressed it into Maggie's hand.

Maggie opened the package and gasped at the gleaming gift. ''Tis very beautiful, but I'm not sure . . . '

SETTLERS HOME

167

'Just think of it as a gift to a good friend. I'll not hold you obliged.

'She felt its smooth heaviness with her fingers, then kissed her fingertips and pressed them to David's cheek. 'Thank you my good friend.'

He took her hand in his and in turn kissed the place where her lips had touched and looked into her eyes. Maggie gently withdrew her hand but held the look between them for a moment more.

'I must go David. Robert is waitin'.'

As he rode away David's thoughts leapt from uncertainty to wild hope. He berated himself for his clumsiness, for not choosing a more suitable occasion, for not being more gentlemanly in his manner. But he relished the feeling that had sprung up between them in the touch of their hands, and once again he raised his fingers to the place on his cheek where Maggie's fingers had so recently touched him. That look. What did it mean?

Part 4

SONGS AND WHISPERS

MARRIED LIFE, 1860 -1900

In time I surrendered to the demands of the task and set about reading all of the letters. At first I thought their matter insignificant, for they were largely about daily activities, 'Today I did a large baking ready for the Church Anniversary,' or 'Father has hurt his knee and will not be able to go to Talbot (30 miles distant) until next week. The mare is lame too.' Then, as I read more, I was caught up in the rhythm of their lives. The planting of the seeds, the coming of the rain, the heat of summer, the frosts which destroyed their vegetables, the cow in the orchard feasting on the summer's fruit.

It is easy from three generations forward to see only the surface of these past lives. Only the parts they wrote of. The parts shown by the photos they posed for. Graceful girls in long dresses, hair piled high, branches of eucalyptus leaves and flowers framing their formal, serious faces. Why did they not smile? Were they unhappy? Was it because they had to be very still in posing for the photographer in the 1880s? Or was the occasion a sad one, following a funeral or some loss in the family?

Amongst the earliest photos are many loose Carte de Visites, those calling cards showing a photo of the caller, popular in the 1880s. These too I love to browse through, speculating about each individual. Their faces show so much. This one is of a thin-faced woman of about thirty, with her sturdy husband standing beside her, his suit coarse and crumpled. Her eyes are downcast, her mouth a grim down turned curve, sorrow in every line of her body. On the back I find written 'Aunt's first child was fatally scalded by a careless nurse while she was abed, having the second.' My skin crawls at the thought of that child's pain. And its mother's. Later I find another photo that I think shows the same woman. Now her face is fuller, she smiles, and three young children stand beside their beaming parents. It is Maggie's sister, Susannah.

I begin to realise that even though they lived only a few miles apart, letters were the way families kept in touch. Just as today there is little time for socialising, so it was then, except that the constraints upon their time were to do with the seasons, the crops, the babies. The demands of every day survival. Even injury or illness would not allow them a day off work. If they did not work, they did not eat.

And as I read I began to know them. Most of all Maggie. It was she who most engaged my curiosity. What had her life been like? I was moved enormously when I found a small bundle of letters written by Maggie to her daughter Annie in 1885. When I saw her handwriting I felt very close to her. It was extremely difficult to read as she had overwritten, as they did in the old days to save paper. She wrote once on the lines, then turned the page 90 degrees and wrote across the first lot of writing and if she was really short of paper, made a 45 degree turn and wrote diagonally as well. But not only this. Maggie's writing was spiky and peculiar. She did not close her a's, or o's and her b's , t's, and f's and p's were almost impossible to distinguish. She used no punctuation, and rarely, capitalisation. She did not know about paragraphs, or even sentences, for she would run on from one thought to another without pause. And of course the manner of language was different then so that if an unexpected word was used it was almost impossible to guess what it might be. Nevertheless, as I read I gained profound satisfaction from her words and thoughts and a sort of connection arose between us so that I felt, even more, that I knew her. And I learned also to read between her lines, the unspoken feelings, the fears, and the understatements.

In reading fragments of their lives I began to realise the synchronicities of my own life. To see the similarities between making patchwork and making history. The joining together of random pieces to make a whole. The way each piece of life joins its neighbour, blending the colours of experience, the subtleties of texture and shape and patterns of life that emerge as I take into my mind these random facts.

I search these letters for clues to their state of mind. I find statements of events - bankruptcy, urgent sale, Essie has sore ears, Willy is gone to Avoca to find work. They tell me much, and yet little.

They are from a generation which did not speak of personal

things. A generation that hid their pain. Even their joy was calm and measured, accepted with thanks to God for His goodness and never thought of as being the result of their own strivings, or the natural outcome of their integrity.

In the chest were three photograph albums. Each appears to have belonged to a particular person but in the front of each were the photos of the man and woman. And in time I recognised them as Maggie and David. Emma was their youngest daughter. Having known her only as Great Aunt Emma, it was at first difficult to reconcile the pictures of the lively girl with the old, deaf woman I remembered from my childhood.

In her album was, very near the front, quite a large picture of a very handsome man. But no name. Later I found another picture of the same man but this time with the name John Whan on the back. I could not recall ever having seen any letters signed John Whan, nor did his photo occur in either of the other albums. The name did not mean anything to me, indeed it almost sounded Chinese which made it seem most unlikely he would be a partner for Emma. Then one day when we were travelling in the goldfields area and looking at the gravestones in one of the old cemeteries, I saw the name Whan, in the Catholic section of the cemetery. Suddenly all the pieces fell together, even the tiny purse. From the first moment I could not understand even its presence in the chest. Our family were staunch Presbyterians. Always had been. But in this little purse when I opened it, I had found a picture of the Virgin Mary and a St Christopher medal. Very puzzling.

Tucked inside the purse was a small hand carved ring. It seemed to be made of some sort of wood. For something so small, it is finely and beautifully carved. And the name carved into it is 'Emma'. Did John Whan make this ring for Emma? Was he a Catholic? If he was, would Emma have dared to marry him? It would have been a bold and almost unheard of thing for her to do in those far off days when Presbyterian and Catholic barely spoke to each other. In fact they regarded each other as religious enemies.

Curiously enough, I then remembered that in the final years of her life, Emma no longer went to church. At the time I didn't understand the full significance of this, but amongst the letters written to Emma in the last decade of her life were a series spanning about five years in which the writer and Emma obviously discussed religious and philosophic matters in great depth. They were signed simply, John. I never saw any of Emma's contributions to this correspondence, only the writer's replies to her. I searched those letters page by page for more clues but never found any more than an occasional oblique reference to some earlier time.

In the face of their religious differences, maybe John married someone else and it was not until later in life, after he was widowed perhaps, that they were able to pursue the intellectual ideas that had appealed to them in their youth. I do know from the tenor of the letters that Emma's attitude to her Presbyterianism changed radically at that time. But by then it was too late.

I fancy I can see the sadness in the droop of her body as she placed the ring inside that precious little purse he had made for her. The way she folded it, then gave it one final kiss before putting it away with firmness and resolve. Just as she followed the strict conventions of her generation and surrendered her happiness to her strict moral convictions.

WRITER'S NOTES: *A marriage Certificate!* So here it is, firm evidence of David and Margaret's wedding. The certificate states they were married on 12th April, 1860 at Chalmers Church, East Melbourne, by the Reverend Adam Cairns. The marriage was witnessed by Susannah McFaden and William Stavers. The certificate is a short wide form about 25 cm by 500 cm. The printing is in red and the signings have all been done with the same pen and ink. It has been folded several times and is worn through at the folds so that it barely holds together.

Cheque of the Oriental Bank, Melbourne, made payable to David Stavers, and signed by Wm.Russell. It is dated 25th March, 1860. Beside the date are written two words - possibly Back Curb or Bank Curb. I am amazed to find this uncashed cheque. Who could afford not to cash in a cheque for three hundred pounds in 1860? That was a considerable sum of money, equal to wages for two or three years at that time. And what might Bank Curb mean?

Christening robe, well preserved, its fabric pure and strong. It is well made, from finely woven, soft linen, trimmed with handmade lace and is tucked and embroidered down the front of the skirt. The stitches are so tiny I have to use a magnifying glass to confirm that it is made entirely by hand. The lace has been added to it afterwards, round the ends of the sleeves and below the bodice and round the hem. It is also hand made. It's beautifully made and I wonder at a woman who, amidst all the labour and hardship of those days, had time to make something so refined and lovely.

MAJORCA 1860

David leaned over the table and wrote 'David Stavers, Gold Broker, Pleasant Creek' and signed his name, then handed the pen to Maggie who dipped it into the inkpot and carefully wrote her name followed by 'housekeeper' and 'Ararat' which she printed with some pride before signing. Then Susannah came forward and signed her name, followed by Will. The Reverend Adam Cairns then added his signature and waited some minutes for the ink to dry properly before he shook hands with David and Maggie, congratulated them, and handed them their Certificate of Marriage.

Maggie had chosen her dress carefully - a skirt of cream bombazine with a matching jacket, trimmed with black velvet - she loved the little velvet bows on the sleeves and at the bottom of the jacket. It was the first time in her life she had had a dress made especially for her. Under the jacket she wore a white lace blouse with a ruffled collar. The lace around the neck she had made herself with a leaf and flower pattern of her own design.

Her feet hurt in her new shoes and she had done her skirt up a little too tightly so that it cut into her waist and she stretched herself a little to ease it, then looked to see if David had noticed. He was so handsome in his dark suit, with his white pintucked shirt and

175

the black silk neckerchief, which she had given him. She was conscious of how stylish a wedding it was and aware of the eyes that turned to look at them afterwards as they all trotted down to the Bourke Street in a brougham for a pot of Indian tea and sandwiches at the Indian Teahouse.

That evening they walked around the gaslit streets of Melbourne until almost eleven o'clock, David too shy and Maggie too apprehensive to hurry to their room at the Criterion. Maggie was afraid. Somewhere deep in her mind lingered a shadowy memory of blood and a baby and her mother's white legs. Many a time she had vowed she would never marry, thinking that Tarleton's assault on her was the way of marriage. So that when they did go to their room and David climbed into the bed beside her, Maggie was swallowing and feeling quite sick.

David's approach surprised her.

'Don't you want to put it in my mouth?' she asked timorously.

David was shocked by the question but excited at the thought in spite of himself. 'Down here will do very nicely Maggie' he gasped as he rather clumsily pressed her thighs apart and attempted to enter her.

Maggie was embarrassed by her wetness, not knowing. But it seemed to help. They struggled together briefly until David fell back with a moan.

Later he asked her 'Maggie. What did you mean before? About your mouth?'

Maggie shrank her head into his shoulder to hide her scarlet face and whispered 'I thought that was the way of married people.'

'And whatever made you think that?'

She wanted to tell David but even now her shame and disgust were too great. Perhaps David would never kiss her again if he knew. Or blame her for a strumpet as Tarleton had called her even though she didn't really know what strumpet meant. In the smallest whisper possible she lied, 'I saw someone do that once,' and was pained to begin her married life with a lie, although in the years to come she never regretted it.

176

Soon afterwards Maggie took up her pen one evening and wrote to her friend Sarah.

Dere Sarah

you will be surprized to here that i am now a marrid woman the man i have marrid is David Stavers who was on the ship and hee is a gold buyer and as a store in Pleasant Creek and we live behind now i am not working as a housekeeper but just sometimes in the store we had a verry grand wedding and you wold not have beleved if you had seen me trotting down the main street in my silk and velvet David as given me a gold locket it opens out and i have put in a lock of me hare and a lock of his

Davids brother hee is living with us but it is not good hee is a man who thinks evry woman is for his taking and as even tried to kiss me when David is not here i hop he soon will go hee is older than David and they argu something terrible but it is the bisness

you can rite me a letter send it to post office Plesant Creek for the post master ther is relible and does not throe letters away my name is Maggie Stavers now.

your loving frend

Maggie Stavers

On 28th March, just two weeks before Maggie and David were married, David had received a large cheque in payment for his latest consignment of gold. He had presented the cheque to the local branch of the Oriental Bank and they had paid him out. This cheque was the bounty on which the beginning of their marriage was based.

As a gold buyer for the Oriental Bank in Melbourne, each week David was responsible for taking down the week's consignment with the Gold Escort. He would carefully pack each parcel of gold, label it with the miner's name and a tally of the amount due to that miner, and then make out a receipt for the miner, redeemable at the bank. It was a procedure he had carried out almost daily for years and one he was thoroughly familiar with.

On a Thursday morning, a week or so after they had married, David walked down to the post office with the intention of picking up his mail. He was in a buoyant mood and whistled as he walked briskly to the small timber post office in the main street. There were several letters for him but he was most eager to read the one bearing the signature on its reverse side of his friend William Russell. When he got back to the store Maggie was just pulling a loaf of bread from the oven. He tossed the other letters on the rough table and sat down to see what news William had for him. Before he began to read he asked,

'Is there a cup of tea to be had, Maggie?'

As he opened the letter, a cheque fell out and fluttered to the floor. David's eyes raced across the page and he read the words 'A Bank Curb has been placed on this cheque as the gold in your parcel of March 15th 1860, assayed at a value of three hundred pounds less than stated in your receipts.'

David bent and picked up the dishonoured cheque in his hand, disbelieving, breathless with rage and apprehension.

'That scoundrel Hamilton. That miserable, conniving, two faced, scheming scoundrel. I knew I should not have trusted him.'

'What is it Davey?'

'We've had a bad parcel. Hamilton must have slipped some bad gold in that last parcel.'

David stormed out to the kitchen lean-to at the back of the store where Will was leaning against a post, his clay pipe clenched between his teeth. David waved the cheque in Will's face.

'He's ruined us. Hamilton! That so-called friend of yours!'

'What are you talking about?' Will took the cheque from David's hand and examined it.

'His was the only parcel I didn't check myself. He must have come in deliberately when we were busy. When they assayed it in Melbourne there was a shortfall of three hundred pounds!'

'You don't know it was him. And you authorised the consignment y'fool.'

'You said Hamilton was a decent man! You recommended him!'

'You should have checked the parcels properly.'

'I can't do everything while you're gallivanting round the place with the local women.'

'You're so damn trusting David. You never learn.'

'I've learned never to trust you again!'

'Don't blame me for your own stupidity!'

'You dare to call me stupid when it's your villainous friends who caused all this? That's the last time I trust you. This is the end. We're finished. You and your shady friends, you've ruined us.

'Well. I'll be well out of it but I'll be wanting my cut of the business David. I'll not walk away from this without my share.'

'There'll be no share, can't you see. There'll be nothing!'

'Then I'll take Maggie.' Will laughed and grabbed her by the arm.

David's rage burst from him. 'Get out! Get out of my sight.' He pushed Will in the chest and the men began to trade punches while Maggie pulled at David's jacket and desperately tried to separate them.

When their anger was exhausted and Will had left, Maggie and David sat at the table, heads in hands, staring at the dishonoured cheque.

'Well. Go with him. I'll not stop you.'

Maggie reached out and touched him on the arm. 'Sure and sometimes I'm thinkin' you're a foolish man. Thinkin' that I'd want to be going' with Will, and him your own brother. Can't you see - that's just his bluster. I've no wishin' to be with Will. You're me own husband. Here with you is altogether where I want to be.'

In his head David could hear Maggie's words repeated over and over *I'll not be livin' in a tent on the goldfields.* He'd failed. Everything was lost. All his effort for the last seven years wasted and vanished. 'But we're ruined. We'll have to live poor again.'

Maggie looked at David, at his crushed and beaten expression. A wave of tenderness swept over her at his hurt. She wanted to hold him. To make him whole again. She could not bear his pain. It was as if it were her own, the look in his eyes, the way he turned away from her to hide his suffering. Ah, me poor man, I never thought I'd see you like this. With a shiver of dread she said, 'We can start agen.'

'We'll have to sell this shop to meet the shortfall. The land and buildings. I'll have to go back to prospecting. That's not as easy as it was a few years ago.'

'Plenty of others have done it.'

David looked at his hands. They had lost their calluses and become soft again, 'I expect I'll even lose my Brokers Licence. I don't expect we'll get anything out of this. Nothing.'

Maggie pushed the still warm bread aside. 'Well Davey, one thing we're knowin', neither of us is afraid of hard work.' Maggie stood up and fetched David's writing case from under the bed. 'The first thing you must do is write to William Russell - he knows well enough it wouldn't be your doin'. He'll advise you.'

Within a couple of days a reply came back from David's friend

Melbourne
7th May, 1860

My Dear David,

I only received your letter this morning and my advice to you is to write a letter to the Manager saying that you consider yourself aggrieved by bearing the blame of Hamilton's bad parcels and also send him the particulars of the Escorts, the same as you sent me. Explain to them that as his gold has turned out badly it is not your buying but his - of course don't say anything about my corresponding with you on this subject as it would not do for it to be known - I am very busy now David so I have no time to write at greater length but I have told you what I think in the matter and remain in haste.

Your most affectionate friend
Wm Russell

The letter to the Manager was written, and though everyone knew David as an honest trader, he could not prove his innocence and he was left with the huge debt of three hundred pounds to make good.

The store and the stock and the land were sold and they applied for time to pay their creditors so that David would not be sent to prison. But he was angry and humiliated that his reputation had been so marred by another's villainy, especially as he had so strictly maintained his honesty. His record with the bank was such that he did not lose his Broker's Licence but it was suspended for six months, which meant he was forced back to mining.

David borrowed ten pounds from James Ennis and with that stake secured a claim and set himself up with a cradle and enough gear to start prospecting again. Maggie went back into service with a family near Back Creek and they had to content themselves with meeting once a week.

They were both glad enough when Will announced his intention to make a fresh start in New Zealand where yet another gold rush was offering hope to thousands. Maggie had waved goodbye with some relief and David and Will had shaken hands but Maggie knew there was no good heart in it as she watched the stiff way they farewelled each other.

Maggie wrote again to Sarah,

> . . . *i was a fool to think it could be lasting we as lost everything Davey as not been so good tempered and as been taking to the drink i won't be putting up with that if he don't stop soon i think i will not stay marrid to him just now when everything is so black the onely time he is forgetting is when we're abed so I am teaching him how to please me..*

Late one day in June, Maggie arrived at the claim for her weekly visit. She had news for David but did not know how to tell him, not being quite sure whether it was good or not. That night Maggie said 'Remember Davey how I always vowed I'd never be livin' on the goldfields in a tent. And look at me now,' she laughed, as they pulled the blankets over themselves that night and turned to each other.

At first, David's silence, his reticence had bothered her. But slowly she began to tell him, about her life, her home, her sisters and the stories of her girlhood. He was amazed at her memory, how vivid it was and how clearly she remembered events even from her earliest years. He was never able to respond, the pain of becoming adult and separating from his family had been too great for him and he would not speak of those things, those times, but he felt drawn into her feeling and was content to be part of that.

That night David mumbled into her neck and pulled her night-dress up and stroked her round hips and pressed himself against her. 'Ah, my beautiful Maggie. My own Nugget of Gold' he mur-mured. And she laughed at him calling her Nugget and beautiful, and wanted to believe it.

She loved the flat planes of David's body, his wiry strength, the silkiness of the skin on his private parts. She was always amazed at how hard he was there. So soft. Then when she touched him, so hard. She remembered her first feelings on the ship, and the waves of pleasure that had washed her as she lay in her bunk.

Afterwards she put her face close to his and whispered. 'Davey. I'm thinkin' they's to be three of us.'

David was aware of the walls of the tent breathing softly, the shadows of trees moving to and fro as the roof lifted in response to the wind, the sound of crickets, a mopoke calling in the distance. He felt himself adrift on a tide of life he could not resist. No busi-ness, his brother gone, their work of seven years wiped out in a moment, his dreams destroyed. And now, a baby. I should have expected it, he thought to himself, but not now. Not yet.

'Ah Nugget, what's to become of us? I should never have asked you to marry me.' And David held her close, as much to reassure himself, as to comfort her.

'And where would I be if you hadn't?'

'At least you'd be living in a house.'

'By meself, as lonely as that old mopoke out there.'

'I'll work as hard as I can Maggie. I promise.'

'And Davey. There's somethin' else. I don't want our babby to be growin' up with a father that's drinkin'.'

'I swear I'll never touch another drop Maggie.'

In the profound silence of the night, when even the mopoke had gone to rest, they lay in their bed and dreamed their separate dreams. He would reach for her, and briefly she thought they might meet behind each other's eyes. Afterwards, she would be filled with a nameless energy and imagined herself running through the moonlight to plunge into the lagoon. And she would urge David to run with her, and tried to imagine him beside her but somehow he was left behind and she plunged naked into the waters, and swam alone below the glimmering surface, with shafts of moonlight illuminating her.

'I'll not have me first born christened without a christening robe Davey. Flour bags is alright for baby clothes, but if I'm makin' a christening robe, I'll be needin' some fine linen. Next time you go to Melbourne will you get two yards for me?'

'If I don't have the mare shod soon I won't be able to get to Melbourne. Linen costs almost two shillings a yard here. Not like at home.'

'I've been sellin' a few eggs. In the spring when the vegetables come on I'll have a few of them to sell too. I can give you the money meself', Maggie said proudly as she tipped a few coins out of a tin she kept under the bed.

In time, David brought the linen and in the lonely nights, when he was away on a trip to Melbourne, Maggie sat in the light of a candle and stitched together the pieces that he had helped her to cut out one day on the kitchen table. As the evenings grew longer she was grateful for the light and sat outside to stitch the scalloped edge of the robe.

At first she had been nervous of his absences, but as the months passed and she grew familiar with the sounds of the house, and the wind and the bush creatures, she grew more confident and even enjoyed going out into the vast, silvery night to pee beneath the sharp and glittering stars.

David had built the house during the winter so that it would be ready before the baby came. It was like many of its neighbours, a simple and honest unlined building, about four metres by four metres. When Maggie closed the door behind her at the end of the day, she did so with a sense of security far stronger than she had ever felt when they lived in the tent where there was always the fear of the slitting cut in the night. Everyone who came to their door was greeted with the same words. 'A hundred thousand welcomes' Maggie would say as she held the door wide and ushered them in to their humble home.

Maggie was proud of her new house. Up to about shoulder height it was made of hand split weatherboards, of a soft, pinky-red colour. These David had sawn, and then split from a tall straight eucalypt. The upper parts of the walls were made from a good heavy hessian nailed across the framework up to low ceiling height. The roof was made from slabs of thick bark, stripped from the felled tree before it was sawn. The slabs of bark were throughly soaked and then weighed down with logs to flatten them.

Later the bark was hauled up to the roof frame, laid in overlap-

SHACK

184

ping layers and tied to the beams with greenhide. Finally four strong lengths of greenhide had been pulled over the top of the roof from front to back and secured to long logs that lay across the whole width of the house. 'To hold the roof down and give it extra strength against the wind.' David said.

In each wall of the hut were horizontally hung shutters, also covered in hessian, which Maggie could prop open with a stick on fine days. Inside, the floor was mostly beaten earth with a section of bricks in front of a small hearth and a corrugated iron chimney. Mostly, Maggie preferred to cook outside on the built up rock fireplace which she whitewashed every week. She was always nervous of fire in her timber house, but when the wind blew, or it was raining, it was good to be able to go inside and stir up the coals and hear the kettle singing while the wind sought a way in through the roof.

Across one end of the room a curtain hung and behind that David had built a greenhide bed with straps of hide woven and stretched across a frame of saplings. Beneath the straw mattress, the leather creaked and sagged a little in the damp weather but Maggie thought it quite the most comfortable bed she had ever slept in.

That night as Maggie sat outside, stitching in the fading light, it was hot with a northerly blowing gusts through the windows. All day Maggie had walked back and forth from the wood heap to the verandah, carrying loads of firewood. She wanted a good supply close by and ready to use in the days after the baby was born. For cooking and the kettle. She knew their baby would come soon.

The baby stopped kicking for a while and Maggie sat and smelled the hot night air. Each armful of firewood had carried a breath of eucalyptus to her nostrils, but now she could smell something else, like hot bark she thought, with the dryness of dust in it. She hoped it would rain.

In the middle of the night, Maggie got up to go outside. As she went out the door she sniffed it - a distant acrid scent on the wind. She looked up at the moon and with a shock saw its face, blood red and huge, looming in the sky above the trees. She looked up the hill to their neighbour's house. All was darkness.

The wind became stronger and gusted violently around the cor-

185

ners of the house. As she went back inside a flurry of burnt leaves followed her through the door and settled on the floor.

Maggie stood and stared at them for a few moments, then realized. Dear God, there must be a fire somewhere. Not stopping to dress she gathered a quilt round her shoulders and lumbered as fast as she could, up the hill to the Petersons.

She pounded on their door and called 'Walter, Walter! The moon is red! D'ye think it's a fire? Is it the end of the world?'

Walter came to the door with Annie peering from behind his shoulder. With a quick look at the sky with its red glow in the north, he pulled on his clothes, all the while giving Maggie and Annie instructions. 'Take our baby Annie, put a blanket round you both and go down to the creek with Maggie. Stay there with them Maggie while I see which way it's heading. I think the wind's got a bit of west in it. Maybe it'll change soon.'

Maggie and Annie clutched each other and stumbled down the slope towards the creek. The child was whimpering in Annie's arms as Maggie tried to guide their steps through the darkness.

'If we wait near the ford we can wade into deeper water if the fire comes close!' Maggie urged Annie, pulling her along behind.

'Where's Walter? Why doesn't he come?'

'He'll be here soon enough.'

Maggie and Annie shuddered as they heard the wind roaring strongly through the treetops and close by a limb crashed to the ground. They clung together, as red flares leapt into the sky, and their noses were filled with fearful hints of smoke.

When they reached the creek they huddled together, their feet in the water at the edge, the baby fully awake now and crying. Glowing cinders fell onto the surface of the creek and rapidly quenched only to be replaced by another and another. Maggie felt a fizz as another cinder fell into her hair and she brushed at it, dipping her hand into the creek and splashing water over her head.

'I think we'd better be wettin' the quilt and holdin' it over our heads Annie.'

'But it's your best quilt Maggie!'

'Needs must' Maggie muttered as she dunked the quilt. Now heavy with water, she struggled to pull it over their heads and they shivered a little with cold and fear as the water coursed down between their shoulders.

Maggie could feel tightness in her belly, and eased herself into a sitting position. She was profoundly uncomfortable. The wind was growing stronger and gusting even more. In the distance they thought they heard Walter's voice but could not make out his words.

'Do you think we'd best go back to the house?'

'No. Let's wait here a bit longer. There's a restlessness in the wind. Dear God I hope it changes soon.'

Maggie wanted to be somewhere else. Wanted someone else to look after Annie and the baby. Someone to look after her. Where was David? Why did these things always happen when he was away? If only he would ride up now. Maggie peered up the track praying he would appear.

And he did, but not until the next day, after the wind had changed, and the rain had fallen and quenched the flames. And Maggie had been in labour for ten hours by then.

Following the difficult birth of their first child Essie, Maggie thought hell could not be worse than that summer on the gold field. When the sun blazed down day after endless day. When the flies worried their eyes and crawled lazily in the house every daylight hour. When dust gathered in their hair and the corners of their mouths, and their hands never lost the feel of grit for more than a few moments. The wind swirled dirt into every crevice of their bodies and chafed them and what little water they had must be saved for washing the gold rather than their faces. And when the sun went down, the heat rose up from the earth and they lay sweating in their clothes all night rather than be bitten by the incessant mosquitoes.

Maggie prayed for it to be cold. She laughed to herself - wouldn't you think I'm a foolish woman now, to be missing the frost. Missing the way it really woke me in the mornings, not slow like here, but nipping me out of sleep with its sneaking cold white teeth beneath the blanket, searing my lungs with its icy breath. I'd like a crisp, cold pinching of me nose and fingers on an Irish morning, puddles cracklin' beneath me feet, a bright sparkle of ice on the briars and strings of diamonds on the grass. And frozen tears at me nose and eyes too, she remembered, as she rose on yet another blinding sunlit day in the summer of 1861.

Soon enough that year, she was pregnant again and, in the summer of 1862, Willie was born. The birth was much easier so that Maggie was well again quickly, in the way of strong women.

A week later, two years after the fateful consignment, David received a large package in the mail. 'It's come at last Maggie.'

'What is it Davey?'

'A Total Discharge of Insolvency. Look at this 'All debts and commitments paid in full'. Thank God. Never again will I go into partnership with anyone.' David vowed. 'I'll not trust another soul.'

'Except meself Davey. I won't let you down.'

'I know that Nugget. But you can't be overseeing the consignments now can you?'

David had begun buying gold again after his Licence was restored and as his reputation was gradually vindicated, the diggers once more trusted him with their parcels and slowly, but regularly, their business increased until once more they could contemplate building another store. Nevertheless there were times when Maggie wondered whether she had made the right decision in marrying David.

One night when Willie was about six months old Maggie heard a terrible ruckus down the road and turned wearily, and tucked the baby down in the curve of her body and pulled the blankets up over their heads to muffle the sounds of shouting. She heard David's voice amongst the clamour and while a moment ago she was mad with anxiety at his absence, sure that he had fallen down a shicer somewhere, now her anxiety turned to fury for the state he was in. She put her pillow to the baby's back, tucked him in securely then rose to stand at the door as David came stumbling towards her.

When he was a few feet away he stopped and crept elaborately towards her but tripped on a piece of firewood and sent himself and several pots and pans crashing about.

I'll not let him in this house in that state he can sleep out there and freeze I'll not have his boozy breath all over me. I hate him when he's like this. Why does he do it, 'Don't you dare to come in here in that state David Stavers.' Maggie held the door and stood at the opening 'You can sleep outside for all I care.'

'Shh Marg'ret. Keep your voice down. I shall be eshtremely quite.'

Maggie smiled in spite of her anger 'Yes. Like just now I suppose.'

David tried to retrieve a bit of dignity. 'I jus' wantto come inan get a blaket. It's a col' night, Marg'ret and I am eshtremely col'.'

David swayed towards her and Maggie put out a hand to steady him. His hands were indeed icy cold. 'Oh come on then yeh great babby. But be quiet.' And she helped him get his boots off and then lay near him while he shivered. But she was still too angry to give him the warmth of her body

They had been asleep only minutes it seemed when he stirred and got up to go outside and pee and fart loudly without even taking the trouble to go to the pit, to Maggie's utter mortification.

Whatever does he get from drinkin' like that? I don't understand it and I don't like him when he drinks. I'm shamed that he's my husband the way he behaves, and everybody knows he's been drinking again and everybody knows I made him swear not to. 'Be quiet David.' Maggie hissed, 'Everybody can hear you,' as he reeled back in.

'I am at leasht in my own home Marg'ret. Not like shome others.' He declared virtuously.

'Shhh! What do you mean? What others?' He's such a fool with that look on his face

David flopped back into bed almost leaning on the baby as he fell. 'Mind the babby, you great lummox!' Willie began to cry in fright and Maggie pushed David away and lifted Willie to her breast to comfort him.

David turned away to shut out his guilt and sank into oblivion while Maggie fumed, barely comforted by Willie's steady sucking.

At first light, while David snored on, Essie was awake and fussing for her breakfast. While Willie still slept, Maggie got up and went outside. She gathered some dried leaves and sticks to put on the grey coals to get the fire going before filling the kettle. We'll be needin' another load of water soon she thought as she leaned down deep into the barrel to dipper the water out then poured it into the kettle. Davey's not helpin' by gettin' drunk like that. He'll have a sore head when he wakes, but I'll not be sorry for him; he doesn't need to do that drinkin', we're gettin' along alright and it won't be long before we can build another store. But goin' out and drinkin' like that it doesn't help at all.

She built up the fire some more and put the kettle on and crouched on her stool by the fireplace while she mixed some flour and water to make damper. She glanced at Essie in the dust by the fireplace with her slow, blue eyes, staring. Essie never cried.

Just then David came outside, shielding his eyes from the light and went to relieve himself. When he came back he squatted on his stool with his head on his hand and wordlessly held out his mug for some tea. Maggie poured the scalding tea into his mug. 'David, we can't go on like this you know. It has to stop. You swore you'd never touch another drop when we was married. And again when Essie was born.'

'I know Margaret, I know. I don't even know why I do it.'

'And again just three months ago.'

Remorse crumpled David's face and he turned away.

'It doesn't help any. An' it wastes money.'

'Stop going on woman. I've said I'm sorry. And that's an end of it.'

'All that brandy in the store. It's too easy for you. We should sell the Licence. Walter Patterson would be glad to buy it.'

David rose from his stool. 'I'll not sell the licence! You know it earns us a good living. If you want a better house forget about selling the licence. You look after the children. I'll decide whether we are to sell licences or not.' And he strode away without another word.

When Maggie was angry with David, when he drank too much and came home reeking of brandy, then she would go into the bush and gather wildflowers and bring bunches of them home which she'd put in jars at the window and on the table. David in his guilty state would chide her for wasting time and she would look at him, reproach in her eyes and he would go to the wood heap and expiate his guilt with the axe.

Later when he carried a load of firewood and placed it carefully beside the hearth, then she would make him a pannikin of tea and they would sit together and silently forgive each other. And in the night he would wash himself before coming to their bed and with his rough workened hands, caress her belly where the child swelled within.

WRITER'S NOTES: *Photogravure*, of what is obviously a school building. It is a symmetrical brick building with four pairs of double windows along its front, divided by a tall central bell tower. Written across the front is Majorca School No. 263. Est.1866. In the school yard, all the children are gathered for the photo. The girls in front wear pantaloons beneath their skirts, some wear a pinafore, others a cape, many wear small hats like little boaters with a black ribbon around the crown. The boys are not so well dressed and most seem to be wearing long trousers and jackets and a soft cap. The crowd of children, there are about one hundred and fifty of them, seems too large to fit into the school building. The other strange thing is that they all seem to be younger than seven or eight years. Certainly they all appear to be close in age.

Faded photograph of a store, showing a group of people outside, and two horses standing with carts backed up to the footpath. There are three men with white aprons, thumbs hooked into their waistcoats, standing outside the door. There is a woman holding a basket over her arm and, beside her, several children playing on the boardwalk. The building is single story, plain brick in construction with a central door and windows on either side. A sign across the top of the verandah says D. STAVERS, WHOLESALE AND GENERAL STORE, MAJORCA and in

191

smaller lettering on the windows, Wine and Spirit Merchants. This building is not nearly so grand as the first store David built at Pleasant Creek. That store had arched bay windows with a recessed central door, in the Victorian manner. It must have all but broken David's heart to lose it, but I imagine this one served well enough. This photograph is dated about 1869. By then David and Maggie had four children - Essie, Willie, Annie and Molly. Written on the back is a list of goods. I am intrigued by the variety of these goods - 24 yards of printed dimity, colour green; 2 boxes white clay pipes; 12 tin washing dishes; 40 gallons of whitewash; 12 pounds of soap; 4 pipes of brandy. I know that dimity is a light cotton fabric, usually printed, but what is a pipe of brandy? I looked it up and find it is a cask or butt, of two hogsheads, varying according to the wine but ordinarily about 105 gallons! That's a lot of brandy. What has happened to my god fearing, upright young man?

Wooden box, about two fitty by one fifty by one twenty millimetres. Inside the lid is a gold insignia with a crown on top that says Benjamin Poulton, 84 Collins Street East, Melbourne, Homeopathic Chemist. Sitting in the box are thirty-six small corked bottles or phials each containing tiny pilules. On each cork is written the name of its contents, Opium, Nux Vomica, Laudanum, Pulsatilla, Digitalis and many others I have never heard of before. Each bottle is labelled with the ailment it is intended for and the appropriate dosage. Baptisia is for Typhoid or Colonial Fever, Ipececuanha is one of the best remedies for spasmodic cough, rattling of phlegm, asthma and whooping cough. Acid Phos. Is good for loss of memory - must get some of that!

Bundle of Phrenology Charts. On top is a sheet with a picture of a human head in profile, devoid of hair, with the various areas of character delineation charted and numbered. These are listed as temperament, social affections, selfish propensities, moral sentiments, self perfecting, intellectual faculties and reflective faculties. These are further divided into many subgroups. Across the top is written MAN KNOW THYSELF and a paragraph to the left proclaims, 'It is woman who trains the young mind, and lays the foundation of man's greatness, hence it is imperative for her to know her own defects.'!

Phrenology was the study of human nature and potential, based on the size and configuration of the head. It was considered a science during the nineteenth century and I'm sure David considered himself very advanced in his thinking when, as I see by the charts here, every few years he took his family along to a Phrenologist to have their characters defined. When I think about how there Phrenologists interviewed people it occurs to me that they were the psychologists of their time and were probably quite keen observers of human nature, So even though the science itself is now thoroughly discredited, I believe the phrenologists observations of personalities and characteristics were very likely quite accurate and perceptive, though not necessarily related to the shape of the skulls they examined.

192

In 1865 it had been unusually dry for two summers and the earth was like dust. Everywhere throughout Victoria the squatters and farmers were despairing, and even in the towns, water was scarce as rivers and creeks dried up and the sun sucked the remaining film of water from the dams. One night late in autumn as they lay in bed Maggie heard an unfamiliar sound.

The light next morning seemed strange, dim, and the air heavy and still. They strained to hear, incredulous at first, the soft pit pit of scattered raindrops. David and Maggie got up and went outside and held their faces up, seeking the pregnant rain clouds.

Young Willie was three years old. He had never seen rain. When he woke that morning, rain was drumming on the roof and he padded out to the kitchen to ask what the noise was.

'It's rain Willie, spillin' out of the heavens it is. Thanks be to God.'

David lifted his son and carried him to the verandah where he set him down and pulled off his night gown. Willie struggled out of his father's hands and ran naked into the rain, his nostrils filled with the unfamiliar smell of water on dry earth. As the puddles filled and the runnels formed he stomped and made splashings in the wetted earth and the dusty water arced around his feet. He rolled and laughed and squealed with delight as rain poured over his body, and he raised his small arms to praise this newly darkened sky.

And when Maggie was older she told anyone who would listen how the rain came that autumn and how young Willie had danced in the puddles. How the sky was black and the thunder and the lightning continuous. And the rain came with the thunder and the lightning and when it came, it poured down like a river from the sky and she could scent the dust and the wind blew and the trees danced and all the leaves sang in the blowing of the wind and the wonderful, beautiful, blessed rain.

It rained for three days, and they were jubilant at the filling of their tanks, and the flowing of the creek and the washing away of the dust. Life was given a new beginning.

Soon they could think of other things and one day Maggie said to David 'You must do something about a school. Couldn't you raise a public meeting to talk about it?'

'You know how busy I am. I'll do it soon. Willie's only three.'

'I want our girls to go to school too, David. I'll not have them brought up without bein' able to read and write. Essie is five, and Willie's almost four. And there may be another boy next time.' Maggie patted her stomach.

'I'll bring it up as soon as I've got time.'

'We have to do something about it now, David.' she looked at him sharply.

'Alright then, the Progress Committee is meeting next week. We've got to take steps to build a dam on the edge of town with a standpipe in the main street. If the talk about that doesn't go on too long, I'll mention it then. Goodness knows there's enough children in the town to warrant it.'

Over the next two years David and his Progress Committee wrote to the National Education Board, the government and to the shire, asking for land, for building designs and for a teacher to be assigned. Meantime, in her own way, Maggie began to teach her own small brood.

She wrote out the letters of the alphabet and cut them out and

SCHOOL PHOTOGRAPH 1881

stuck them on the wall outside, in the shelter of the verandah. At first the children didn't show much interest, and when she recited the letters over and over to Essie and Willie, they would repeat them in their sing song voices but their eyes would drift away to look longingly at their favourite tree or notice a rosella as it darted through its branches. But Maggie persevered, making simple words with the letters, until they could spell their names and some of the words. Maggie was determined they would not have to wait until they were twelve before such learning came to them.

When Annie was about three, one day she picked up a piece of newspaper that had been wrapped around a parcel of meat. She had been playing with it for a while when she pointed to the word ball and said, 'Ball!' and toddled outside only to come back in with her toy, a soft, round sphere made from leftover sheepskin scraps which Maggie had sewn together.

'Mama, look! Annie knows Ball.'

'Show Mama Ball, Annie' Willie and Essie urged her.

'Look, she did it again.'

Maggie knew it was no accident, Annie had been chattering since before she was one year old and was certainly the brightest of their children.

Each day after that Maggie included Annie in the spelling lessons and before long she could sit down and read the one or two simpler books belonging to Essie and Willy.

'It's come Maggie! It's a letter from the Board of National Education. They've appointed a teacher to us. He's to commence in January, next year.'

Maggie was just pouring the last of the parrafin into the candle moulds as David spoke. She pulled each wick up to make sure it was straight. 'That's surely grand David. We'll have to get that buildin' finished then. And arrange an openin'. What's still to be done David?' Maggie took the moulds outside to set firmly and placed them high on a shelf out of reach of the children. She flicked the scabs of paraffin from her hands where it had splashed and solidified.

'The walls have to be hard plastered yet. And then all the painting of course. And we'll have to get some desks and forms.' David was jotting notes down on the back of the Board's letter.

'And the floors waxed.' Maggie insisted. 'We've got a clear three months to do it all. If we get everyone helpin' every day after work and a big workin' bee every Saturday we should get it altogether finished before Christmas. We'll have to build privies too of course, and we'll need a water tank.'

'At last count we had over 150 children enrolled. It'll be too much for one teacher - what do you think about Gertie Pearson? She'd be a good helper, and perhaps Edward Dutton? I've heard him say he would like to teach. What do you think Maggie? Would everyone contribute sixpence a week to cover their wages? If they did there'd even be a little left over for chalk and some reading books.'

'I think so. And I'm sure those that can't pay would be helped somehow.' Maggie considered for a few moments, 'and as far as Gertie and Edward are concerned, it would be better if the Board approved them. Then they could get their training at the same time.'

'We've still got a good balance in the School account so we should be able to afford everything we need. Getting that teacher appointed is the best thing that could have happened. Now it'll be an official school.'

On the day of the opening of Majorca Common School No.263, in January it was cloudy and overcast. But that didn't diminish the excitement in the town. The children assembled at the standpipe and marched in rows down to the school, with the new head teacher Mr O'Connell Lane leading them, followed by members of the Progress Committee carrying a banner that the ladies had made for the occasion. The banner said 'GRAND OPENING' and was decorated with drawings of books and pencils and inkpots and rulers. All the women and younger children stood on either side of the road, clapping and cheering. Young Annie tried to wriggle out of her mothers restraining hand and join the parade herself. Maggie longed to let her go; she would easily fit into the youngest grade even though she was only four and Maggie wondered how long she would have to hold her back.

When they arrived at the school, all the children were lined up in front of it and the photographer, who had come up from Ballaarat for the occasion, arranged his camera on its tripod, pulled a black sheet over his head and the camera and, crying 'Hold Still Everyone!' took several photographs of the occasion. Mary Philpot spoiled it a bit by bursting into tears when the cameraman fired his sulphurous flame but was soon comforted by Gertie who really looked the part of the young teacher in her striped blouse and dark skirt. Very stylish she looked, with that long woollen coat, Maggie said later.

It was late spring and there had been copious rain over the past weeks and the surrounding land was lush and green. Even the mullock heaps on the barren outskirts of the town were showing signs of green on their rough surface. On that October morning it was fine and warm.

David and a wagoner had been unloading goods from the wagon for the last hour. They had carried eight barrels and twice as many sacks of produce into the storeroom at the back of the shop. They were both sweaty and hot. As he came to the door, David tossed his hat, quoit like, onto a peg on the wall. 'Nugget - a drop of tea for us if you please,' he called.

Annie and Molly were playing under the tank stand, building tiny fences from twigs and leaves in the moist earth. They called 'Look Papa - we've made a stockade.'

David squinted at the wobbly little structure and suggested that the miners might need a stronger wall to shelter behind. 'Be sure to keep that wall strong.'

Maggie heaved herself up for the dozenth time that morning and went outside to the kitchen lean-to at the back of the store, to stir up the fire and add some more sticks to it. She topped up the black kettle from the tank then hung it on the crane and pushed it back over the fire. Immediately it began to sing. She stood back for a few moments to make sure the fire had caught properly then returned to the tank and scooped out another dipperful and carried it to the verandah where she poured it into the bowl in the washstand ready for David and the wagoner to clean up. They splashed their faces with water, dried their hands on a towel hung from one of the verandah posts, then noisily entered the small room behind the store.

Maggie carried a large pot of tea inside and put it on the table and set out some cups beside it. She also fetched a jug of milk from the Coolgardie safe and set it beside the pot in readiness, dipping her finger in and tasting it as she did so to make sure it hadn't turned.

By the time David and the wagoner sat at the table to drink their tea there was barely room to move. Molly was under the table, bumping the legs and making the tea slop. Maggie bent down and pulled her from under the table and sat her in the corner and gave her a crust of bread with a bit of honey on it. Thoroughly cross at being moved from her cubby, Molly threw it away and began to wail. 'Hssht now!' Maggie straightened and put her hand to her back and wondered how she was going to manage another babe so soon.

When the wagoner had departed she said 'Davey do yeh think we could be buildin' another lean to on the side of the shop? When the babby comes I'll have to put it in a drawer. There won't be a corner for it at all.'

David looked at his offspring and his amiable Maggie and wondered how many more mouths there might be to feed in the coming years. But we're managing all right and perhaps she's right, we could do with a bit more space. 'Yes, well then. We'll have to think about that Maggie, but we are managing well enough for now. What would you think if we built another house on our land on the edge of town?'

Maggie plumped down on a chair at the table and lifted Molly onto her lap. She looked at Essie and Willie through the door and tried to imagine having space for them all to move. Somewhere to put a cot for the baby instead of a gin box on the floor where the mice might worry it. She shifted Molly to her other hip, 'I'm thinkin' that would be grand Davey. But then I wouldn't be able to help in the shop. Wouldn't it be better if we just made the store bigger? If we could just have a bedroom for us and maybe we could have a kitchen off the side and a bench where I can do the washin' instead of just a tub on the ground . . . '

'Well, first we'll be needing a small sitting room now that I am on the Council.' David took a pencil and paper and began to sketch the rooms he thought they would need. He drew an oblong and divided it into two and then added another half square onto one side for an extra store room.'Ten feet by ten feet should do for each room,' he added.

'But what about a kitchen, David?'

'Oh yes. Six feet by six feet should do for that. I can close in the verandah on the west side.'

'But the sun shines so hot on that side David.'

'I can't fit it in anywhere else.'

'If you moved the sitting room to that side, the kitchen could be on the east.'

'But then the sitting room wouldn't be at the front. Really Maggie. I can't have councillors coming in through the kitchen! You stick to the cooking. I'll plan the rooms. Ten feet by ten feet' he muttered and scribbled at the page 'and six by six for the kitchen. We can have verandahs at the back and the front. Essie and Annie and Molly can have one room and Willie can sleep on the verandah.'

'And the baby can go in with the girls too. Do you think I could have a one-fire stove in the kitchen? They're very safe. Especially if you have a stone chimney instead of corrugated iron. We could still use the old bread oven outside.'

'I don't think we'll be having a one-fire stove. It's safer to keep the cooking fire outside. I'll have to sit down and work it all out, but providing it doesn't cost more than twenty pounds, I think we might be able to manage it.'

A few weeks later, just before their fifth child was born, David decided to go prospecting for a few days. As he gathered together the familiar tools of his mining days he felt a lift of excitement at the thought of once more camping, digging, and the constant flash of hope that came with every pick stroke. 'Maggie, I'm going fossicking with Atchison tomorrow. If we have some luck it will help us to build on the house. It must be three years since the last time I went.'

'I'll be puttin' up some food for you then. But I hope you'll be enjoyin' yourself diggin' because that's all you'll be gettin' out of it.'

'I think I'll take Willie with me.'

'Ah, he's too young David. Don't you think, another year?'

'It's time he learned to do a bit of digging and washing - it won't hurt him.'

'Well don't be too hard on him, he's only seven Davey.'

'Oh stop fussing woman. You'd keep him a sop forever.'

David, with young Willie and his neighbour Atchison, set out at first light the next morning and rode for several hours to the perimeter of the latest rush. David and Atcheson pegged out a shallow claim early and were rewarded within days by several good-sized nuggets, the largest of 18 oz.

'What say you, we stay a few days longer Atch?'

'Prospects look good. I vote we stay on - what do you say young Willie?'

Willie looked up at his father and Atch from the mullock heap where he was fossicking for any small colours they might have missed. 'Look Papa, I've got some nuggets already! Will Mama be alright without us?' he asked a little doubtfully.

So in spite of young Willie's doubts they decided to stay a little longer and secured a claim in deeper ground and soon bottomed out. Their first three loads of wash dirt yielded more than 60 ozs.

Young Willie proved handy in fetching and carrying for the two men and their exuberance at their good fortune was so infectious that when they arrived home they were full of good cheer and optimism. In six days they had found more than enough gold to build themselves new houses.

'This will change our lives Maggie. Now we can build a good house and get ourselves really established. After all our expenses are paid and divided between us we've got over a hundred pounds each!'

Maggie sank onto her chair and gasped. 'I can't believe it at all,

Davey! What good luck! Now we can . . . Would you think now we can build a proper kitchen with a wood stove?'

Winter extended right into spring and even in November when David Atchison Weir, known as Atch, was born, it was still drizzling. Everything was damp, even the timbers of the new house seemed to have sucked in the moisture and breathed it out again each evening when the fire was lit. At night, the blankets felt cold and damp when David and Maggie and the children climbed into their beds. Colds and earaches had plagued Essie and Will all winter. Annie had whooping cough and even Molly, who never seemed to catch anything, had succumbed to a couple of bouts of fever.

Maggie was standing at the bench kneading the bread and watching the raindrops accumulate and run down the windowpane. She had been awake since first light, pushing up the bread between spasms. Molly woke first and toddled out to the kitchen, hair tousled, to stand at her mother's side, pulling at her skirt till Maggie gave her a crust to chew on. When Maggie thought she could wait no longer she went back to the bedroom and said, 'David, you'll have to get the midwife. Essie'll be lookin' after the others.'

As David hurried away Maggie lay on the bed waiting for the next pain. Between contractions she could hear Annie coughing and the note of panic in her indrawn breath. 'Willie, get Annie some Ipec. Mind you only put one pill into the bowl and get a towel to put over her head, tell her to breathe slowly. I'll get the kettle.' Maggie tried to get up but was grabbed by another contraction. 'Dear God, don't let her have an asthma attack. Not now.'

'Willie!' she called again, 'You'll have to get the kettle yourself, mind you, don't burn yourself at all.'

When he came back into the room, she grabbed his wrist and gasped, 'Go to the gate and see if Mrs Wrightson is comin' . . . Tell her to come quickly . . . Papa's not in the store. Papa . . . ' Maggie panted quickly for what seemed a very long time to Willie '. . . unnh . . . unnnnnnnnnnnnh . . . you'll have to look after it.' Seven-year-old Willie felt very important. Maggie thought she might have been better to leave David at the store and keep Willie here; he was such a dependable little boy.

Essie peered round the doorway 'Are you all right Mamma?' she asked gently, terrified of the power which seemed to be wrenching at her mother's body.

'It's comin' fast. I wish the midwife . . . uuuuuuunnnnnnnhhhhh!' Maggie panted briefly before another huge spasm. 'Quick Essie. Get the scissors . . . make sure . . . they's clean . . . there's cord. . . . inthechest! Aaha-aaha-aaha-aaha-aaha- . . . uuuuuuunnnnnggghhhh! Aaagggggghhhhh! . . . .

'There it is now.' Maggie sighed with relief at the feel of warm slippery flesh between her thighs. She lay back on the pillow and tried to find the energy to reach down to the wailing infant. At last she could hear David's voice from a long way away and Mrs Wrightson bustled into the room. 'Ah medear. I'm late I see. There now, I'll be fixin' this Essie. Your Ma's fine. Just get me some water and I'll be washin' your Ma and seein' she's comfortable. Sure an it's a fine boy you've got there Maggie.' And the capable Mrs Wrightson quickly cut the cord and lifted the quivering babe into a swaddling cloth and passed him to Maggie.

Maggie smiled with content. Davey will be pleased, he needs another son to help him.

When Maggie was washed and presentable, David stuck his head around the door. 'Ah 'tis a fine son you've given me Maggie my girl. I thought I'd have to get the laudanum out for a while there my little Nugget.' Maggie could see he was smiling fit to bust as he came into the room and took the tiny bundle into his arms.

'I'll name him David after me, Atchison after my friend next door, and Weir after poor Sam Weir which was shot.'

'That's surely a lot of names for such a small lad Davey.' Maggie smiled again, I hope they's not too much for him to carry.'

'We'll call him Atchison. It's a good name and you're a good wife Maggie - you're surely the best Nugget a man ever found.' And David waltzed round the room with his newest son in his arms, then took him to meet his brother and sisters.

Reading for Mr David Stavers.-
May 1868.

Mr Stavers, the following is our impartial sketch of your character but you would require a full study to do you justice in all your peculiar points You are by constitution active, fiery and excitable and by the form of your brain you are eager, industrious, impatient and clever and enterprising. Your hope has been depressed, your spirit has been often worried and your temper sorely tried partly by your own irritability & partly by vexations from without. Therefore sir, I advise you to take things as easily as possible, rush as little as you can, avoid all sorts of tippling and irritation. Sleep as much as possible avoid irritable people, have no partners in business and strive as far as possible to be contented and to govern your temper and all must yet be well with you as you have intelligence, ingenuity, industry, enterprise and great observation. Strive to keep down your combatativeness, eat wholesome food and never neglect your meals. You are a little too blunt & open - strive to modify this. Read hopeful works, take bright views of religion and avoid much controversy and avoid all boring, slow & lazy or dull people. You will in all things seek to have your day and in most things strive to have your way. Good memory, ready in language & argument but a little too fast & apt to feel & think & to say that others are dull & stupid. You are hard to please, kind to children, pure in affection & faithful in love but sometimes very impatient - active in imagination & a man of many . . . (last few words unreadable)

The last of the readings was the one done for Maggie which was in 1876, eight years after the previous reading and two years after

203

their last child Emma, was born. David had a reading on that occasion too, but was so disgusted by it he immediately screwed it up and threw it away, in spite of it having cost him fifteen shillings.

Madam Stavers   *Delineation of Character*
by John Benj. Thomas,
Phrenologist, Majorca, April 18th 1876.
This lady's Phrenological developments are of a very superior nature. Her brain is large, powerful & active. Her reflective faculties are very powerful in their influence & will act as a guide & a light to the other faculties inasmuch as they have the power to balance every thing that passes through the mind through which her lady ship will possess sound judgment & wisdom in a very high degree. This lady's mental ability would be very great indeed had it been fully cultivated. The social affections are ruling in their influence inasmuch as it has a tendency to make her agreeable, graceful and elevated in character, feeling & purpose. Has great command over her temper & will possess a calm thoughtful & a reasonable mind, but will be very sensitive, very much so indeed. Yes. Will be a very affectionate parent yet be very firm with children & possess stability of character & moral courage to a very great extent. Will be very honest & conscientious in all her dealings & would be tormented with the mere suspicion of having done wrong. Her moral sentiments denote an elevated tone of mind through which her ladyship will despise & detest meanness & shrink from it & assume an appearance of dignity & firmness. Has an excellent memory & can call to mind things that occurred many years ago as though it took place yesterday. Will be very orderly & systematic will have every thing in their respective places & will be annoyed by confusion & disorder Her desire to possess is not very great yet will know the true value of money. This lady has good ability & would make a Physiognomist (descriptor of science/nature) of the first order. Her ladyship will express important ideas in a peculiarly felicitous & a happy style and have thoughts enough handsomely to

fill the channel through which they flow. This head is capable of guiding its possessor through the path of virtue & duty.

Afterwards, David was close lipped and silent all the way home. When young Molly and Atch began to laugh and play in the back of the trap, he turned to them and snapped 'Sit up and stop that nonsense!'

'Now then David, they're not hurting anything at all.' Maggie remonstrated.

'Behaving like fools!'

'They're children! Having a bit of holiday from rules.'

'Time they were grown up then. And I'll thank you not to undermine my authority.'

He's more of a child than they are, Maggie thought to herself. Such a stickler for being in charge. But he's right; I shouldn't have said anything in front of the children. I wonder why he can't see that he just makes himself look foolish. He's got enough presence to hold his own anywhere but then he goes and undermines himself by being so sure he's right. Which he mostly is, but he'd be more impressive if he believed it himself instead of having to push it down others' throats. Maggie turned to the children in the back 'Here's some string - play cat's cradles the way Moorangi showed you.'

'And what are you encouraging them in those heathen games for?'

'Really David, you're altogether cranky this afternoon. What's the matter?'

'Nothing.' But he was in fact humiliated. Maggie's chart, so full of good character and qualities. His own, damned by his own impatience and ill temper.

When they were almost home David said, 'I'm going to have an ale. You can go on home with the children', and without another word he handed Maggie the reins and jumped down from the trap.

They were all relieved when he got out, and continued their journey laughing and singing songs.

'Why is Da so cranky Mama?' Essie asked as she and Maggie

205

washed the dishes that evening. David was still not home and Maggie was herself a little angry with him. Drinking again. That was no solution.

'Well, you know Essie, he has a lot of things on his mind. A lot of responsibilities. Being Mayor is a great honour.'

'Yes I know Mama. But why can't he be patient and steady like you?'

Maggie laughed. 'Patient and steady he's never been Essie. But he has other qualities. He has good ideas and lots of energy to carry them out. And he's a very loyal man. They're all strong qualities. You must remember to humor him when he's in a bad mood. It's better in the end. Now, can you be puttin' Emma to bed Essie, while I set the bread.'

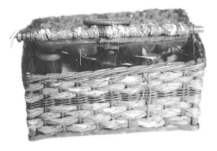

WRITER'S NOTES: *Sewing basket*, made from rushes, loosely woven on a frame of light cane, mounted on a light wooden base. It looks rough outside but inside it is lined with sky blue silk. The lid is padded and buttoned and has bands to hold scissors and a place for needles. In the bottom are wooden spools of faded cottons and silks and a silver thimble. And so many buttons! Bone and mother of pearl and pressed metal and hand carved wooden ones. And a tumble of lace bobbins also made from bone, or wood, and carved into spindle shapes with a loop of tiny glass beads on the heads, or some with little gum nuts, and seedpods and even silken tassels. These probably held the cottons used in lace making.

Leather bound family bible, within its pages, between the old and the new testaments, there is a carefully written list of names. It is dated December,1885, the month of Maggie's death and so the youngest child Emma would have been eleven, ranging through the teens to Essie twenty four. The first name on the list is David's. Above the names is a declaration that all the signatories will 'Abstain from Indulgence in all Spirituous Liquor.' Dramatically, a pen stroke has been drawn through David's name.

Whose anger so defaced the family Bible? In various letters written by his daughters there are hints . . . 'father's behaviour is most vexing' . . . 'money and father do not agree . . . '

Small bundle of letters, written by David to his daughter Emma between 1892 and 1894. He writes with gentleness and wisdom to his youngest during the time she went to the city to be a governess with a family in Camberwell.

206

Painting of D.Stavers. What I thought was the bottom of the chest is in fact a loose sheet of tin. I lift it up and find a wonderful surprise. It is a painting of David! I am delighted by this for I have seen only two photographs of him, the one which was on top of the chest when I first opened it. The painting shows him seated in an armchair reading the paper. His youngest daughter Emma painted it and I think it is probably a passably good likeness of him. She has chosen to paint him in profile and his expression is calm and concentrated. He appears formal, straight-backed, but not stern. He has a full grizzled beard. Even though the painting is in profile, Emma has caught an expression that is firm, but a little sad. There's something about this painting, which makes me think his daughter Emma must have loved him dearly.

<hr>

David had kissed the top of Maggie's head and retired early to his bed. He was leaving for Melbourne before dawn the next day, his lunch already packed in his saddlebag.

Maggie watched his compact frame as he walked from the room; limping slightly from the time he fell down the shaft and broke his ankle. It was only noticeable when he was tired and suddenly she saw how the years of unremitting labour had bent his body. He was a good provider she thought, but it was strange how whenever things were going well he always seemed to set himself against something that made it all unravel. She hoped the court case in Melbourne would work out well for him this time.

She set down the candle on the table beside her and sat facing the back of another chair. She took her cushion and tied the top of it to the back of the chair and rested the bottom of it on her lap. One by one she unpinned the thirty bobbins from the cushion, letting them hang from the length of lace she had already worked. She arranged them in order. A small forest of pins held the design in place. It was to be a lace collar for Essie's twentieth birthday. Maggie had worked out the intricacies of the pattern in her head, making the design of maidenhair fern as she went along, her fingers flying, twisting threads, placing pins deftly at each twist. Maidenhair fern - so right for Essie, Maggie thought. I don't know how I'd manage without her if ever she decided to get married. But maybe I won't have to - she's such a homebody and so shy, I can't imagine her even meeting a young man. And she'd make such a good wife too - so loyal and kind. Maggie's hands were deftly weaving - twisting the slender threads in and out, over and under, a double twist here, a loose link there, looping and pinning rapidly. Whenever Maggie was unhappy, working the bobbin lace occupied her mind completely. If she did not hold her concentration she knew she would find a mistake later and it was altogether too fine to allow that.

Although Maggie loved to make lace, she was always a little reluctant to begin. Somehow the rhythm of it and the concentration of her mind on the twisting, looping cottons, made her unwary. The moment she stopped weaving, while she was still concentrated on the bobbins, a door in her mind opened and memories of Richard slipped in. Always unsettling even after all these years. She sighed and shifted her weight a little, loosened her waistband and probed at her side where it pained. She closed her eyes for a few minutes.

Instantly she was there beside the lagoon with Richard, the moon's light casting shadows around them, its shimmering body reflected in the water. They were in a world that excluded all else, whose boundaries were as close as their breath and as distant as infinity. Richard had just loosened her hair and she turned to him, her body imbued with an excitement she had never before felt. She looked into his eyes and it seemed her whole life flowed through that gaze into his mind, and his into hers. Like looking into his eyes and seeing meself, she thought. Richard stroked her face, then his hands slowly untied the ribbons of her blouse. Her own hands were busy too, finding his buttons, his belt, burrowing under his shirt, feeling, touching, stroking, gripping.

In that timeless, boundless space, they lay in a patch of sweet grass, their bodies silvered by moonlight, melded into one by touch and tongue, scent and taste. They breathed each other's souls in their mingled breaths, aware of no other, until it seemed they breathed and moved as one. In their brief moment, in the deep silence of the eternal, a chrysanthemum of white light blossomed, expanding them infinitely in time and space.

Maggie, warmed and moistened by her dream, stirred and smiled gently to herself. She slowly put away her bobbins and lace and went quietly to her bed, taking no candle, but undressing silently in the darkness, glad that David was asleep already. She took off her clothes, aware of her body beneath her cotton nightie, and the thought came to her that whatever wounds of mind and body she had endured, at this moment she felt entirely complete. She lay her head on her pillow and fell into a dreamless state of love so profound she knew it would last her for the rest of her life.

While David was away Maggie decided she would pay a visit to the Benleys, her old employers, and take the opportunity to look at the lagoon again. 'Willie, will you harness up the trap for me. I'm going to Bentleys for today and I'll be back tomorrow. Essie, you can look after Emma, I'm sure. I'll not be late back.'

'She can sleep in bed with me tonight.'

David and Maggie's oldest and youngest daughters had formed a close bond despite the thirteen years that separated them. Emma, now five, adored Essie and followed her everywhere. Somehow she always managed to make herself understood to her almost totally deaf sister.

As Maggie trotted along in the trap, she thought about David and their children. I've given my life wholly to my family; I'll not reproach meself now for either the past or the present.

Maggie always enjoyed a visit with her lifelong friend. At dinner that night, after exchanging memories and family talk, Maggie excused herself early and Mrs Bentley took a shawl and folded it lovingly round Maggie's shoulders. 'Now don't you be staying out there all night,' she said as she patted Maggie on the shoulder. They had never spoken about Richard since his death, yet there was no one else in the world that better understood Maggie's feelings.

By one of those synchronous and magical events of life, the full moon came from behind the clouds as Maggie stepped down from the verandah and lighted her path to the lagoon just as it had that night so many years ago. More profoundly than ever before, she felt Richard's presence there beside her, as if the reality of her life with David and their children was the dream, and the brief days of her time with Richard were the solidity of her life.

MARGARET STAVERS

She sat on the fallen tree and loosened her hair. It fell round her shoulders, warm, like a cloak.

Annie had been disturbed when she read her mother's letter.

5th December, 1885.

Dear Annie,
I received your letter on Sunday which was a plesant surprise as I never begin to look for letters so early in the week I had one from Atchie today but I have not heard from Molly this week yet I am afraid she finds the work hard and the hours long do you think she will be abel to stand it I think she will have to be carefull about her meals she could make some arrangement up near the shop to have a hot dinner for the summer at any rate you know her chest is not strong and if her systim gets low a cold would very easi settil on her that would be hard to get rid of I look to you to sea after them both I can sea you are all right while madam is so sweet I have just been down getting Mrs Armitage away to hosptal Willie is got to drive her in Troon's cart she is lying in the sitting room on a bed I dont think she will ever come out again the doctor does not think she will but she might linger a long time so he ricomened her to go to the hosptyal I had a letter from Mrs Wellimson she says she feels the death of her husband far more than she thought possible after looking for it so long Dear Annie I miss you very much I feel very tired so you must excuse this
I remain your loving mother M.Stavers

Maggie had written it the night before and was panting and had a pain in her side by the time she got to the post office.

'Good mornin' Mrs Stewart.'

'How are you today Mrs Stavers?'

'I haven't heard the coach, it's not gone has it? I've got a letter for Annie.'

'No, it's just coming now. You're looking a bit breathless this morning.'

'Ah I'm well enough, thank you. I just want this letter to get to Annie before the weekend.'

'How is she liking it in Talbot?'

'She likes the work well enough, but enjoys coming home for a weekend now and then. I have to keep her up to date with everything happenin' here. She'll have a good laugh about Andy McIvor fallin' down the pit like that. Wasn't he lucky he didn't break his neck entirely?'

'I don't suppose Mrs McIvor found it all that amusing, waiting all night for him to come home, but really you can't help laughing about it, specially as he didn't really hurt himself.'

'I wonder if they had as much rain in Talbot. Annie didn't say anythin' about it in her last, but her letter might have gone before the worst of it. I don't suppose she'll be missin' mopping all the water up. It's always comin' into our house when it's as heavy as that. We had to put tins under all the leaks and even then we had some moppin' to do. Ah well, the tanks'll be full and we won't have to be carryin' water for a while.'

As she picked her way home again round the puddles and muddy ruts, Maggie wished profoundly that Annie was back home. It was not that she needed help, Essie was doing most of the work and Emma was always willing. It was more that Annie always seemed to understand most clearly what Maggie was telling her. She seemed able to see behind the words to the feelings. And Maggie wasn't feeling right.

What with David being a Councillor of Majorca and soon to become a Magistrate, there was much to do. Maggie couldn't have said what it was, but with so many visits and houseguests to look after, she always felt tired. She told herself it was just that she was getting older; after all she was fifty-one.

After tea that evening while the men were talking in the drawing room, Maggie went to the kitchen and sat at the table, holding her side and breathing deeply.

'What is it Mama, do you have any pain anywhere? Do you want me to get the doctor?'

'No Essie, I'll wait till your father's finished. There's no real pain in me but I feel like I couldn't even lift meself out of this chair.'

'Should I get some laudanam?'

'If I tried to swallow anything I'd just throw it back up again. Just leave me be Essie, you're a good daughter. Go to your bed, I'll stay here in the kitchen.'

Maggie sat in the doorway, to catch the last of the evening breeze and tried to think about its coolness. She eased her skirt undone at the waist and as she did so, her stone fell out of her pocket onto the floor. She looked down at it. It seemed impossibly far away down there. She put out her hand and bent to reach it.

A sudden pain gripped her and she fell from her chair, panting. To hold the stone seemed to be important, as if it was the only connection between her body, and her inner self.

Or was that God?

As Maggie lay in the doorway, unable to move, unable to speak, the pain deepened. She stared at the doorjamb, at its grain and texture; remembered the very tree David had cut to build the house, the way it fell, how he cut it in the sawpit, then sawed the pieces for the windows and doors, they rhythm of his saw, cutting into the heart of the tree. Why should I be thinkin' of that just now, she wondered.

Something was pressing into her temple. Gathering her strength, she lifted her head a little and moved it back from the hardness. It was her stone. Now she could see it - close up to her eyes - like a landscape into which her mind wandered towards a distant horizon.

After his meeting David farewelled his fellow councillors and closed the front door. It's almost midnight, Maggie must be in bed, he thought as he went to the kitchen, to get a glass of water. The candle had burned down very low and he didn't see her at first, but heard her breathing. She was sprawled in the doorway with the hem of her skirt still caught on the chair where it was rough. 'Maggie! Maggie! What is it? Maggie, speak to me.' Maggie gave no answer and David called for Essie and Willie to come quickly. 'Willie, fetch the doctor as fast as you can. Essie, help me get her into bed.'

David and Essie struggled with Maggie's inert body, carried her to her bed and made her comfortable. David tried to rouse her with cool compresses and massage but she did not respond. Even Dr Grant was unable to offer any help and declared her condition grave.

Willie decided to ride immediately to Talbot to fetch Annie but was spared the twentyfive miles when he met her on the road in the darkest of the night, not five miles from home.

She was riding along the lonely road with her head low.

'Goodnight stranger.' Willie said quietly.

Annie was immensely relieved to hear her brother's voice. 'Willie! Is that you? What is it? What's wrong?'

'Annie, thank God you're here. Mama's ill.'

'I knew something was amiss. I had such a bad feeling when I read her letter this morning I decided to come home straight after I finished work. She never writes like that.'

As she walked in the door, Annie bent and picked something up.

'Look Essie, it's Mama's stone.' She mouthed the words to Essie. 'I must give it to her.'

Annie hurried into the bedroom and knelt beside her mother's bed. 'Mama. Here's your stone.' She took Maggie fingers and closed them around the ancient stone, and held them there, willing her mother to live. But when Annie at last released her mother's hand, Maggie's fingers fell open and the stone slipped to the counterpane.

'I hope she's not in pain,' Annie whispered to Willie as they sat beside the bed, watching Maggie's breathing as it became shallower. Occasionally she groaned and they leapt to her side. But no light of consciousness came.

David joined their vigil. Annie had walked from the room and stood outside watching the first faint glimmers of light in the east, not wanting the finality of her mother's death, but waited for it, knowing it was inevitable. When she returned to the bedroom her

213

mother lay still and silent. Annie saw that somehow the light from her eyes had dulled.

David stroked Maggie's hair. 'Ah Nugget' he sighed. 'She's gone, Annie,' he sobbed.

Essie and Willie, Annie and Molly, Atchie, Emma and David, one and all, they gathered around the bed. They knelt, heads bowed, hands clasped in prayer. David spoke, his voice strengthened by the familiar words. 'The Lord is my Shepherd. I shall not want . . .

Later, it was Emma who found Maggie's stone and quietly she slipped it into her pocket. And like Maggie before her, she cut a lock from her Mother's hair and folded it round the stone and put it away in a small velvet purse.

Gentle mannered Essie was furious. For the third time that week her father had come home the worse for drink. It was not the drinking so much, she thought, but the way he behaved, smirking, and smart answered, making a fool of himself in front of everyone. Essie was mortified. After all, he is a Magistrate and a councillor. God forgive me but I'm glad Mama is not here to see him and I'm glad I can't hear what he's saying, it's bad enough watching him, goodness only knows what stupidity he's spouting. I just wish he'd go to bed and get out of my sight so I can put away those wretched bottles and glasses.

When Annie came home from work at the millinery shop the next evening Essie still could not contain her anger.

'Father didn't get up until ten this morning. He's been thoroughly unpleasant all day and now he's sitting in the office, snoring like a pig. I'm really disgusted with him Annie. Since Mama died he's been drinking more and more - he still reeks of brandy! Even now!'

Annie leaned close to Essie and cupped her hand round her mouth 'Well Mama tried often enough to get him to swear off it, I doubt we'll be able to do any better. There's a Temperance Meeting next week, we might be able to get him to go to that, particularly as he's standing for Mayor again.'

'Standing the mare?' repeated Essie, bewildered.

'Standing FOR Mayor' Annie shouted into Essie's deaf ears, despairing of Essie ever being really in touch with the real world. Annie believed that if they'd known about onion juice and vinegar when they were young, perhaps they mightn't have all been deaf the way they were. When she recalled the hours of agonising pain they all suffered she winced. But still thought herself lucky not to be as deaf as Essie.

The following week at the Temperance Meeting, eleven-year-old Emma was the first to sign the declaration in the family bible. Followed by her sisters and her brother Atch and finally her father.

It took a lot of persuasion to get him to the meeting but by good fortune Mr Everton the Minister had called just at the right moment and David was too embarrassed to refuse. He signed his name with its usual flourish and stood back proudly as if he was already a teetotaller in spite of having had his last drink only two hours previously.

'I don't believe him Annie. But if he lets us down this time I don't believe I'll ever speak to him again.'

'Why is Essie so angry with Papa, Annie?' Emma asked as she and her sisters removed their bonnets and shawls while David was still outside unhitching the horse from the trap after the Sunday service.

'It's nothing for you to worry about Emma. He's always sweetness itself to you - you're his favourite. But sometimes he doesn't behave so well with Essie and me.' Annie said.

Perhaps it was unfortunate for David that he was once again elected Mayor of Majorca only a few days later. In celebrating his election he forgot the vow so recently made and arrived home from his council meeting more than a little worse for drink. This might have gone unnoticed if he had he not brought his fellow councillors with him. They drank and argued in David's office for several hours while Essie sat in the kitchen, dozing by the fireside, waiting for them to go home so she could clean up. She fumed and raged at his thoughtlessness and in the end went to the parlour and taking a pen and ink, opened the family Bible and dragged a line across his name; in a pen stroke so hard that the nib spread apart and dragged a double line across the page almost tearing it.

'Please Papa, sit still.' Emma stood back from her easel and looked at her father as he sat in his favourite chair. As always she was nervous of upsetting his present calmness which she knew could errupt into impatience in a moment.

'Yes, yes, child. If I am to sit still, I must have a paper to read.'

'Oh dear! I do hope I can paint it.'

'I'm sure you'll manage perfectly well, Emma.'

David sat very still for the next half hour while Emma first sketched, then painted in the main features of her painting. She knew exactly how she wanted it to look and had been able to persuade David, as only she could, to put on his best vest and jacket and his white cravat, which she had tied for him. David had felt a pang of grief as she arranged it, remembering how often Maggie had done exactly the same for him before he attended a council meeting or one of his many duties.

After her death, his world had fallen into chaos. He had tried to sell the store but the whole State of Victoria, after the years of abundance, was in recession and in spite of advertising sales and reducing his prices on several occasions, he never had so much as one enquiry.

When he looked back, he knew that drinking was not the way to solve anything, but it had given him oblivion often enough. And pain and hurt for his family too. Emma was his only consolation.

To David she embodied everything that was good, of both himself and Maggie. She was beautiful and lively and had a quick intelligence. That phrenologist had been perfectly correct in his reading of her. She had fulfilled every forecast that he made for her. When she gained the appointment as a governess for the Turners in Camberwell, David was proud beyond measure. Even though his pride was tempered by humiliation that he must depend on his daughter's small salary to survive.

She was the only member of the family who had proper employment in those years of recession in the 1890s. Willie and young Atch had gone prospecting, while Essie remained at home. Annie and Molly were barely able to make ends meet

with their millinery and dressmaking. He wondered at the futility of all his years of striving and working as he sat and waited for Emma to finish her painting.

'That's enough for today Papa. I'll have to finish it next week. I must pack now, to go back to Turners.'

'Just a moment. here's something I want you to have.' David reached into his inner pocket and pulled out a thick envelope. 'I've made my will, Emma. I want you to have a copy of it, and make sure everything works out as I have written out here.'

'But Papa, you're not going to die!'

'Everyone does, child. But listen to what I have done. I have left the family home, two blocks of land, three water tanks, the bedroom furniture, the sewing machine and mother's picture to Essie. She has cared for us all our lives and when I go she will need a place to live. You will always have a place with her and I trust you will look after her.'

Emma's heart trembled at the thought of losing her father, but she replied firmly, 'I will Papa.'

'I've left the horses, buggies and workshop to Will and Atch. They can provide for themselves. And Annie and Molly have the means of supporting themselves with dressmaking so I've left Annie the piano and Molly the family bible.'

'Molly will be married soon, and I know she will treasure the Bible Papa, and Annie the piano. She plays it so well.'

'Now, for you my dear, I have left the rest of the furniture. But more importantly, the things which are most precious to me. My books, the small trinkets and necklets which belonged to your mother, and for practical reasons, Pet the cow.'

'You know I'll always treasure them, Papa. Especially Pet!' she laughed and hugged her father. In that brief moment David knew why it was that Emma occupied first place in his heart.

David was never a vain man. During his whole life he had rarely looked in a mirror, so that it surprised him when he saw himself portrayed in Emma's painting, as so straight and upright. The struggle of his life had left him bent and battered, or so he believed. When the painting was finished a few weeks later, David was delighted with the image his daughter had made of him. 'You've made me very upright! Do I really look like that?'

'That's how I see you Papa.'

'I must trim my beard, it looks a bit ragged. And you've got my forearm a bit short there.'

'Well, you might be able to trim your beard, but you can't grow your arm! And in any case, I was concentrating on your face. It's more important than your arm.'

'I'm going to hang it here in the parlour, where all our guests will see it, Emma.'

Davide made a sign to Essie that he was going to the post office. He had a letter to post to Emma but more importantly, he hoped there was one waiting for him. Each week a letter came from Emma containing a pound note and it was this small contribution that supplemented the family's homegrown vegetables, eggs and chickens. But it was not the pound note David longed for. His needs were small. After Emma's departure for Melbourne, David had missed her more than he could have imagined, her laughing presence, her fondness, her quick intelligence. Her absence was like another grief to him, and as much as he was able, he opened his heart to her when he wrote.

Each letter he wrote begged details of the Turner family. Mr Turner's profession, their religion, their circumstances, how many servants they employed. All of these were possible threats to his precious Emma. It had taken him several months to be easy in his mind about her living with the Turners. He thought her innocent of life and warned her constantly that the world was a dangerous place.

The letter in his hand began

Majorca, 9 Sept 1894

My Dear Emma

I recd your letter of Tuesday last with your kind and thoughtful birthday gift. Re mining So far we can only call it prospecting but I think we will have a trial crushing within a fortnight. Willie will not be able to travel any this year for want of money but I am writing to a large number of farmers hoping to get orders for phosphate.

The garden is too wet it is only green and that embraces the whole of its beauty.

I am anxious that you should continue your studies to pass your matriculation but how do you go to Mrs Lasts? Do you walk or go by train? You say you do not like to stay long after tea as you will have to come home alone, it is not well for you to be out at night alone and Mrs Turner should always know where you are.

You speak of Mrs Turner being fond of dancing and teaching her children. I have never been able to see any harm in dancing it is a good and graceful exercise provided always you are careful about your associates. Objectionable people may be met with in public ballrooms but as a rule this does not occur at private parties.

I fear Atch is giving too much time and attention to his Mary. It is neather less or more than an act of stupid folley for they two to be betrothed when he can with difficulty only manage to keep himself. How can he keep a family?

I often wish you were at home that I might have someone to speak to When I look at your paintings hanging on the walls it gives me still further longings.

Your loving and affectionate Father.

Re the birds They can hear each other but not together the parit is in the yard at the kitchen and the cannerrey at the side door, out in the day and in at night. It sings almost continuous and a strong voice.

Due to the long recession of the 1890s things hardly improved and during the next two years Emma stayed in Melbourne. Back at Majorca David remained with Essie in the silent family home while the other members of the family lived as best they could, the sisters sewing and making hats, the brothers prospecting, labouring, doing whatever they could to survive. They lived in neighbouring towns, always keeping in contact by letter. The news seemed to be a bit more encouraging in 1896 when once again a letter remains from that time.

Majorca 26 Nov 1896

My Very Dear Emma

I recd your very long letter but the most interesting part was the first where you decide to remain at home for a time after Christmas and I trust it will not be necessary for you to go away again until you go to a home of your own as I would like to see you all settled before I go and not serving strangers yet I have little doubt it has done you a lot of good I am quite sure you can see things now in a very different light but when you went it could not be avoided as I was very ill and poverty stricken and I was troubled to see you self supporting before I left you but God has been pleased in his judgement to spare me longer than I expected although I have suffered very much in mind in consequence.

Sunday. Molly has been very ill. She did not say anything was the matter but I noticed she seemed low-spirited and had no apatite and last Tuesday at dinnertime I asked her what was the matter and she asked what was the meaning of a pain in the right shoulder. I told her it is inflammation of the liver then she told me all paticulars. I have been giving her homeopathic medicine and several mustard blisters both back and front. I have forbidden her to do any housework at all as I fear typhoid

Monday morning. Molly is much better, she continues to improve although she completely lost the use of her right arm but now she can use it freely without pain.
Your most affectionate father.

On the 18th August, 1900 it was Emma's twentysixth birthday. On that sad afternoon she received a letter from her sister Annie.

Talbot, 18th August, 1900

Darling old Em,
I know you are experiencing the saddest of trouble but Oh Em what a happy peaceful ending to the world's sorrow our father's passing was.
Em dear, I feel so sorry for you and should have liked to send a token of my love and sympathy in the shape of flowers but could not get any. I know you will understand.
Dear old girl, please pardon this poor attempt. I have had so many interruptions and know that other work is waiting for me. With my fondest love and Em, my prayers are for you. I will be home tomorrow.
Yours lovingly   Annie.

HOUSE BUILT BY DAVID AT MAJORCA CIRCA ~1880

I sit back and recall my feelings when I first opened the box. How I almost threw away most of what it contained. Slowly I replace the photographs and letters, the cards and newspaper cuttings, the writing box, the pistol in its rosewood case. How precious they are now. In delving into the chest I have found a goldmine of history. Like my great grandfather before me I have dug and sifted and washed, and from the lodestone of the chest have emerged real people. No longer shadowy and distant but strong, passionate, determined people. People with frailties, weaknesses, prejudices, but people nevertheless with a belief in themselves and the strength of self-reliance in a strange and new land. People who by their will and their strength have helped to make my Australia.

As I close the lid, I realise that both Maggie and I found the family we so longed for.

The Diary

David Staver's diary of the voyage of the Miles Barton departing Liverpool 25th April, 1853 and not seeing land until Cape Otway was sighted 20th July. Disembarked Melbourne 26th July, 1853 where he proceeded to Melbourne town and had a good cup of tea and some beef stake.

25th April 1853. At last we was able to board and an Agent came this morning and passed the ship ready for sea after being declared full. He then had the Carptr commence works erecting a good many additional bunks, and extra passengers were called on board this afternoon. Immediately there were called a meeting of the Passengers to make an objection and to adopt measures to have the extra passengers taken ashore and the bunks taken down. Also a lady taken into custody from the cabin for elopement with another lady's husband who left seven of a family.

26th April 1853. The agent caused bunks to be put up in a different part of the ship! Myself and others were engaged at undoing what the carpenters had done. The majority of the passengers combined and opposed them and proposed a collection to raise funds to enter a lawsuit against them if they would not send the overplus of passengers ashore as it was likely to prove injurious to the well being of all on Board for so long a voyage. The majority was determined upon preventing them from making any further alterations and so the work was all ordered to be undone. We then had a lecture of thanks to the Capn and crew and groans for the Agents.

There was nine I believe who missed their passage by being ashore merely through drunkenness. The anchor was then drawn up and we sailed from the Mersey at 4 pm. The pilot left us at 9pm after having all our tickets examined and a search made for stowaways but found none. The Evg. passed with music and dancing.

28th April. Capn read the rules and regulations.

That all ventilators and portholes be opened at 6 o'clock am till 10 o'clock pm, weather permitting.

That every passenger shall cause his bedding, blankets etc to be aired on deck once a week and the berth cleaned. That between decks shall be scraped and scrabbled every morning and swept out after every meal.

That smoking be strictly prohibited between decks.

Men are requested to wash on deck (weather permitting) and women are requested to clean the floors and see to washing.

That all goods be removed from under the berths once a week and the flooring cleaned.

That all slops be emptied every morning before breakfast and any person found not obeying this rule his allowance of water will be withheld.

That all music and singing or noisy amusements shall cease at 10 o'clock pm.

That all water closets be cleaned out every morning.

That any person found in the possession of anothers property shall be punished as the Captain wishes to direct.

That information be given to Cap Groves of all articles lost or found.

That the Sabbath day be strictly observed.

That no clothes or cloths of any kind be washed below.

29th April. Had a fine gale and passed every sale that appeared in sight but sorry to say that it was then that the groaning commenced. Everyone obliged to groan for themselves and I for myself too.

30th April. Gale continued and a great many of the passengers are yet sick. We were within a few minutes of coming into collission with another vessel at about 9pm but by good management and the assistance of God there was no harm done.

1st May. The westerly wind still very strong. Going about 12 miles per hour. Got very rough in the evening. Took a lee lurch at 10pm when the sea was running fore and aft on the main deck and down the hatchways and shipping heavy seas all night.

5th May. After three days of gale force winds and huge seas we are now in calmer weather; and cleaning up. I am much relieved to see that the ship sails so well. She is like a living thing. She bucks and rolls and pitches with the sea but always she answers the helm and the wind. The Captain and the sailors are every hour busy at putting up sail, or taking it down, or adjusting the set of the sails. You can feel her quick response to a gust of wind, or her gentler motion when the wind is slight. She groans and creaks and the sails pull and the ropes stretch until you think they will snap. It is very strange to be swinging in a hammock.

7th May. The gale a little stronger after the birth of a female child by the wife of J.Filles - named Emilia Barton by request of the Captain in honour of the ship. Also a fight between two men, one accusing the other of theft. The case was immediately brought before the Captain who made a Court of Inquiry. They decided not to put them in irons it being the first riot on board if they would shake hands which they did but I would say their hearts were a bad colour towards each other.

8th May. A fine day with a pretty strong breeze and a great many of the passengers are yet sick but glad to say I have my sea legs. We were within a few minutes of coming into collission with another vessel at about 9pm but by the assistance of God there were no harm done with the exceptance of a seaman who fell from the yardarm but not dangerous hurt. Still continuing to pass every sale that appears in view.

Sunday 9th May. A good gale but sorry to say that the day was not spent as a Sabbath should be. A very great increase of heat.

May 18th. Very calm and excessively hot. Two sharks were caught and hauled on board. The first one when hauled upon the quarterdeck leaped up and knocked down two men and leaped over the top of them. The second, being the largest measured six and a half feet in length. We saw also large shoals of Blackfish each about 12 cwt. And the little fish called the Nautilus with its little sail spread out to catch the breeze. Slept outside with a single sheet over me.

May 20th. An intense burning sun and dead calm. 114 degrees in shade.

May 28th. A good breeze and not quite so hot. At 8 am a tub of burning tar was dropped overboard to deceive the passengers that it was lamps on the Equator. Neptune and his wife came on board dressed in sheepskins and was drawn along the deck on a slide to the quarter deck where he shook hands with the Captain saying he was come on board to pay him a visit and shave all his children. The Captain was very pleased to see him and hoped he would use them decently as his children was of a superior breed and brought up at the boarding schools of England, Scotland but mostly Irish. The Captain asked them to pay another visit and bring with them a Silver Raisor and some of her Majesties double refined scented soap.

May 29th. Neptune was inclined to have one of the seamen for breakfast this morning. And was going to be put in irons for being so carnivorous. It is a beautiful day with a fair but light breeze.

30th May. A fine day, going on well. We expected to be shaved but the Captain would not allow it lest there should be any-one hurt.

2nd June. The breeze continuing. A fight in the morning between two passengers when the second mate took the liberty of

226

striking one of them for which he was dismanded. At 11am we saw a vessell in sight. We signalized her and she answered and turned towards us. It was then like a writing school for a few minutes. A great many had letters already written in expectation of meeting a vessell and sorry was I that I had none. We only got then about ten minutes to write. I wrote a few lines to my brother and a few to my Father. We gave loud cheers when the letters passed over.

Thurs. 9th June. Lost the trade winds last night. Calm today and warmer. Saw some birds today one they call the Albatross a large white bird with brown wings about the size of a goose. And a cape pigeon which is a beautiful bird nearly all white with a black head and a little of the wings and tail dark.

Sun. 12th June. A pleasant heat and had a Methodist Meeting on board and I think it was better spent than any Sabbath since we came on board. The passengers all looked healthy and respectable and the Seamen with white trousers and blue shirts which according to my estimation I think very becoming.

Wed. 15th June. Wind same as yesterday. Course S.E . Dist. in the last 24 hours 262 miles by obs. Lat 40 deg South >Long 20 deg West. We have the first quarter moon tonight and how strange you would think it to see going up in the opposite side to what you have her. Our new one being just like your old one and our old one like your new one.

Thurs. 16th June. Morning dark and hazy with wind same as yesterday. Sailing SE. We had a fight between decks at night.

18th June. Good wind continuing. A run of 14 miles from 5am to 6 am by which the Capt won two pounds of Capt Williams as he was convinced no ship could do it. Distance made from 12 yesterday to 12 today, 310 miles. Course ESE.

Mon. 20th June. Strong gale with very heavy sea. Last night so rough that the bullworks was running under water and the sea running on the lee decks. Passed Cape of Good Hope about 2pm. Strong winds and heavy rains. Had fight between decks at 9pm.

23rd June. Westerly wind with heavy rains and hail showers. Frequent squalls going about 12 miles per hour. Got very rough in the evening. Took a lee lurch at 10pm when the sea was running fore and aft on the main deck and down the hatchways and shipping heavy seas all night. Shower composed of ice particles at 8pm. Very cold.

24th June. About 6 am Capt came and called for the North Country gold diggers to get up and help them to hoist sail as the gale was over. Squally all day but not so rough as yesterday. Wagers of 13 to 1 offered that we will be in Melbourne in 3 weeks from this date.

July 1st. Continuing on direct course 67 deg.E. Breeze same as yesterday when we had a strong gale from the west increasing up to 9pm Sunday. Continued to about 4 am. She was shipping very heavy seas over each side which was running down the hatches at each continuing roll and so deep between decks that the water would have run over the top of a boot. Also a great many enjoying themselves and the idea of the rapid progress we was making of about 16 miles per hour while others praying for themselves expecting every moment to be their last.

Thursday 20th July. Caught sight of Cape Otway light about 3 o'clock this morning and about 8 o'clock were close by it about a mile from the shore sailing on the wind. It surely caused great excitement and was considered as a beautiful scenery appearingly quite wild and uninhabited with scrogs and woods to the very water edge and some of it has white sandy banks.

5 or 6 miles of the entrance at 2 o'clock pm on account of the strong head gale was obliged to tack about and laid to during the night.

Friday 21st July. Got a lt breeze about 3 o'clock this morning but drifted so far back with the wind and tide that it took us to 10 o'clock to come up as near to the entrance as we were yesterday evg. When the deep water Pilot came aboard. Soon after we were becalmed and was obliged to come up as near to the entrance to stay there or drift with the tide untill we would get wind to take us up the Bay.

23rd July. About 1 o'clock a lit breeze sprang up when we got inside of land heads and cast anchor and was obliged to stay there untill we would get another pilot. Although we had a fair wind the pilot came on board at 9 o'clock am who cleared us of the light ship. Was again becalmed about 11 o'clock am the tide getting ahead about 6 o'clock pm, lest she might drift back, cast anchor for the night. During the day saw several little hutts and tents with the naked eye and a great quantity through the glass. Also cattle and they was as fine as ever I saw a sight in summer at home and the moon arose so beautiful on the unfurled water. It was most delightful.

24th July. Weighed anchor at 5 o'clock am had a very light breeze in the morning and dead calm during the day. Came again to anchor at 5 pm about 10 miles from Melbourne after being about 4 days over the past 40 miles. Had several inspectors on board during the night. The Capt went ashore and arranged a schooner and a lighter to take the passengers and luggage ashore The schooner came alongside in the evg to get in some luggage and will be here all night. A fight on board although a woman on her expected death bed within a few yards every hour expecting to be her last.

Tuesday 26th July 1853. A great confusion all day getting all luggage cleared out. Left the ship at 3 o'clock pm and arrived in Melbourne about 5 pm. 10 of the seamen has turned out today and is of work. And here I end my voyage with a good cup of tea and some beef stake. A woman died on board about 13 minutes before we left.